LEGION

'Fear the Eighth'

D1347648

by

Geraint Jones

To the Royal British Legion

Prologue

I was watching my friend die.

He was slumped back against a slab of rock smeared red with his blood. Right hand held against the torn chain mail and flesh of his stomach, left arm hanging useless by his side. When he pressed against the spear-wound, dark liquid seeped between his weathered fingers.

I wanted to make him laugh before he left us. 'You're doing a shit job of dying, Brutus.'

'Piss off,' he tried to snarl, but his grey eyes were smiling.

Alone, we sheltered between rocks in an arid canyon between scorched mountainsides. The stink of smoke, blood and shit teased our nostrils – nearby a small village burned. From the sound of drawn-out screams, my friend was not the only one whose flesh had become a home for iron.

'Haven't you done this before?' I tried to joke, desperate to show indifference to the desolation and his wretched state. Desperate to be the warrior that he had taught me to be.

The old soldier grimaced through what was usually a brilliant smile. 'Don't worry about me. I'll be all right.'

I wouldn't have expected Brutus to say any different. Fifteen years a legionary, he was more than just my section commander. To me he was a friend, a teacher, and a father – or at least as close as I had to one.

'I'm sorry,' I confessed. Sorry because my soldier's mask was slipping – my hands were shaking. I was scared.

He saw it and shrugged it away. It was as if his own matter of life and death was an afterthought, his sole attention given to the young soldier in his charge. 'You saved my life.'

I shook my head. 'You're dying.'

'Let's not split hairs,' the veteran wheezed, and his words caused us both to burst out in laughter. A brief moment of defiance against the absurdity of it all, before the angry red pain in his stomach gripped my friend once more, and he cursed every god that he could name.

'Fuck off before you make me laugh again.' He winced. 'Go check on the others.'

'I shouldn't leave you.'

'I'm still your section commander, lad. Do as I say.'

I held the man's iron stare. I wanted to disobey him. I almost did, but then he grinned, and told me, 'I won't die without saying goodbye.'

It was a ludicrous thing to say, and yet I believed him. I stood and turned my back on my friend. I caught the eye of a knot of soldiers. Two were young, eyes wide with shock, but the others were solid, and I knew that they would see to the comfort of the veteran in our ranks. Then I left the sharp rocks where I had dragged my friend to safety, and moved out on to the canyon's floor, guided to my half-century by the crackle and hiss of thatch as a mountain dwelling burned furiously. A few other huts stood unmolested for now, but they too would be ash before our withdrawal, of that I was certain. First they would be stacked with the dozen local dead, and I watched as Roman soldiers carried the leaking bodies of the enemy to their final resting place.

Enemy. It was such a trumped-up term, I knew. The people we had killed that day had been thieves and brigands, nothing more, but they had opposed the rule of Rome, and for that they had died. Some had even fallen to my own sword. They had been my first. I was a killer, I now realized. That morning I had just been . . .

Me.

I rubbed at my eyes. How had things changed so quickly in just a few hours? The day had begun with peace, a slither of orange light painting the mountaintops with such majesty that no man had spoken as we readied to march. The dawn which followed that natural splendour was cool, at least compared to the oppressive heat of the mountains in summer, and there was no clue in the air that the hours ahead would see blood, and guts, and shit, and screams. But then, as we shouldered our burdens and staggered up into the stony heights, our section had chanced upon the seemingly deserted camp of brigands operating in the area. We had been looking for them of course, but then we were always looking for outlaws, and never finding them. This was their homeland. These were their mountains. They floated in and out of the ravines like ghosts, and we blundered and sweated our way through the passes with the grace of elephants. Simply finding a recently used camp was cause for celebration, and none of us had expected that the mountain-people would be within miles of our small patrol of forty men, let alone a spear's length.

That had changed when Brutus had led our eight-man section to look for water. Who knows why the brigands chose to make a stand that day? Maybe they were simply tired of running; maybe they hated the sight of our uniforms so much that they could no longer keep their blades sheathed. Whatever the reason, they fell upon us with spear and sword, and so unexpected was the ferocity that for a moment it had seemed as though we would be overwhelmed through sheer surprise and violence of action.

One man had saved us.

He reacted with such force and viciousness that he almost single-handedly beat back the enemy's first attack. As others had stood wide-eyed and panicked, this soldier had been consumed instantly by a need to kill and maim, and it was with such reckless disregard for legion sword drill that he had even decapitated one bandit with a single wild swing of his blade. In the face of this battle-tyrant the enemy had lost all spirit and fled, but javelins had spitted their exposed backs like game, and now their bodies lay scattered and pathetic, the mountain's insects swarming on their spilled blood and flesh. Taking in the scene of the carnage, I now wondered at the savage man who had turned the tide. The man who had welcomed the chance to kill. The man who had run to the legions in search of the promise of such brutal death.

I wondered about myself.

I was broken out of my painful thoughts when a hand landed on my shoulder, heavy as a bear's paw. I turned and looked up into the face of my comrade Varo, his older features as blunt and forbidding as the terrain in which we had fought that day. 'Come with me.'

I followed.

He led me to a legionary laid out on his back, stripped of his chain mail. Beside the wounded man, two soldiers offered water and comfort. One was Priscus, a kindly veteran with as many years' service as Brutus. The other, Octavius, was a handsome youth who had come through training beside me. I looked at him, and saw that I wasn't the only one with shaking hands.

I turned my eyes to the man in their midst. He was a young soldier of our section, Fano. He'd taken a spear-point in the initial attack. The Italian's skin looked waxen and the colour of dried ash. He was nearer to death's world than our own. I knew in that moment that he would die far from the coastal town that had given him his name. A town that he had spoken of with love, and pride. He would never see the sea again. He would never see his mother. Fano had told me that she had cried when he enlisted. How would she weep now?

'Thought you would want to say goodbye,' Priscus offered, ever wise.

'Goodbye, Fano,' was all that I said. What else was there?

Priscus looked at Varo, and motioned to Octavius and myself. 'Take these two and put the rest of the bodies into the huts.'

We moved away. Varo sensed I had a question burning.

'Why doesn't he look to Brutus?' I asked.

Varo made no reply. Instead he pointed to a young brigand who lay in a pool of dark blood. A handful of guts protruded from the dead man's stomach. His eyes were open and staring at an empty blue sky.

'Yours, wasn't he?' Varo asked me.

He was. My blade had gone clean through him. I could feel the resistance of it now, and recalled the heat of the man's blood on my hand, and his choked breath on my face.

'Your first?'

I nodded. 'Then another two.'

The lump grinned, clapping me on the shoulder. 'If you didn't kill anyone before you joined up, how did you know that you'd like it?' Growing up a big lad in a big city, Varo had come to violence early.

I said nothing, and looked at the lifeless corpse at my feet. Had I enjoyed killing him? I certainly hadn't hated it. Looking at the body caused no emotion in me, either good or bad. I was simply numb. In the moment of killing him, all that had existed was rage, and the desire to protect Brutus.

'We walked into a trap here.' Octavius shrugged, looking at the steep-sided hills and rocky outcrops that scorned our well-drilled tactics. 'We're lucky we're all not like Fano.'

'That's because this lot are nothing but criminals,' Varo scoffed, grabbing my kill by the hair and dragging him towards a hut; the dusty ground was streaked red in their wake. 'Not warriors. Just thieves. This was a tavern brawl on a mountainside, lads. It meant nothing.'

It meant something to Fano.

'He's dead,' Priscus told us after we'd put the last of the Pannonian bodies inside the hovels, and set them alight.

'What about Brutus?' I asked.

Priscus said nothing. Varo put a hand on my shoulder.

'You did well today,' the older soldier told me.

'What about Brutus?'

The veterans looked at me with patient eyes.

'You did well, Corvus,' Priscus said. 'Let's get that blood cleaned off you.'

And then he led me away from the smoke, from the shit and from the bodies. He led me away from the place where I killed for the first time. Where I lost a comrade for the first time. Where I fought like a dog in a pit for the first time.

Had I known what was to become of my life, I would have lain down and stayed with the dead.

PART ONE

❧ ◆ ❧

❧ 1 ❧

Five years later

There was a rumour of war.

It was a breathless rumour, carried by merchants, spread by whores and whispered by slaves.

It was a guarded rumour, hushed by officers, denied by diplomats and savoured by soldiers.

Savoured by *us*, because it was a rumour of *our* war.

'We need to celebrate,' Varo declared, the slur in his speech announcing that the big man's celebrations had begun hours ago.

'I'm not objecting.' Priscus shrugged. 'Octavius?'

'I'm up for it. Can't take it with us, can we? If it's time to die, then I want to leave some rich whores behind. What do you say, Corvus?'

What did I say? Not a lot. I was known for my temper, not my tongue, and my head was full of war. I didn't want rumour, I wanted battle. Real battle, against a real enemy.

'He's got that look again.' Varo pointed an accusing finger at me. 'Brooding bastard.'

'I'm thinking,' I replied.

'About what?'

'How long it would take to dig a grave for your fat arse.'

My companions laughed, and the thinnest of smiles crept on to my face. Octavius saw it and feigned falling from his stool.

'Did you see that, lads? Did you see that? A little more and I'd have worried his face was going to tear in half.'

'Makes a change from worrying about your arsehole tearing.'

'Gods.' Priscus shook his head. 'You really are in a good mood. What's up?'

I shrugged as if it were obvious. As if there could be no better explanation for smiles, laughter and an excited anticipation for tomorrow.

'War,' I told them. '*Our* war.'

We walked into the town with puffed-out chests and raised voices. We were confident bastards, soldiers in our prime. In the years since I had first killed, my friends and I had grown into new positions, but we had not been separated. We each commanded a section in the Second Century of the Second Cohort of the Eighth Legion, which we whittled down to the Second of the Second of the Eighth when talking to those in the know – soldiers and camp followers alike. The century of eighty soldiers was our family, the cohort our village, and the legion our tribe. Priscus, Varo and Octavius were my brothers, and we formed a tight band. Not without pride: we knew that we were good soldiers. The opportunity to fight in a war had eluded all of us except our oldest comrade Priscus, but, none the less, we were trusted by our commanders and respected by our fellow legionaries. When battle did come – as it seemed that it soon must – we knew that other men would look to us when it was time to hold the line, or lead the charge.

'It'll be Tiberius who commands the army,' said Priscus as we negotiated the town's streets, the white walls reflecting the sun into our narrowed eyes. Like many settlements across the Empire, this town had sprung up alongside a fort built to house a legion, the site strategically chosen to best support the imposition of Roman law and order on to a new dominion. The province of Pannonia was a recent addition to the Empire, and Priscus had fought as a boy soldier in the final months of the campaign to claim it. We loved and looked up to him for it.

'He's a great general,' Priscus went on, still referring to Tiberius, careful to step over a pile of horse dung on the dirt street.

'What makes him any different?' Octavius asked, his eyes trailing a slave girl who walked by with her master.

'Well, he loves us for a start,' the older man mused. 'He's not like other aristocrats. He walks and rides with his men. He eats at the table with them.'

'I don't care where he eats,' Varo put in. 'He can feast with the shithouse rats as far as I'm concerned, just so long as he wins.'

'He does that,' Priscus confirmed with the confidence of a man who had seen that victory first hand.

Personally, I knew little of Tiberius, and nor did I care. What I did know was that the general had proven himself in battle, that he had at first been a stepson to the Emperor Augustus, but a few years ago had been adopted as a true son in order to provide Augustus with legitimate heirs. Men such as Priscus, who had served under the general, and so had some bond of shared valour, seemed to to follow the developments in his life with some interest, as these pieces of information slowly and surely made their way out from Rome, via both official and unofficial channels. For the majority of the soldiery, however, our biggest concern in times of peace was not who would govern over us, so long as they were paying us. If the pay chests arrived on time and brimming, we cared little whose face was stamped into the coin.

'Today's on you,' I told Octavius, with such thoughts in mind. 'You owe me for the other night.'

A scowl crossed his handsome face. 'I don't remember that.'

'Exactly. You were shitfaced and kept dropping your drinks. I probably had to buy three for every one you managed to get into your mouth.'

Priscus and Varo laughed at the memory, and Octavius shrugged, admitting his likely guilt.

'Home sweet home,' said Varo then, grinning as he spotted ahead of us the vines that marked out the Black Sheep Inn, favoured watering hole of our brotherhood and the cohort at large.

'All right, lads!' a veteran greeted us by the door. 'Heard the news?'

Varo held up his huge hands in protest. 'I told your wife already: it's not mine.'

The old soldier laughed, and the tang of the wine on his breath slapped me in the face and made my nose wrinkle. 'Not that, you prick. The news about the war! Tiberius is coming, and he's going to gather the biggest army in a generation!'

I looked at my comrades. I imagine what they saw in my eyes was the mirror of what I saw in theirs – unbridled excitement, like a child seeing his first toy.

'Where'd you hear this?' Varo asked, sceptically, knowing how prone soldiers were to inflating numbers.

The soldierlegionary jabbed his thumb behind him into the inn. 'There's a couple of clerks in there from the legion staff. They've been spilling their guts for a drink.'

'Where are we going?' I asked quickly.

'North, across the Danube! King Marabodus is due a good Roman shafting!'

I watched Priscus's face as he absorbed the news. For the first time, I saw a little hesitation amongst the jubilation.

'He's King of the Marcomanni,' our old head finally ventured. 'That's a big tribe.'

'Exactly!' the veteran slurred drunkenly. 'Enjoy your night, boys! We'll either be rich or dead by the end of summer!'

'I know which I'll be.' Octavius smiled as he pushed his way to the bar and waved for the innkeeper's attention.

'You could find King Maro-what's-his-name's own horde and you'd still owe us money, you tight bastard.' Varo smirked. 'So what you think, Priscus? You've gone quiet.'

'It's a big tribe,' repeated the old soldier.

'Who did you think we were going to invade?' Varo shook his head, irritated that his friend's mood had slumped. 'Not gonna get rich turning over a couple of farmers, are we?'

Priscus held his tongue, instead helping himself to a cup of wine that Octavius held out.

'And what about you?' Varo asked me. 'What do you think?'

I said nothing.

'Well, you two are great fucking sport,' Varo snorted, draining his cup in one.

But the big man had misinterpreted my apathy for disinterest – I didn't care *who* we fought, I just wanted to *fight*. Not since that day in the mountains had my sword been pulled from its sheath for anything other than drill and training, and I thought back to those few short moments of combat with a yearning usually reserved for lovers. The truth was that I didn't care if I was fighting against King Marabodus or General Tiberius. I just wanted to fight. To draw blood. To kill. To lose myself in that moment. The only moment where I had really – *truly* – forgotten the reason that had driven me to the legions in the first place.

'Hey!' I heard the innkeeper shout. 'Hey, Corvus: don't be starting fucking trouble again tonight. I'm warning you!'

I was known in the Black Sheep, and the proprietor had seen the dark mood that had laid itself across my features like a shroud. He knew what that portended. So did my friends.

'Don't,' Priscus begged me, taking hold of my arm.

But it was too late.

A drunken soldier stumbled into me, and I had my excuse.

Less than a heartbeat later, the inn became the scene of a riot.

Thick swarms of flies buzzed about me as I dropped to my knees in the sewage and cursed my lot in life. For starting the fight in the inn I had been awarded extra duties, and now I had the task of unblocking a pipe that led away from one of the cohort's latrines. I tried not to gag as I dug away at the blockage, the tool in my hand coming away thick with shit that splattered up my forearm.

'You're a natural,' I heard from the bank above me.

I turned, and found myself looking up at the Roman ideal.

Marcus.

If it were possible for a man to outshine his armour, then he did so. The Greeks would have adored him for his perfect symmetry, and the Spartans for his noble, effortless bearing. Marcus resembled a statue of Achilles made flesh, a fact that I was keenly aware of since we had grown up together as young boys, and he had been the envy or want of everyone in our town. He was, in all ways, perfect.

I threw a lump of shit at him.

He dodged it without effort, of course. So clean was his aura that I doubted my friend ever needed to squat and crap like the rest of us mortals. He was an optio – the second in command of a century in the Sixth Cohort – and as such we were often separated, even when it was only by a short distance within the camp.

'What do you want?' I growled by way of greeting.

'I heard you were in the shit.'

'You're funny.'

'And you're an idiot. Another brawl?'

I shrugged, wiping my filthy hand against the dusty earth of the bank. 'He started it.'

Marcus shook his head, but with fondness. 'Let me guess. He bumped into you.'

'He was looking for trouble.'

'Well, he found that, didn't he?'

He had. No sooner had the man touched me than I dropped him with a headbutt. My face was far from the unmarked beauty of Marcus's, and the scars on my forehead and tilt of my nose told a story of other drunkards, and other fights.

'Why do you do it, Corvus?' Marcus asked me, looking down from atop the bank. 'You could be a centurion one day if you weren't so hostile and aggressive.'

'I'm an infantry soldier,' I grunted, surveying the length of pipe that I still had to clear. 'I'm supposed to be hostile and aggressive.'

'Not to your own side.'

And he was right, I knew, but rank and station had never been my ambition. I had joined the legions for one reason. If I couldn't be given an enemy to do battle with, then the soldiers of my own empire would do.

Not so Marcus. He had left our home town two years before me with a head full of grandeur and glory. He was going to expand Rome's borders and bring the barbarians to heel. He was going to bring enlightenment to the dark corners of the world. He was going to build an empire that

9

lasted for thousands of years. He was going to do all this, and he wanted me to be beside him when he did it.

'Why are you laughing?' he asked me now.

I couldn't stop myself, but nor could I tell my friend the reason behind it, and risk hurting his idealistic feelings – all that noble talk, and yet here was the reality: Marcus had never wet his blade in battle, and I had a legion's shit on my hands.

'Just thinking about the good old times,' I said instead. And there had been plenty of those. Times when we had run over the hills. Times when we had dived into the clear blue sea. Times when we had fought for each other, lied for each other, taken hidings for each other. We had been born to different families, but we were destined to be brothers. No day had that proven truer than when I had run away from home, and towards the legions.

'What's wrong?' my oldest friend asked me.

My smile had slipped. 'Nothing.'

But there was no lying to Marcus. Within a moment he had slid down the bank, his immaculate sandals now buried in the sewage of the overflowing pipes.

He smiled at me. 'Let me help you with this.'

How could I not grin back?

'Always in the shit together,' I snorted.

'Always, brother.'

❧ 3 ❧

In the days that followed the fight at the inn, two things of note occurred.

The first was that my friends began to call me turd-lover, and accused me of getting into trouble deliberately so that I had an excuse to indulge my disgusting fetish. The second was that news of the coming campaign began to trickle its way through the fantastical machine known to the soldier as the 'rumour mill'.

'We're marching with ten legions,' Octavius said confidently as we leaned against the wall of our barracks, enjoying the spring sunshine that warmed the skin as comfortingly as the prospect of war warmed my soul.

Varo creased his thick brow. 'Where'd you hear that?'

'Rumour mill.'

'Ten legions, my arse.' Varo shook his head. 'Priscus?'

'I don't think it will be that size,' the oldest and wisest of us decided.

'The size of ten legions, or Varo's arse?' Octavius smirked.

Priscus laughed; then he continued: 'There comes a point where an army gets too big, and its size becomes its weakness, making it too hard for the commander to control. Communication is difficult. Manoeuvres get sloppy. Gaps open for the enemy to exploit. Think of wielding a sword. You wouldn't want one a mile long, would you?'

'Speak for yourself.' Octavius grinned, grabbing his crotch.

I laughed with the others. The promise of campaign ran through my veins like fire. I was *happy*. There had been joy in my life before – no, bliss! – but to think on it caused me nothing but the darkest rage, and so I pressed those memories down into the pit of my soul as if I were drowning a thrashing beast.

'What was that?' I asked, because the eyes of my friends were expectantly upon me. I had drifted from their conversation and into the wandering river of my thoughts.

Priscus shook his head. He knew what I was like. 'I said, we were thinking about going to see *him*. Are you all right with that?'

I knew who *he* was, and why they were asking me.

I shrugged. 'Of course I am.'

I wasn't.

'All right,' said Priscus. 'Let's go.'

Priscus rapped his knuckles against the wooden door. We were in the town's warren of narrow streets, the space made claustrophobic by Varo's bulk. It was not the most desirable neighbourhood, downwind of the legion's fort and in lower ground that was prone to flash flooding during the heavy rainfall of the harsh winter. Detachments of soldiers patrolled the streets to prevent crime, which was often violent and sometimes deadly, and a grubby young boy seemed to mistake us for one of these as we waited for the door to be opened.

'Excuse me,' he said, looking up with awe at Varo, the titan among us. 'Some boys stole my bread. Can you help me get it back?'

The big man grinned. 'No. No handouts, you little shit. You want something in life, go and take it yourself.'

The urchin's shoulders dropped at the words. Priscus looked at his friend with narrow eyes. 'I'll remember that the next time you need bailing out. Here,' he said to the lad after reaching inside a slit in his belt and removing a small coin. 'Go buy yourself some food.'

He tossed it to the lad, who dropped it in his excitement, and had to retrieve it from a dirty gutter.

'You shouldn't do that.' Varo shook his head. 'People don't learn that way.'

'It's my money,' Priscus replied, before knocking again at the door. 'Doesn't look like anybody's home.'

I felt a surge of relief at that notion, but then instantly became ashamed because of it. I turned to Priscus to suggest we leave, but at that moment the door opened, and I looked into the grey eyes of a man whose life I had once thought that I'd saved.

Brutus.

'Lads!' exclaimed the veteran. 'Come on in. What a nice surprise!'

I hung back as the others moved forwards to greet the bearded man who stood in the doorway. I fought not to look at the left arm that hung limp and useless by his side.

'How are you, Corvus?' He beamed at me when the others had moved inside.

'Good. I'm good. You?'

'Never better.'

I followed my former section commander inside the tiny building. The space was Spartan: a bed in the corner and a chest beside it, atop which rested the shining helmet that Brutus had worn as a soldier, before wounds had driven him from the ranks. Wounds that I should have prevented.

'Go out the back,' Brutus insisted, and our troop followed the light of the sun, and stepped into a common area shared with Brutus's neighbours. There was a woman there, dark-haired and a decade younger that Brutus. She smiled to see us.

'Good to see you, Lulmire.' Priscus grinned back at her. 'How's Brutus behaving?'

'Very good,' she answered, her Latin thick with a local accent.

'Do us a favour, darling,' Brutus asked. 'Can you go get us some wine, please?'

'No need for that.' Varo shook his head. 'Brought some along. Here, try this piss.'

He held out the skin to Brutus, who took a long pull and then smacked his lips dramatically. 'I detect a hint of goat. Fine stuff.'

He held the wine out to Priscus, and the skin passed from hand to hand as we arranged ourselves in the small courtyard, leaning back against the walls or sitting on wooden stools bleached pale by the sun.

'There's a war coming,' Priscus said simply to his old comrade.

Brutus nodded, and for a moment I caught a flash of sadness in his grey eyes. 'I wish I was coming with you,' he said, confirming what I had seen. The words struck me like a blow, and suddenly I felt claustrophobic in the small space.

'What have you heard?' Varo asked.

Brutus pulled at his beard. There was white in the corners of it. He must have been forty by now. Had he come away from that mountainside uninjured, he would have been into his second enlistment of twenty years. Brutus had been a loyal soldier, and dreamed of becoming one of the few men chosen to bear the legion's eagle standard. A dream that had been denied when we were ambushed, and I was too slow in coming to his aid.

'King Marabodus is a powerful bastard,' he began, with more touching of the beard. 'He'll be able to bring a big army to bear, but from what I hear, Tiberius isn't messing around either. It's going to be the greatest army any of us will have ever seen. At least five legions, and as many troops again in auxiliary units.'

Varo whistled – it was some force. At full strength a Roman legion stood at five thousand men. If what Brutus said about the auxiliaries was true, then Tiberius would ride at the head of fifty thousand soldiers.

Brutus acknowledged the fact with a solemn nod of his head before continuing. 'They've already started levying units from the locals here in Pannonia, and in Dalmatia.'

I sat up at that news, though it shouldn't have surprised me. Dalmatia had once been my home, a place only colonized by the Empire a couple of generations past. All peoples within the province were considered Roman subjects, and answerable to Rome's laws, but only a few held the title of citizen. I had inherited my title from my father, which was why I could serve in the legions, rather than the auxiliary units that were now being raised. For those men, citizenship would be an award for completion of their twenty-five years' service.

Of course, they'd have to survive it first.

'What do you think the war will be like?' Octavius asked of the most salted veteran we knew. Like myself, Octavius's experience was limited to the solitary skirmish in the mountains. Brutus had marched on campaign even before Priscus had stood beside him.

'It'll be different to what I saw back then,' the veteran acknowledged. 'For us, it was always hard to bring them to battle. It was a case of sweeps, and blocking forces. Pushing them into our traps, and most of the time failing. Just one ravine or pass was enough for them to escape, and they knew the land because it was their own.'

I'd heard it all before, and yet I hung on every word of war. It was what I dreamed of. What I *needed* to be a part of.

'Every time we did get the better of them we thought that would be it, but then they'd spring back up, rebellion after rebellion. I got lucky, and on the odd occasion they did choose to stand in the plains, I was there. I stood in the ranks. I . . .'

The man trailed off, and I saw the look of awe pass over his face with the memory. Recalling the moment, he suddenly looked ten years younger.

'We fucking slaughtered them on the plains, and we thought it would be done then, but they took to the mountains. I had friends in the centuries that we sent after them . . .' Brutus remembered. He wasn't smiling now. 'I never saw most of them again.'

We were all silent. What was Brutus seeing in his mind in those quiet moments?

'Your war will be different,' our friend finally concluded with sadness. Sadness, I imagined, because he would not be a part of it. 'The lands of the Marcomanni lie on the plains north of the Danube and they are vast. There'll be a great battle, maybe a couple, but that will be it. Be happy, lads. Yours will be a glorious war. You won't be ambushed in death traps in the mountains. You'll face your enemy down, and crush them. You'll push Rome's borders further than ever. They'll talk about this campaign for hundreds of years.'

And that's when he said it.

'It kills me that I'm not coming with you.'

The words were like a sword in my guts. I looked at my hands in shame. It was my fault that this born warrior would be denied shared glory with his comrades. I opened my mouth to speak.

But nothing came out.

'Let's get a drink,' Varo suggested. 'Let's toast our war.'

The other men stood, grinning like feral dogs with the scent of meat in their nostrils. Brutus led for the door, and smiled.

'A drink with the boys sounds fucking good.'

We drank, and we listened. Brutus told stories, and we lapped up the blood of the enemy dead like a cat with milk. When he spoke of the loss of a comrade, it was

17

always in terms of the highest honour and glory. Brutus was a true servant of Rome, and nothing in his eyes was more to be celebrated than death in combat on behalf of the Empire.

'You're quiet?' Octavius noticed of me.

'Just trying to stay out of trouble,' I told him, which was true enough. Marcus had found a way of keeping me from throwing my fists around at the local inns – he'd put the idea in my head that I could miss the coming war if I was sanctioned, or imprisoned, and such a thought had scared me into good behaviour. As much as I wanted to throw a punch at the strangers around me, and lose myself to rage, I made myself wait and be patient for the true delirium of combat.

'We'll walk you home,' Priscus eventually told Brutus.

Of course, it was more of a stumble, and twice Octavius had to stop to puke. The second time, Varo kicked him in the arse and sent the younger man head first into a ditch. The rest of us had been near death with laughter.

But we weren't laughing now.

'I always thought this would be my war,' Brutus confided as we neared his home. 'I knew it would come one day. It had to. You just have to look back, and see how the wars fall over time, pushing out the borders. The Empire's like a snake, and it has to shed its skin and grow a new one. All my career I dreamed I would be the one to carry the eagle when that day came but . . .' He shook his head. 'Gods, to have it all end because of some sheep-shagger in the mountains?' He spat.

'Life can be cruel,' Priscus allowed.

Brutus shook his head, as if convincing himself otherwise. 'No, no. Life is good, my friends. I'm just being a sour old bastard. I had a good sixteen years in the legion. I saw war, if only for a little, and I love my wife. I'm happy.'

We'd reached his door. The veteran stopped on the threshold. 'Come see me before you go,' he made us promise.

Afterwards, we were silent as we walked back towards camp. Silent until we saw a dark shape whimpering at the edge of the street.

It was the child whom Priscus had gifted with a coin. His face was battered and bloody, his young nose spread across it. He had been robbed. He recognized us, and ran away.

Varo snorted. 'You see where kindness gets you?' he told his friend. 'You've got to be hard, Priscus. With what's coming, it won't pay to have any weakness. We look out for our own, and no one else.'

For a moment, Priscus said nothing. 'We could all be dead soon, couldn't we?' he finally ventured.

No one replied. We knew it was true, but each man fancied himself immortal – it would be others that died, not us.

'We could,' Priscus insisted. 'So let's enjoy ourselves while we can.'

Varo raised a thick eyebrow. 'What do you have in mind?'

❧ 4 ❧

It was to a brothel that Priscus led us. As we approached the doorway, the smell of sweat and sickly perfume assaulted my nostrils. I slowed my pace, and watched as a soldier stumbled out of the building with a wide grin.

'Have fun stirring my stew, lads!'

'Piss off, you dickhead,' Varo rumbled, and the man chortled to himself as he made his way up the street. Usually, I would have used the stranger's words as reason to flatten his face, but Marcus's caution was still fresh in my ears.

'Coming in or not?' Varo asked me, Priscus and Octavius having already disappeared from view.

'I don't think so,' I replied, coming to a stop in the street.

'Gods.' The big man shook his head. 'Five years and I've never seen you with a woman. No wonder you're so bloody angry.'

'I'm not angry,' I lied.

'They've got lads if you're feeling Greek?' he offered helpfully.

I reached up to grasp my friend's shoulder, and bid him a good night. 'I'm just going to head back to camp. Check on my section.'

'Your section will be out having fun, you idiot, but suit yourself.' Varo turned and ducked beneath the doorway. Within a moment he had a whore in each arm. His was a ferocious appetite in all things.

I turned on my heel and began the walk back to the fort. It wasn't from any sensibility that I refused the invitation – my friends were free to spend their coin as they liked, and the whores were free to take it – but the presence of the women made me uncomfortable. A legion of Rome was an all-male affair, of course, and within the ranks it was easier for me to avoid the reminders of what I had left behind. The scent of perfume. Dark hair cascading over narrow shoulders. A woman's laughter. These were all things that reminded me of a past life. All things that reminded me of *her*.

But just by trying to avoid them I had acknowledged the memories, and now there was no escaping the tendrils that grasped at me from the deepest recesses of my mind. By trying to run from the ghosts of my life I had given them form, and now they fought to be heard. Fought to be remembered.

I gave in, and let them take me.

I'd been staring for hours.

'What are you looking at?' the man asked me.

I turned back from the window.

'Nothing,' I lied, facing my tutor.

His name was Cynbel. He was a Briton with hair as fiery as his eyes, and I liked him. I liked him because he had a funny accent, a sharp wit and a head full of wisdom. I liked him because, though my family's slave, he talked to me as if he were my equal, and not a dog, in the way the other slaves did. I might have only been a child but I was old enough to know that I admired him, and beyond all that, I was deeply grateful to the man. More grateful than he could ever imagine.

And I could never tell him why.

Now I frowned. 'I don't want to do maths.'

'Well, that's what your father wants.'

'Tell me a story instead,' I asked, forcing myself to move away from the window, and the secret that had kept me staring.

Cynbel knew me well enough to know when he was about to fight a losing battle, and I knew my tutor well enough to recognize when he was on the edge of capitulation. The truth was, Cynbel loved a story as much as I did. I was young, but I was perceptive. My father said that it was something I had inherited from my mother.

'Tell me about the cliffs again,' I asked. 'The white ones. You said that they're bigger than the tallest building in Rome, but I don't believe you. Convince me.'

The man laughed and waved away my suggestion. I tried a new tactic.

'You don't like maths either, do you?'

He said nothing, but the battle he fought to control his smile was answer enough.

'So why did you learn it?'

Silence, but I was getting close.

'How did you learn it?'

Nothing, but I knew the man – a good man – and now I dealt my killing blow.

'Who taught it to you?'

Cynbel took in an intake of breath. He narrowed his eyes and looked at me, and I thought I saw some pride in them for my guile – we both knew that there was no way this honourable soul could pass over giving due recognition to those to whom he owed a debt.

'His name was Demetrius,' Cynbel began, giving in. 'When I was a slave, newly taken from Britain, we found ourselves in the same household. I was there to labour in the kitchens and the gardens. To work, and to look attractive and exotic for my owner's guests.'

I tried to imagine what a younger Cynbel would have looked like. He was still broad of chest and his hair was almost as red as flame. He had told me once that he had seen war, which was as far as he would go to explain his enslavement., but his mind had always yearned to work the land.

'Demetrius was twice my age, maybe older. He had been made a slave in Egypt, and had even lived in Rome. He was wise, and experienced. He told me that, as a slave, I had a simple choice. I could accept my position, and work to become indispensable, or I could wallow in self-pity, and I would be passed from master to master, likely to finish my days in a mine or field when I was no longer of any value.

'I chose to accept,' Cynbel told me. 'I chose to learn.'

'Demetrius taught you maths?'

'Maths, philosophy, Latin. You must understand that at this time, my grasp of language was almost non-existent. Before I could learn anything else, I had to learn the Roman tongue, but from there everything became easier. After a few years, I myself began to teach other slaves in the household.

'And then, one day, Demetrius heard one of our master's guests talk of how he was looking for a tutor to take with him to Dalmatia, where he was to take up a government appointment.'

'My father?' I asked quickly.

'No.' Cynbel shook his head, and I sat back a little in disappointment – my father's past was as unknown to me as was my own future, and I yearned to know more of it. 'But Demetrius brought me forwards,' Cynbel went on, 'and our master was delighted. You must remember, he had bought me as just a tool, but now he could sell me as a teacher. He made a profit. I was sad to leave the home, of course, and to say farewell to Demetrius, but I knew that this was a step to becoming a freedman one day. By accepting my fate as a slave, I had actually made progress towards my freedom.'

'Do you think my father will free you?' I asked pointedly.

'Not if you keep tricking me into stories instead of lessons.' He smiled. 'What's wrong?' he then asked, frowning, because I was not smiling with him.

'Nothing,' I lied. 'Nothing.'

And then I thanked the man. I thanked him outwardly for his story, but inside my heart I thanked him for something far greater – the reason that I had been staring out of the window. The reason that I yearned for Cynbel's freedom as if it were my own.

I thanked him for the love of his daughter.

I could barely stand still.

Save for a skeleton guard force and a few detachments policing the nearby towns, the entire might of the Eighth Legion stood in ranks of iron upon the parade square, almost five thousand armoured warriors united as part of the most lethal infantry formation ever to walk the earth. We were the weapon of empire. Rome's blade. To see such power – and to know that I was a part of it – filled my veins with energy and excitement at the thought of what we could achieve. We were an unstoppable force. An irresistible tide.

My morning had not begun with such grandeur in mind. The night before, after turning my back on the brothel, I had been roused from my sleep several times as the young soldiers of my section staggered in drunk from their revelry. I shared an eight-man bunk room with the men that I commanded, part of a building that held ten identical spaces for the sections of our century. Each section was also provided with an equipment room, and at the end of the building was a larger quarters for the centurion, and a lesser one for his optio. It was a standard template laid out across the Empire, and I felt as at home in the barrack room with its stale farts and snoring as I could have done anywhere else in the world. The truth was, I welcomed the interruptions to my sleep, as the realm of dreams was not a happy place for me. After I had given in to memory that night and thought of my childhood days on the Dalmatian coast, I had needed the help of a wineskin to put me into a deep slumber. Though already in my bed, I was probably as drunk as the soldiers who crept giggling into the room to collapse on their bunks. Upon waking ready to wash and shave for the day ahead, I had felt as though Hannibal's elephants had been stampeding inside my skull.

That had all changed when the order had come to form up as a cohort, and to march to the open square to parade as a legion. Such moments of total gathering were rare, and there was not one among us who did not grasp the significance of this assembly.

It was time for war.

I had barely kept my smile hidden from my section. I wanted the young soldiers to think that this was just another day for me. Not one of them was over twenty years old, a fresh draft from Italy having replaced the old heads in the legion. They were awed by me because I had seen combat. I knew that it was just one pathetic skirmish, but to them I was Scipio. I had no intention of breaking that illusion by showing myself as excited as a child at the prospect of campaigning.

As we had marched to the parade square, our sandalled feet tramping the dirt with vigour and purpose, I had chanced to catch the eye of Octavius with his own section. It was all I could do to keep the roar of pure joy from bursting from my lungs, but in my head I screamed: *This is it! This is our war! Our time!*

Gods, but I was fucking ready.

And so was the rest of the legion. I could feel it in the air. We were a crouching lion, ready to pounce and tear, claw and kill. We were a sharpened blade, ready to puncture, slice, gut and maim. We were young, we were willing and we were ready.

We were soldiers.

'Thank you,' I found myself uttering before I could stop myself. 'Thank you.'

I don't know if I was thanking the gods, the Emperor or my comrades. I just knew that, for the first time in years, I felt truly happy.

'Thank you,' I whispered.

And then I saw him.

He rode out on a horse so dark and magnificent that for a moment the splendid beast eclipsed the man who sat astride it. He was almost a reflection of the animal itself, the limbs that protruded from his gleaming armour strong and vital, their power obvious even at the distance from which I viewed him. There are some in life who are gifted with a presence that heralds their arrival on scene with greater drama than any host of musicians and standard-bearers could ever achieve. Marcus was one such man. Here was another.

'It's Tiberius,' I heard a young man whisper.

'Silence in the ranks,' a veteran voice growled.

The rider paced his horse before the formation. He seemed to grow in the saddle, as if the sight of armoured files before him nurtured his martial soul. The horse stamped and its muscles quivered, nostrils flaring as the beast recognized the charged air of the parade square. Finally, its master deigned to speak. His voice and manner reminded me of a proud oak. Powerful yet patient. Magnificent and immovable.

'I am Marcus Valerius Messalinus. Governor of Pannonia, and servant of Rome.'

He paused then, and stood in his stirrups, voice rising with his height. 'I am also the luckiest man alive,' he declared, 'because I will be leading you warriors to war!'

There was no holding back the cheer that burst from every part of my body. With thousands of others, I let loose a feral roar of pure ecstasy. There was no longer any doubt – we were going to war! – and relief and excitement coursed through my body like lava.

'The rumours are true!' Messalinus went on, after our centurions had called a dozen times for quiet. Now, we listened intently to the man who was a general in rank by virtue of his position in society, which was neither truly a civil post, nor a military one, but demanded time and talent in both. 'Tiberius is assembling an invasion force south of the Danube,' he told us. 'It will comprise five legions, and more than twice as many men again in auxiliary cohorts! At this moment we are raising *a hundred thousand men* from Dalmatia and here, in Pannonia! Our enemy is King Marabodus, who is soon to give up his lands, his women and his treasures to you men of the Eighth Legion! What do you say to that?'

What did we say? There were promises and threats to our enemy within the cheers, but mostly we roared like animals in the arena. We had been given the scent of our prey, and we were bloodthirsty beasts intent on killing. Now, we simply needed to be released from our cage.

The governor might have had some final words, but they were drowned by the din of the legion, and this time not even the calls of our centurions could hold back our fervour. I watched impressed as our general made his steed rear in an act of martial showmanship, then raced her from the parade ground, and our sight – Messalinus had done his job. His hounds were ready for the hunt.

We were ready to kill.

Never have I known such a feeling of purpose as we were marched from the parade square and back to our cohort's section of camp. Our centurions and optios barked at us to hold back on the pace, but I could hear the excitement in their own voices. Every man among us wanted to reach our barracks as quickly as possible so that we could fall out and find our friends. This was a moment of shared glory, and we had yet to even take to a battlefield! What must it feel like to conquer an enemy? I felt as though every part of my body was made of feathers. All the doubts, anger and resentment in my mind were gone. I could almost sing with pure joy.

And then, someone did!

'Oh, how I am fed up with Egypt, the land of sin, and pox, and shame . . .'

Within a moment, the familiar marching song, brought back from when the legion had been posted in the East, spread through the cohort like wildfire in Rome.

'Where I lost my good reputation, and only the army's to blame!

Oh, bury me out in the desert, where the hawks may pick at my bones,

With a couple of wineskins beside me, so I won't be so very alone!'

And so it went, verse after verse, song after song, a legion reciting the tales and traditions handed down from soldier to soldier, from campaign to campaign. By the time that we were finally called to a halt outside our barracks, I could not have been more proud to have been a soldier of the Eighth Legion soldier had I hatched from an egg laid by our eagle.

'Cohort!' First Century's centurion bellowed. 'Falllllllll out!'

The simple right turn was carried out with pride and precision. A split second later, men were running and bumping into one another as they greedily sought out their closest comrades.

Octavius was the first friend that I found, and we embraced like long-lost brothers. As we broke apart, I noticed there were tears in his eyes. Tears of pure joy.

'We're going to war,' he announced as though he had just birthed his first son.

Varo found us a moment later. Then Priscus. There were jumbled words, and promises, and bluster, and bravado. There was laughing, and singing, and handshakes, and happiness.

My life had taught me to be wary of such bliss.

I should have listened.

❧ 6 ❦

The augur of the storm was inconspicuous, a simple dispatch rider who rode to the fort's headquarters that night. We didn't know it at the time, of course, but our sentence had been delivered in the darkness, and in the morning, our cohort stumbled out with sore heads, oblivious to the executioner's axe that was poised above our necks.

Blind to what was to come, the atmosphere on parade was growing thick with excited anticipation, and not even our officers made much of an effort to kill the eager chatter in the ranks.

Then, when our cohort commander appeared, no man needed to be told to hold his silence. The officer's demeanour did all the talking needed. Usually a man of proud bearing and vigour, he stepped forth before our ranks like a victim of plague.

At the sight of the veteran's distress, I knew what was coming before the fatal words fell from his lips.

'We're not going.'

The statement hung over the assembly like a curse, dark and venomous. In seconds I went from elation at the prospect of war to feeling as though the very essence of my body was being pulled from my bones.

'The legion commander got the word last night,' our leader explained against the mournful silence. 'Orders came from Tiberius himself. Cohort's One to Five are

31

staying here. Six to Ten will march out with the governor and join Tiberius.'

No one spoke. No one moved.

'The legion commander wants you to take pride in knowing that the Eighth Legion will still be represented on this campaign, and that the glory won by the Sixth to Tenth Cohorts will be shared amongst us who remain here. Glory for one soldier of the Eighth is glory for all.'

He tried. He really tried, but his words were as empty and grey as ash. We all knew the reality. Why else would my stomach feel cold and knotted? Why else were my fingers trembling? Why else did I want to scream out in rage that it could not be so?

This was supposed to be *my* time. *My* war.

I thought of Marcus then. As second in command of a century in the Sixth Cohort, he would still be going to war. His dream would be realized. I should have been happy and proud for my brother, but I felt only bile and bitter resentment.

'This is fucking bollocks,' I spat, unable to help myself.

'Silence in the ranks!'

'Why us, sir?' another voice called plaintively, soon to be followed by others before the officers could hush them.

'They should draw lots, sir!'

'We're the best cohort in the legion, sir!'

'Sir, please, speak with them, sir!'

'SILENCE!' the commander bellowed, his grey face now lined with anger as well as grief. 'It's done!' he boomed. 'Done! These are orders from Tiberius himself, and we are soldiers! We follow *orders,* not our own desires!

It is only because I recognize your yearning to serve the Empire in war that I do not punish every single one of you for daring to question these commands, but they are *orders* and they will be obeyed, do you understand me? *Do you understand me?*

'Yes sir,' came the murmur from the ranks, the words as pathetic as a sickly child crawling in the gutter.

'General Tiberius is one of the greatest military minds ever known to Rome,' the senior centurion concluded, seeing the martial spirit fleeing from his men and attempting to retrieve it. 'Do not think that you are in a position to outthink him. Instead, think of how you may best serve the general, and Rome, by being obedient to his commands. Now fall out.'

And with that order, five centuries of men fell out of their ranks, and into the pits of their individual despair.

7

When Marcus found me, the knuckles of my right hand were red and bloodied.

It had been a comment from a man in Octavius's section that started it. I'd overheard him say to a friend that he wasn't too sorry about the news – at least this way he knew that he'd be alive come the winter.

It wasn't the kind of thing that I wanted to hear.

I don't know if it was a hatred of cowardice that made me hit him, or just because I was so selfisharrogant that anybody whose thoughts did not align with my own was likely to enrage me. Whatever the reason, it hardly mattered once I'd crashed my fist into his nose and begun to kick his prone form when he collapsed to the ground. Octavius and others had pulled me away, and my friend had been furious with me for what I'd done. Varo and Priscus, already aggrieved at the news of our exclusion from campaign, had shaken their heads at me and walked away. So it was that I had been alone in my barrack room, having ordered my young section out. After seeing the murder in my eyes, they hadn't needed telling twice.

'Octavius has every right to be angry,' my visitor Marcus told me gently, having heard how I'd come to throw my weight around. 'Those are *his* boys. He's got to live and die for them.'

'Except he hasn't, has he?' I answered with poisonsnidely. 'We're not going anywhere.'

That fact hung in the air like a flaming ember. If it landed in the wrong spot, it could cause fire, and carnage.

Marcus sought to extinguish it by appealing to logic. 'Think about this, Corvus. Tiberius is one of the greatest commanders that Rome has ever been blessed with—'

'That *you've* been blessed with.'

'Let me finish, brother. He's a great commander about to embark on a campaign. Do you think he takes the decision to leave half of a legion behind lightly?'

'No,' I finally conceded, beaten into answering by my friend's patient gaze.

'Exactly. There *will* be a reason for it, and where legions are concerned, the reason is usually war.'

'There's no war here,' I grumbled.

'True.' Marcus shrugged. 'But look east, brother. The Dacians are a constant threat. Tiberius is pulling a force together for war, and those troops have to come from somewhere. It won't go unnoticed. Maybe an enemy sees the chance to grab land, or quick plunder. You will be the force that stands against them.'

I scoffed. 'You said Tiberius is a great general, Marcus. You can't have it both ways, saying that he's overextending himself. He's left enough troops on the frontiers to put off the Dacians. You know that.'

'Then why do you think you're staying here?' he asked me, holding up his palms.

The truth was, I had no idea. My rage was clouding my judgement. I could only see the result of our omission from the campaign, and not guess at the reason.

'It really doesn't matter anyway, does it?' I eventually spat. 'The fact is I'm staying here, and you're going to war.'

'I'd trade places with you if I could.' My friend spoke earnestly.

'I know you would, you bastard.' I was still simmering with wrath. 'You're too fucking nice for your own good.'

He smiled. 'Well, we even each other out, don't we?'

'We *did*,' I replied, despondent, realizing that there was more chafing at me than simply being left out of the campaign. I was about to be separated fully from Marcus, the one constant from my old life that was with me in the new. The one person that knew my every secret, and who had stood with me at his own peril in my darkest moment.

'It kills me that you're going without me,' I finally admitted, looking at my feet.

Marcus said nothing at first, and simply nodded. I felt as though he was waiting for me to turn my gaze up from the floor. Reluctantly, I did so. His eyes had not changed as we had grown older. Where mine had become narrowed and angry, Marcus's were still open and kind.

'You know I always dreamed of campaign,' my old friend said, and I had no need to reply. We both remembered the childhood days where Marcus would recite tales of long-dead generals, or when he would pay limbless beggars in the streets to describe the battles that had shaped and scarred their lives. Marcus was ambitious, and that ambition was martial in its essence. He wanted glorious conquest. To bring noble enlightenment to the barbarian. Not me. I had only wanted one thing, and only when it was taken from me did my mind become enraptured with the idea and adventure of war.

Marcus knew as much.

'Never did I expect to see you as this, brother. A soldier, and a great one at that. Now that I do, my own dreams of war seem tainted. No matter the honour that my cohort will find in battle, it will be sullied by you not having been there by my side.'

The words were well meant. An expression of my friend's deepest love.

I laughed all the same.

'You always were good with your words, Marcus. Just promise me you'll be as good with your sword, and better still with your shield. You're the only thing I have from our old life. If I lose you, I lose the only thing left of . . .'

They were hard words for me to utter, and I looked at my hands as I did so. I felt, more than saw, Marcus get to his feet.

I knew that I had to follow the gesture.

I stood, and looked into my friend's noble face. 'You already look like a fucking hero. Don't try too hard to prove it.'

And with those words I threw my arms around my brother.

The next morning, Marcus and half of the legion marched to war.

8

I watched from the battlements as the Sixth to Tenth Cohorts marched forth from the fort in all of their brilliance, two and a half thousand armoured men shining in the spring sunshine like the serrations of a blade. A blade that was now aimed at the throat of Rome's enemy. A blade that would not return to its sheath until it was bloodied and covered in glory.

It didn't enter my mind for one moment that there would be any other conclusion but victory. Roman heavy infantry was the best in the world; it was as simple as that. I didn't see it as hubris – I just felt it as fact. Legions would march, enemies would fall and the Empire's borders would grow. It was as predictable and as unstoppable as the rising of the sun.

But we would lose men, I knew, and that knowledge gripped at my guts. Watching them go from the battlements, I accepted the truth that I would rather see every other man fall so long as Marcus returned alive. Likewise, if the legion lost only one man in the coming war, and it was my brother, then I would take no solace in the sparing of other lives. In the five cohorts of soldiers that tramped their way from the fort, shoulders back and chins held high with pride, there was only one life that mattered to me.

'Don't die, you bastard,' I hissed, looking for him in the mass of sword and iron and shield. 'Don't die.'

It was not from choice that I watched this procession of men on their way to war. Some cruel joke had seen to it that my century was tasked with guard duty as others marched nobly on to the campaign trail. Crueller still was that my post was close enough to the gates to see them leave. To feel the excitement. To smell and taste the dust kicked up by the feet of more than two thousand hungry killers, their footsteps followed by the iron hoofs of auxiliary cavalry, big Germans in the saddles, chests as broad as their predatory smiles.

'Not easy to watch, is it?' I heard from behind me.

I turned, and was surprised by whom I saw.

'It's not,' I replied. 'How are you inside the fort?' I asked the civilian as he gave me his hand.

'Centurion Justus is an old comrade.' Brutus shrugged. His grey eyes were like a lonely wolf's watching the pack depart without him.

For a long time, I said nothing. We simply stood and watched together as the last of them marched through the gates. They carried sword, and shield, and javelin, and packs, but did they also feel the weight that they carried from those who were left behind? The weight of expectation. The weight of yearning. The weight of jealousy.

I didn't need to tell Brutus that I wished I was going with them. He didn't need to tell me the same. As the man stared at the rear of the column pulling away into the distance, I chanced a look at the arm that hung useless at his side. Had I acted more quickly that day . . .

Brutus suddenly swung his head, and I followed his gaze. Through the gate were returning the standards of the legion. At their head came a man swathed from head to waist in the skin of a bear. He would have been a formidable-looking man even without the snarling beast for company, a warrior picked for his courage and skill. It was the position in the legion that Brutus had always wanted.

We watched as the glinting standard was carried towards its altar at the centre of camp. To me, the standard meant nothing – it was to the flesh and blood of a handful of comrades that I was dedicated – but to Brutus, the eagle was a symbol of Rome, and as such, he was near-religious in his worship of the totem that had been touched by the Emperor's own hand.

'Magnificent,' he murmured.

I said nothing.

We stood like that for some time, our eyes vacantly looking out over the battlements. I wanted to tell him that it was my fault he was a crippled civilian, and not the soldier he had been born to be. I wanted to tell him that there wasn't a day that I didn't replay the skirmish in my mind, and think of how it could have been different. How I could have saved them. Brutus could have gone on to carry the eagle. Young Fano could have lived.

I had failed them both.

We stood until the end of my watch. The fort felt like a sea after a storm, an oppressive calm settling heavily after the vigour and industry of a column making its way to war.

'You said goodbye to Marcus?' Brutus finally asked me as I was relieved by the next sentry, and we walked from the step.

'I did.' We both knew that the goodbye could be final.

'He'll come back in glory, that one.' The veteran smiled. 'Some people are born for it.'

From the look that he gave me, I knew that he was including me in that statement. 'Glorious guard duty,' I snorted.

Brutus shrugged what had once been broad shoulders, his muscles reduced from inactivity. 'Some people find war, and other times, war finds people.'

I felt the corner of my mouth pull into a smile. 'Didn't have you down as a philosopher, Brutus.'

'With enough miles under your sandals, every man fancies himself Plato.' He winked. 'Marching. Guard duty. That's a lot of time to think.'

Something I had no desire for. 'I just want to fight.'

'You're as much of a hothead as when you first came into my section,' he agreed. 'And you've never told me why.'

And neither would I. A look was enough.

Brutus shrugged again, and ran a hand over his beard. He might not have seen as much of me since his injury, but he was right: I hadn't changed. I was angry. I wanted to forget. The only way I could lose myself was by fighting, and I had just watched the greatest chance for that march out of the gates.

'I didn't join the legions to sit on my fucking arse,' I growled, feeling the tide of bitter resentment rising again.

'You're six years into your twenty,' my old friend tried to comfort me. 'You'll see plenty of war, Corvus.'

If Brutus's prophecy was to prove true, then I saw no sign of it in the week that followed half of the legion's departure. The days crawled by as if caught in tree sap.

The only chance of relief from the monotonous routine came when we were given a night to go into the town's inns and brothels to drown or fuck away our sorrows. I was far from the only hot-tempered soldier on these nights. Many were sour at being denied a chance of campaign, and I doubt if there was a bar stool left intact after the fighting between would-be comrades and allies. As Varo was fond of saying, 'The crime's in getting caught,' and of that I had certainly been guilty. I was trying to put a cavalryman's head through a door when a centurion and the men of that night's watch got their hands on me.

My actions cost me a week of being confined to camp, and now I lay alone in my bunk room; the young soldiers of my section had disappeared: either they were enjoying the local inns responsibly, or else they had been scared away by my quick temper. I thought about those troops now. I knew each by name, but that was as far as my knowledge of the men extended. I had learned the hard lesson in life that to care was to set yourself up for untold pain and misery, and so I had space in my heart for only a handful of people. Brutus. Priscus. Varo. Octavius. Marcus.

Marcus. Where was he now? I wondered. Had they reached the Danube and the marshalling grounds of Tiberius's grand army? Was he at this moment surrounded by a force so large that I could not even conjure it in my mind? Of course, our legion's command in the fort would have such information, relayed by a string of messengers on swift steeds, but we in the ranks thought of ourselves as mushrooms for a reason – we were fed on shit, and kept in the dark. The only hope of information I could expect would come through the rumour mill, and where the safety of my oldest friend was concerned, I did not trust to gossip. I would have to wait for the reports and ledgers that would be communicated to our legion after the coming battles. I would have to wait to see if my friend was among the fallen, injured or recommended for an award. Knowing Marcus, I was sure that he would be on those lists one way or another. He would be recognized for his gallantry, or die in the pursuit of that triumph.

'I should be there,' I growled aloud.

I stamped my foot against the wall like a petulant child, and put my hands to my face, digging the heels against my eyes.

In an attempt to distract my mind, I thought back to that day on the square when Governor Messalinus had spoken to us. I thought of his power, his presence. I tried again to picture the force that he described. Five legions, and more than a hundred thousand auxiliary soldiers raised from Pannonia and Dalmatia. These would be light infantry and cavalry, and they would come from the same lands that I had once called home. I wondered if there would be familiar faces in those newly assembled ranks. Men from Iader, the coastal town where I'd been raised. Boys that I had seen on the streets, on the beach and in the harbour. Did they now march to war? Surely, with a levy of such size, there must be some known to me who had now been pulled into service of Rome. Iader had been colonized by Roman settlers, but the majority of its peoples had moved there from the mountains, and were not themselves citizens. It was from this population of Roman subjects that the conscripts would be drawn.

I cursed fate at that moment. Had I not run to the legions in search of war, I could have remained in Iader and had it come to me. True, I was a citizen, but which recruiter ever cared for the truth? I could have volunteered and put myself in an auxiliary cohort, and at this moment I would be marching to the very war that I was being denied in the legions! I was under no illusion that I had enlisted into the Eighth for anything other than my own selfish desires. I left honour and eagles to Brutus and Marcus, and men of their mould. All I had wanted, and still wanted, was to fight, and by running in search of war I had missed it.

I stamped against the wall once more. 'Bastard!'

Of course, I knew in my raging heart that there was no way I could ever have remained in Iader. Not after the anger had consumed me, and I had beat my broad-chested father down as if he were a toddler. Not after I had brought my sandals down on to his face, and seen the broken teeth shatter from his mouth. Not after I had been caught in the act of savagery by his slaves, and been forced to escape over the garden's walls. Not after I had run to the one person I had left – Marcus – and confessed to him that I was at least an attempted murderer, and of my own father no less. If he died, and I were caught, then my fate would be grisly: sewn up into a leather sack along with dogs and cats and tossed into the water, where drowning would be a welcome relief after the panic-stricken animals had bitten and clawed me to ruin in their attempt to escape the leather tomb.

I rubbed at my eyes again. Marcus's face that day was as clear to me now as if he were sitting on the end of my bed. I remembered how he had looked at the bloodstains on my toga. How he had seen me desperate, ragged, wild and grief-stricken. He was already a soldier, home in Iader on leave, and perhaps that was why he was able to deliver his words with such calm detachment.

'What can I do?' is all he had asked.

'Run with me?' I'd said.

We ran.

My heart thumped as I recalled that day. How we had broken into the hills like hares before a hound. How the heat had baked us as we climbed higher, leaving behind the skeletal trees and following rugged trails that wound between jagged rocks. Thirst and fatigue were our enemies, but fear was a strong ally, and it drove us on into the darkness, and beyond. It was dawn when I had finally collapsed, and began to weep.

It was only then that Marcus had asked me, 'Why?'

I got up from my bunk in the barracks, and fetched a wineskin from beneath my bed. I would drink myself into oblivion. I pulled hard at the skin like a newborn at the teat, greedy to forget.

'You fucking bastard,' I swore, thinking of my father, and regretting only that I had not had a moment longer to slit open the cunt's throat. 'You fucking bastard,' I snarled again, this time because I had drained the wine, and could not find another skin. Knowing that I could be punished severely for leaving the barracks that I had been confined to, I dropped back heavily on to my bunk, and uttered a prayer that one of my section would return soon so that I could dispatch him to a merchant's.

Then, movement caught my attention.

It was a fly on the ceiling. My eyes followed the creature as it crawled and hopped on the concrete. It was trapped, unable to navigate, incapable of working out the simple puzzle of the open window through which a warm breeze was blowing. The concrete was barren, and the fly would toil against its surface until it expired.

I watched it for hours.

Initially I was cheering the creature, encouraging it to find its freedom as I was denied my own. The window was there, so close, fully open! Go!

Then, as time wore on, I began to resent it. I began to hate it. How could a creature be so stupid? How could it not see the opportunity? How—

It was then that I smelt the smoke. Not the ever-present camp smells of cooking, but the thick noxious type that came from burning timber and plaster.

'Stand to!' someone shouted from outside, 'Stand to!' and I leaped from my bed as I had been trained to do, automatically pulling on my armour.

'What's going on?' I asked no one and everyone. 'What the fuck is going on?'

It was then that I heard the trumpets.

It was then that I heard the screams.

9

Fully armed and armoured, I ran into the sunlight.

The scream came again.

It was long and mournful, almost animal-like in its raw torment. If not for one simple reason, I would have believed the sound was coming from a badly slaughtered beast.

But animals do not cry for help, and those words punctuated the screams like cold nails.

I looked about me. Just under a dozen other men from my century were stumbling wide-eyed from their barrack rooms, the broke and the boring who had remained in camp while others went into the town to drink and fuck. They were all young, members of the last draft from Italy. Their gaze picked me out as a 'veteran' of the unit, and looked to me for guidance.

Seeing clouds of black smoke beginning to drift across the sky, and hearing the cries of alarm from the other parts of camp, I could only think of one order to give. Something Brutus had told me were the only two words a real leader needed to know.

'Follow me.'

I broke off at a sprint, my shield banging against my arm and shoulder, cheek-plates rubbing against my face. I did not turn to check on the progress of those behind me. I simply put my head down and ran to our cohort's assembly point at the western gate.

I pulled up thirty yards short, and looked at my surroundings. Beyond the wall, somewhere in the town, thick columns of noxious smoke were disfiguring the bright blue canvas of sky. I heard rather than saw the panting figures that had followed me come to a stop at my back. At the gate, men of that day's guard ran on to the battlements. There was perhaps a century's worth of them, and I sought out the transverse crest of their centurion.

He found me first.

'You!' I heard from my left. 'What unit?'

I turned and saw the officer. He was an older man, probably into his second enlistment, and if he feared the distant screams and smoke, he didn't show it. His eyes displayed only anger that order had been broken.

'Second of the Second, sir.' I saluted.

'These men with you?' he asked with a sweep of his vine cane – a symbol of his rank – indicating the young soldiers behind me.

'They are, sir.'

The centurion paused then, and seemed to take me in for a moment. He looked at the battlements, at the smoke beyond, and then spat.

'I can't take my guard force off the walls until I'm relieved by a tribune,' he explained, and I could see how his soldier's mind was struggling to balance the need to follow orders at all costs, with the very real problem that was spreading beyond the walls.

'The fires,' the centurion went on, 'they could be out of control by the time a tribune gets here. Take your men and do what you can. Dump your equipment here and go. We'll be behind you as soon we can.'

It doesn't do to hesitate in carrying out any order, but in this instance I had already come to the same conclusion as the officer, and I was dumping my shield and stripping my armour before the words had left his mouth. The young soldiers in my charge followed suit.

'Not your swords!' I told them. There were still screams in the town, and something inside my gut told me that there was more at work here than flame.

It was the position of the pillars of smoke, I realized. They were spread across the town. If this were an accident, then they would be raging outwards from one location. As it was, I could make out at least a half-dozen of the sooty columns rising menacingly beyond the wall.

I turned to the centurion to tell him, but he was gone. The man was long in the tooth; he must have realized the same thing.

'All ready?' I asked the wide-eyed faces that looked back at me.

I saw a couple swallow back their fear. The others stared like rabbits.

'Let's go.'

Panic.

There is no better word to describe the effects of fire than panic.

As we ran into streets beyond the fort, I could smell more than just the burning plaster and wood. I could hear more than the crackle and pop of flame. I could *smell* panic. I could *hear* fear. I saw it on the faces of children standing frozen. I saw it in the way adults shouted at one another as they dithered and delayed in taking action. I even saw it in the cats and rats that forgot their long-running war and united in fleeing an enemy that was more deadly than any other.

Using the nearest pillar of smoke as our guide, we rushed through the streets of slum housing. Here, non-citizens lived aside and atop one another in decrepit homes sitting on narrow and filthy streets. One of these proved to be a dead-end, and with no time to waste I ordered the soldiers up and over a low rooftop. For a few brief seconds, the added elevation carried the sound of crying and screaming and oaths and orders.

It carried the sound of panic.

It carried the sound of murder.

I found them in the street. Rounding a corner, I almost tripped over the two off-duty soldiers laid out like drunks, but it was not wine that ran red into the gutter.

'Draw your swords,' I ordered, and I heard steel pulled free of scabbards. I looked quickly for bloody footprints and trails, but saw nothing. Then the thick cloud of black smoke fought to regain my attention.

So did the screams.

The dead would have to wait.

We ran on.

We ran on, and I considered that I had been wrong. That what I was hearing and seeing were *not* the signs of panic.

They were of *terror*.

And perhaps fear *was* taking hold of the streets, but there were some who resisted the spread of the emotion that could be as deadly as disease, and as we arrived at the source of the nearest blaze I took in the dozen sweat-soaked civilians who were fighting with buckets of water to quench the flames. One section of the two-storey building was already lost, its structure gutted and visible like a blackened skeleton. Now the fight was to stop the fires spreading to the apartments that adjoined it.

'Gods,' I heard beside me. I followed the young soldier's eyes upwards.

There was a woman and two children in a window, a baby in her arms.

'Please!' she shouted to the civilian men in the street. 'Please!'

I realized what she intended to do: she wanted to throw the baby.

'I'll catch her!' a solid-looking man promised, and perhaps he would have done, but at the moment the woman went to toss her precious child into the arms of a stranger, a supports of the building cracked and splintered in the heat, and the whole edifice tilted to its side. Time seemed to slow as I saw the mother juggle the baby in her hands, her eyes and mouth stretched open in pure terror, and then the young life tumbled into the hungry flame below her.

I don't know if the baby screamed as it died. Nothing could be heard above the torment of its mother. Even the spitting and hissing of the fire seemed muted against her wails.

I turned to the men who had followed me, welcoming the distraction. 'You two, get us buckets. Kick down doors if you have to, just find buckets and get back here. Go!

'You! Get back to the fort and report on what you've seen. Run!

'The rest of you, form a chain with the civilians. They're using a fountain behind that building,' I told them, having seen red-faced women and children stagger from that direction with filled buckets and cooking pots. 'Go!'

I turned my eyes back to the scene. The civilians were doing their best, and now there were an extra seven sets of hands, but there was no escaping the truth that was in front of me – the flame would devour the upper apartments before we could beat back the fire. Smoke would choke the mother and her children to death, and then their bodies would be consumed.

'Where are you going?' a man shouted at me. The hair of his beard was singed.

I didn't answer, but used the wooden shutters of a window to climb on to the building beside the apartment. I was a floor too low, and separated by a yard-wide alleyway, but I thought I had a way to the family.

'Get me a ladder!' I shouted down. 'Quickly! A ladder! Go!'

The man with the singed beard quickly grasped my intention. 'We need a ladder! Who's got a ladder?' he called, running to find it as I assessed my plan. It was a good one, and by that, I mean that it was simple. I would rest the ladder across the narrow alleyway and against the slowly tilting building. I would climb it, and then haul myself up on to the rooftop. From there I could offer my arm to the window below. I was certain that I had the strength to pull the two young children free and on to the rooftop. From there I could put them on the ladder across the alley to the lower roof. The mother, well . . . she would want her children saved, of that I was sure.

'I've got the ladder!' the man shouted, and he passed it up, helped by another. 'Please get them!' he pleaded.

I met his eye, and gave him a look that I hoped would reassure him. With the screams of the woman and her children in my ears, and smoke choking my throat and stinging my eyes, I placed the ladder across the gap of the alleyway, and began to climb.

It was as I put my hands on to the rooftop that the building collapsed.

10

I awoke on my back. There was no flame, but I tasted soot and smoke in my throat. My eyes itched and scratched. I moved to sit up, and winced at a deep pain in my side and head.

'What happened?' I asked the man with the singed beard. He was kneeling by my side. All was quiet save for muted conversation between groups of people that I saw out of the corners of my sore eyes.

'The fire burned out the supporting timbers,' he told me, spitting dark fluid on to the dirt. 'Whole thing fell in on top of itself.'

The last that I remembered, I was about to haul myself on to the roof of that building. The man must have sensed my question – how was I not amongst the ruins?

'As it started to go you pushed off the wall and jumped back,' he explained. 'Like a cat, except that you didn't land on your feet.' There was no humour in his voice. I imagined that the people in the building had been known to him, and it was more than smoke that had made his eyes the brightest shade of red. 'You landed hard on the lower roof. I expected to find your head split.'

'It feels like it is,' I confessed, but my helmet had saved me. 'The family?'

I should never have asked the question. The answer was obvious, and I saw it drive a dagger of pain inside the man's heart.

'Thank you for trying though,' he told me as he left.

I pushed myself to my feet. I felt eyes upon me. It was the young soldiers of my century. They looked at me as ewes eye the sheepdog.

'Report.' I spoke to no one in particular.

The natural leader among them piped up. He was square-jawed and thick-set. 'Fire's out, section commander.'

I shook my head. 'I can see that. I mean what the fuck's happening in the rest of the town? Has the lad I sent as runner got back from the fort?'

'I don't know, section commander,' the soldier admitted. 'And no.'

I rubbed a hand over the back of my head. The skull felt intact, but my head was throbbing. I'd suffered hard hits to the head before – sometimes as a child who climbed too high in trees, sometimes as an adult who provoked fights in inns – and I knew that the most severe pain and consequences could come later. I did not want to lose consciousness again with this troop of green idiots as my guardians. The fact that I had woken to the care of the singed man spoke volumes as to the competency and confidence of the young men.

Still, they had followed me, and now they looked to me for orders. What would Marcus or Brutus do in such a situation? What would they say?

'Good work,' I told them, having no idea whether or not it was true. 'Now let's get back to camp.'

The gates were shut when we returned, but we were soon allowed in by the same old centurion who had sent us out. He eyed my dishevelled appearance, but made no comment on it.

'You put that fire out?' he asked me, jutting his vine cane in the direction of where a remnant of smoke hung lazily in the air.

'I think it put itself out, sir,' I admitted. 'Building collapsed, and the flames didn't make it across the alleyways.'

'Any idea what it was?'

I shook my head. 'Apartments and some kind of shop.'

'Excuse me, sir.' The square-jawed soldier in my charge spoke up. 'It was a baker's, sir.'

I bridled, and stared daggers at the man. I did not appreciate being made to look stupid in front of a superior. When we returned to the barracks, I'd put my fist through his stomach, the fat-headed prick.

'A baker's,' the centurion mused, as if trying to convince himself of something. 'So it could have been an accident . . .'

We both knew the flaw in that assumption. What chance was there of multiple accidents causing several fires across the town at the same time?

'Easy place to start a fire, sir,' I ventured. 'If someone had a mind to.'

The officer nodded. 'What's your name?'

'Legionary Corvus, sir.'

'Second of the Second, right?'

'Yes, sir.'

The man nodded. 'I had my lads put your kit by the wall.' He pointed. 'I've had a guard watching it, so it's all there. Report back to your century, Corvus. I expect that we're in for a long day.'

11

I collapsed on to my bunk like an empty wineskin, drained of everything that I had. I thought of the centurion at the west gate, and how he'd been wrong when he guessed that we were in for a long day.

We'd gone all night, too.

The light of dawn was creeping in through the bunk room's window now as the young men of my section dropped on to their beds with satisfied moans. Within seconds they were oblivious to the world. I wanted to fall into that insensible slumber myself, but my mind would not be still. It replayed the events of the day and night, and each blurred recollection birthed questions. Truly, I was at a lost as to what I had witnessed.

I could recall it easily enough. Upon returning to the century we had been thrown quickly into a makeshift task force sent out to tackle further blazes. We had gone from fire to fire, at times acting as part of a bucket-passing chain, at others as grim-faced sentinels to hold back crying and angry civilians – there were some parts of the town that simply could not be saved. Homes and businesses were pulled down to starve the flames of fuel. Some smaller districts were completely condemned. Need I tell you that these were the poorer neighbourhoods? Need I tell you that an entire cohort was dispatched to secure the splendid villas that sat unmolested on the town's highest hills?

But nobody said that life is fair. Certainly I had seen enough evidence of that in the past day. Entire families taken. Businesses and homes lost. Murder in the streets.

It was the murder that kept me awake now. The *why* of what I had seen. There was no doubting that the two off-duty soldiers I had come across had been killed intentionally: their throats had been opened into grotesque smiles. Violent death was a part of town life, but the coincidence of several fires occurring at once was already stretching my imagination. Murder atop of that? What was going on that I didn't know? What madness had gripped the town? And was it over now that the final embers had been extinguished? Two cohorts patrolled and guarded the settlement against any resurgence of flame or bloodshed. We would relieve them at noon. The air was thick with more than simply soot. There was confusion. Fear. Accusation.

'Bastard,' I growled, knowing that sleep would elude me.

And so, despite my aching muscles and throbbing skull, I swung my feet on to the cold floor and went in search of my friends, and answers.

By the light of the coming dawn, I found Priscus and Varo leaning against the short wall that was the head of our barrack block. There was no sign of any other man, and deep snores rang from inside the bunk rooms, punctuated by the occasional coughing fit of a soldier clearing soot from his lungs.

'What are you doing up?' I asked my comrades.

'The same as you, I imagine,' Priscus answered. 'You look like shit.'

I instinctively ran a hand over the back of my head. 'Feel worse.'

There had been no time to talk before; the century had hastily formed and run out into the chaos – those who had been drunk were soon sober, having puked wine over their mail and feet – and now I told my friends all that had occurred from the first moment I'd heard the trumpets and screams, to the moment I had come to stand with them and watch the rising disc of a blood-red sun.

'We saw bodies too,' Varo grunted, pawing at his scarred chin. 'And not dead from smoke. One had his guts hanging out.'

'Soldiers?'

'Civvies too.'

'What's going on?'

Varo shrugged his massive shoulders. Priscus kicked the dirt. 'Justus has been called to HQ, so maybe we'll find out.'

Justus was our centurion, and a thirst for knowledge explained why my two friends were waiting beside his quarters at the end of our block.

'Maybe Octavius knows.' Varo yawned. 'And that's why he can just sleep, the bastard.'

I smiled. Our comrade was a good soldier and a better friend, but he did not concern himself with such things as 'why'. For the three of us standing in the dawn, it was something that pulled and nagged and never stopped. It wasn't enough for us to simply react. We wanted to know the cause of our actions. We wanted to try and predict the next move in the game that was our life.

'You two can get some sleep if you want,' Priscus offered. 'I'll wake you up when Justus gets back.'

'I won't sleep.' I knew it. Varo echoed the sentiment.

And so we waited. We waited as the sun climbed above the mountains to perch dominant and abrasive above the town and valley. We waited as the air warmed, and the cool night's breeze died, to our discomfort. We waited as our eyelids – bright red and chafed with smoke – grew ever heavier. We waited and, eventually, we wished that we hadn't.

What we would have paid for a few more hours of blissful ignorance.

Centurion Justus was white when we saw him. There was the slightest tremble in his hands, and a look of almost wild disbelief in his eyes.

Never a man to mince words, it was Varo who spoke first. 'That bad, sir?' was all that he said, and I felt my throat begin to tighten.

The officer simply nodded, then looked at each of us in turn. I felt as though he was trying to remember our faces, as one does when a family member is on their deathbed, and all hope is lost.

'The auxiliaries have mutinied,' he told us simply. 'A hundred thousand of them.'

❧ 12 ❧

I had thought that I wanted war. Now that it had come in the form of a rebellion of a hundred thousand auxiliary soldiers, I was already recognizing myself a fool.

For a while, not one of us spoke. When words came, they fell hard and heavy like an executioner's sword. 'There's two and a half thousand of us,' said Priscus.

'Not great odds,' Varo replied, anxious to maintain a reputation as a fighter, and a diehard.

Justus shrugged. 'Not great.'

'Not great,' I agreed. What else was there to say? I might have been confident, I might have been cocky, but I was no idiot. Outnumbered forty to one? They could fight like children and still overwhelm us.

'How did this happen?' Priscus then asked.

'Does it matter?' I snapped. Only moments before, I had been so desperate for the 'why'. Now that I had it pointed at my throat, my curiosity was giving way to fatalism.

'It matters,' Priscus insisted. 'How did this come about, sir?' he asked our centurion.

Justus rubbed a hand over his jagged face. He looked whipped from the news, a condemned man in the arena, but retelling what he had learned in the legion headquarters seemed to give him some sense of purpose and energy. I imagine that, as the storyteller, he momentarily felt disconnected from the entire situation, forgetting for a few blissful seconds that he was the one at the sharp end.

'They were being raised for Tiberius's campaign,' Justus began. 'A hundred thousand light infantry and cavalry to accompany him across the Danube. Only, I suppose, the general had forgotten one thing. This is a new province. Maybe Tiberius has a short memory, but the locals don't. It's less than twenty years since the last war here. You were there, weren't you, Priscus?'

'I caught the end of it,' the veteran replied.

'So you remember what happened then?'

Priscus took a deep inhalation of breath. Clearly, the cause of revolt was now becoming clear to him. 'We sold their young men into slavery,' he said quietly.

Justus nodded, and then spat. 'Seemed like a good idea at the time, didn't it?'

'Funny how a family holds a grudge when you take their sons and brothers and sell them off as animals,' I said.

'It's a part of war.' Varo shrugged, almost affronted that the defeated side should take it so personally.

'Of course it is,' Justus agreed. 'But then so is revenge.'

We let those words sink in for a moment. My head still throbbed from my injury. My mouth was dry, and I tried to tell myself it was from a day of fighting fires, not fear.

'So that's what it's all about?' I asked the men. 'Revenge?'

Justus worked his tongue around his gums, then sucked on a tooth. 'Revenge. Power. Choice.'

'Choice?'

'Rumour mill says that the biggest tribe involved in all this are the Daesitatae. Their leader's called Bato, and he put forward to the Dalmatians a simple choice, apparently.

He said, "We're going to fight a war, one way or another. Do you want to fight to expand Rome's borders, or for your own homes?"'

There wasn't much any of us could say to that, except: 'How didn't we see this coming?'

No one had any answer for Priscus. Varo looked at the mountains, as if expecting the enemy to swarm over them at any moment.

'Did he really say that?' he asked Justus.

The centurion nodded. 'A couple of Romans who were there to oversee the raising of the auxiliaries saw the writing on the wall, and got out before heads began to roll.'

'I imagine the rest of the liaison officers are dead?' Priscus asked.

'A good handful, military and civil. There's more, too.' Justus grimaced. 'There was a settlement of retired veterans in the area. They'd been given farmland around there after they saw out their service.'

I didn't need to be told how this story would end. Justus spelt it out anyway.

'They've been butchered to a man.'

'So what now?' Priscus finally broke the silence. 'We attack? We fall back?'

Justus shook his head.

'The massacre of the veterans is the last enemy action that we know about,' the centurion confided. 'We've dispatched cavalry scouts into the plains, but for the mountains . . .'

He let his voice trail away. I watched as Priscus's lips tightened in near pain, and Varo's pulled into a sickly smile.

'Let me guess,' the big man snorted, 'your next sentence contains the word *volunteer.*'

Our officer said nothing. Silence acknowledged the truth of Varo's words. Volunteers to go into mountains that could kill a man through thirst and fatigue. That harboured murderers, brigands and wild beasts. And now, perhaps, were also refuge to an army of well-armed rebels.

I spoke. 'I'll go.'

What other choice was there?

I had begged for war since the moment I had joined the legion. Now was the time to fulfil that ambition, however bleak my prospects of survival.

'I'll go,' I said again, meeting my centurion's eye.

'First Cohort's sending men today.t men out already.' The veteran shrugged, recognizing a dead man walking. 'You've got a day to reconsider.'

I shook my head. 'I'll go,' I said, unblinking. 'I want this.'

They were the truest words I had ever spoken.

Later that day, a patrol went up into the mountains.

One man came back.

He died before he could tell us what happened.

❧ 13 ❦

I didn't know much about war, but one thing I was learning quickly was that pillars of smoke were not a good thing to see. From my vantage in the mountains, I saw them reach across the landscape like tendrils stretching upwards from a verdant sea floor.

Another lesson I had been taught was that words mattered. When our cohort had been gathered together before being marched towards the nearest mountain range, our commander had gone to pains to make us understand that this was a simple uprising. We were to refer to it as a local insurgency, and not a war. The troublemakers that had started fires and murdered soldiers should be thought of in the same vein as brigands, and thieves. They were criminals, and no army.

'A hundred thousand criminals still sounds like an army to me,' Varo had snorted as were dismissed.

I wished the big man and his solid presence was with me now, but I was alone with my section. I had been hasty in volunteering myself for scouting duty, giving little thought to the implications it would have for the seven men beneath my command. I had expected – I had *wanted* – to seek out the enemy alone, but Centurion Justus would have none of it, and so my section scaled a ridge ahead and to the left of where the century followed in the lower ground. Justus had also refused my suggestion that we leave our heavy kit with the main body of troops, and so we sweated and swore as we followed the narrow trail between rock and scree. I had long since tied my helmet off on my equipment, and it was all I could do to keep my gaze up and searching ahead for ambush, sun and fatigue beating my head down relentlessly.

I turned to look back at my seven charges. None had questioned my choice of route, or any other order. I knew there was a reason for that blind obedience other than their shortage of breath: they were scared of me. They knew of my reputation. I had never beaten a man under my command, but that was not out of any sensibility. The young soldiers I had led in the past had simply had the good sense to keep their mouths shut.

'We'll rest here,' I told them, seeing a flash of relief pass over their faces.

'Vitus. Severus. Take watch front and back,' I ordered. They were the fittest of the seven, and I trusted them to keep a lookout while the others gathered their breath and gulped from skins. Whether they carried wine or water, I did not care. So long as they kept up. So long as they would fight.

I sat, grimacing as the hard edges of the ridge dug into my backside. There really was no comfortable way to sit in these jagged mountains, but I forbade my men to sit on their shields – who knew how that accumulated strain would affect their defence in battle? I didn't want to die because someone's arse was too precious to sit on.

I looked into the distance, and thought of Marcus. Where was he now? Surely Tiberius could not continue with his planned war? Surely he – and my greatest friend – would be returning with haste to the land that had burst into flame at their backs?

'Section commander?' one of the young men ventured carefully. His nickname was Gums, because that was mostly all that was in his mouth. He'd told me that his teeth had been kicked out by a horse, and I'd told him that I didn't give a shit. He hadn't tried to speak to me much after that, and now I could hear the nervous edge to his wet words.

'What?' I growled.

Gums didn't speak. He just pointed. I followed the finger, and twisted to look over my shoulder.

More smoke. And close.

'Shit.'

It was a farm, or at least it had been. I didn't know if I was supposed to investigate such things, but the burning buildings weren't far. It seemed like the right thing to drop down the hillside, and to approach the gutted buildings.

I was doubting that now.

It was the smell that did it. Looking at the four blackened corpses, I felt nothing. Not even when Gums pointed out that they were holding each other, a final act of love and desperation.

No. It was the smell. It was the smell of roast chicken, and as we had approached the smoking ruins of what had been a family's life, I had embraced that smell, and pictured food and drink with my friends. My stomach had rumbled at the thought, and I had hoped that maybe some animals had been spared the destruction so that we might spit one on the end of a javelin.

I hadn't thought that it would be the parents and their two young children that would smell so good. As soon as

I realized what had caused my hunger, my stomach turned to concrete.

'Do we bury them, section commander?' someone asked. I don't know who – most of my section sounded the same, young and bleating – and I made no reply. I simply looked into the mountains, then put a hand on the shoulder of the nearest body, and felt at the heat.

'They can't be too far from here,' I told my section, 'the corpse is warm. Be vigilant.'

As soon as I said the words, I realized how stupid they sounded. My section's eyeballs were bulging from their sockets. Knuckles were white where they gripped their javelins. They could not have been more alert.

'Do we bury them, section commander?' the soldier asked again.

I turned to face him. He was short, and his helmet was too big for him. Beneath the rim, his face was red from exertion and stress.

'Do you see any tools with us, Spurius?' I asked.

He did not. We would not be digging marching camps into the stone of the mountain. Shield and javelin would be our defence. The previous night, Justus had wisely positioned us in an outcrop of rock, nature providing us with a formidable rampart. There was no shortage of such bastions in the Pannonian mountains.

'It just feels wrong to leave them like that,' the well-intentioned youth ventured.

I said nothing. My eyes had been drawn to a new atrocity.

'They killed the dogs,' Gums said angrily.

Of course they had.
But who were they killers?
And where were they now?

I stood beside my comrades. No one spoke a word as we watched the red disc of the sun slide behind the mountains to the west, the air about us cast into a dusty orange glow.

'This job has its perks.' Octavius spoke up, breaking our trance. No man disagreed with him.

I had rejoined my century as dusk was threatening the mountaintops and reported on what I had seen to Centurion Justus, who approved of my investigating the smoke.

'We're here to find rebels,' the man had told me, wiping a day's sweat from his brow. 'If we follow enough smoke and bodies, we'll find them eventually.'

I was about to salute and take my leave, but the officer wasn't done with me. 'There's a small village at the end of this little valley. Varo's section found it. It's still intact – and there's people there.' He looked at me as if that was important, then became irritated that I did not grasp the implication.

'It means they're on the insurgents' side,' my centurion said definitively. 'Why else would their homes be standing when there're fires all over the horizon?'

I'd had no answer. Only one question.

'Will we have someone to fight, sir?'

Justus had smiled. He was as eager for blood as I was.

'We'll find our enemy, Corvus. Tomorrow, we'll find them.'

❧ 14 ❧

We came in the dark.

There were three sections of us, with Centurion Justus at our head. The rest other fifty men of the century – Octavius and Priscus with them – had taken blocking positions on the overlooking ridges and across the trails that led out of the mountain pass.

Our leader's words were simple, and ominous: 'Nobody gets out.'

It was a dog that first noted our approach through the pre-dawn gloom. Its bark was savage and caustic. Then it was nothing but a whine. After a few seconds of that, all was silent again but for stumbled steps, and the bump of shield and body.

'Did someone kill the dog?' a young voice whispered.

'Shut your fucking mouth,' I snarled as quietly as I could.

I knew the dog's assassin. Varo had gone ahead of us with a few trusted veterans. They were stripped of all equipment but their swords. They were to find sentries, and silence them. I envied their task. I carried my shield in one hand, javelin in the other. The cheek-plates of my helmet chafed my face. The lip of the brow rubbed against my forehead. It was not a thing of comfort, but perhaps, in the coming moments, it would save my life.

'Wall,' I heard passed quietly from mouth to mouth in the darkness. 'Form on the wall.'

I came to it in a moment. It was a pathetic structure, no higher than my waist. Good enough for keeping out pests, maybe, and keeping in a few sheep. No good against the soldiers who stalked the night.

I looked to the left and right of me, seeing the silhouettes of two men of my section. 'Stay low,' I whispered.

They crouched. My eyes looked on into the darkness. Into a void that I knew held homes of stone, and thatch. And, maybe, our enemy.

We waited.

The stillness of dawn in the mountains was absolute. Atop the nearest ridges, a pale light appeared and began to spread downwards like mercury. The village below was still shrouded in shadow. Behind the low wall, soldiers watched, and waited.

The first dark shape that I saw was the dog. At first I thought it was a rock, but as dawn crept closer, its features grew clearer. Its head lay almost flat back against its spine. Varo and his men had taken no chances. The beast was nearly decapitated.

Slowly, as if cloth were pressed against my eyes, I began to make out more shapes. They were low and rectangular, built from the same stone that surrounded us. I saw four of them, but the gloom made it hard to tell. I wondered whom they housed. Whom they would disgorge. The air was still, and promised no violence, but I thought back to the skirmish five years ago. How a seemingly deserted hamlet had turned into a place of death. How it had surprised us all. How it had surprised *me,* and led to the crippling of Brutus, and the death of Fano.

Not today. Today I would expect death at every turn. Today I would be prepared to give it freely. All that mattered was the safety of my friends, and my selfish desire to be lost in the lust of combat.

I looked to the left and right of me, ready to use the tip of my javelin to rouse a weary soldier. I needn't have worried. The young troops sat poised like hares with the scent of wolf in their nostrils. Their muscles were tight, senses alert. They were ready to spring forward. They were ready to be led.

I felt rather than saw the dark shape that made its way along the wall. Then, he was beside me. Centurion Justus.

'The one on the far left's yours,' he told me, meaning one of the dwellings. 'Let's go.'

It was time.

We crept out over the wall.

I stepped as though I was walking on a thinly iced river, each precious footfall carrying the potential to end my life. My mind told me that I was quiet, but my heart beat faster and told me that I was crashing towards the hut like an elephant. Behind me, I felt the presence of three men of my section. The other four were going to their own hut. We had discussed how we would conduct ourselves the night before, and our plan was simple.

Surprise the enemy.

Kill the enemy.

We reached the hut. There was no door in the entrance, simply a mass of heavy sacking. I waited against the wall, and heard the sound of soft snoring from within. I looked back to where we had come from. Fifty yards away, the low wall and the dead dog were becoming clearly visible, one section of men studded along its length as a reserve. I looked at each of the four huts, and saw the same thing at each – a knot of Roman soldiers tight-faced with anticipation. My centurion caught my eye, and nodded, the movement exaggerated by the crest on his helmet. I looked at Gums beside me, and motioned to our shields. Gently, we placed them against the stone of the hut – they would be nothing but an encumbrance for what was to come.

Then, after a final glance at our officer, I held my breath in my chest, took hold of the cloth sacking of the doorway, and pulled it quickly aside.

The warmth and smell of half a dozen sleeping figures hit me immediately. I tried to pull the sacking totally free of its hanging place to clear a killing lane, but the material snagged on my javelin, and immediately I went from a soldier committed a fluid and perfect operation, to becoming as trapped and useless as a gladiator caught in the fishing net of a retiarius.

'Bastard!' I blurted from frustration. 'Gums, push through!'

The young soldier barged by me as I thrashed and swore, expecting at any moment to be gaffed like a netted trout. Only a few seconds had passed since my last glance at Centurion Justus, but now the high-pitched screams of women and children shattered what had been left of the night.

'Shut up!' I heard Gums scream.

Somehow, at that moment, I wrenched myself free of my self-imposed captivity and stumbled fully into the hut. The motion was violent and I tripped. I saw a blur of startled and terrorized faces, and then I was on the floor.

'Are you hurt?' I heard Gums shout at me.

Was I hurt?

I pushed myself on to my hands and knees, rage pounding in my temples that my actions had been so ignoble. So laughable.

Was I fucking hurt?

'I'm fine!' I snapped, and looked at the cowering figures that had pushed themselves into the corner of the hut like bleating sheep.

'Shut the fuck up!' I yelled at them, further enraged.

Their crying redoubled, and I cursed fate. There was no one to fight in here. There were nothing but women and their disgusting snot-faced children. Not for a moment did I consider that, had there been one half-capable fighter in the room, I would have been found dead and tangled in the door's sacking by my friends.

'Get them outside,' I growled.

The point of Gums's shaking javelin did the rest, and I stepped outside to a valley full of shrieks.

'Shut up!' someone else was shouting. 'Shut up!'

They wouldn't.

They screeched. They cried. They begged. There were two dozen of them, maybe more. Women. Children. A handful of trembling old men. I saw one of these try to stand in supplication. A fist sent him to the ground.

Surrounded by the wolves of the legion, the press of bodies formed a pathetic huddle on the cold earth.

'Double-check the huts,' Justus ordered. 'The rebels must be hiding.'

'Either that or they slipped away,' a veteran agreed, but I had faith in the positioning of our blocking forces, and there was no sound of a clash from higher in the valley.

'They must be hiding,' I repeated to my men. 'Get back in and search the hut. Pull it apart. Go.'

The dwellings of the terrified villagers were small and spartan. It wasn't long before we knew that our empty hands would remain that way.

Justus cursed, and balled his fists. I met Varo's eyes for the first time that morning. He looked angry, and gave a sad shake of his head.

We'd missed them.

'Not a single fighting-age male, sir,' I said , approaching my centurion.

A thought of the villagers' possible innocence entered my mind. I had been so eager to fight that I had not entertained the notion that this village had been anything other than a base for insurgents. Now, however, the truth seemed to be revealing itself. These were women, children and old men. There were no rebels here. I said as much to my commander.

'Exactly.' Justus smiled sickly. 'They've already gone. They're probably the ones that burned that farm yesterday.'

He looked at the elderly men, then. One of them met his gaze, marking himself out as the village elder. Justus motioned him to his feet.

'Where are all your young men?' Justus asked in Latin.

The man shrugged apologetically. It was no surprise that he didn't speak the Roman tongue. Even now that they were under the Empire, there was little need for it in the mountains.

'I'm from the coast, sir,' I offered my centurion. 'I think I'll have enough of a common tongue to get by.'

Justus shrugged, and I took that as my permission to continue.

'Where are your young men?' I asked in the language I had learned when playing on the streets of Iader.

'Gone to war.' The elder spoke quickly. 'For Rome.'

I told Justus as much.

The officer thought on it a moment; then he stared at the elder in contempt. 'Which means they're now rebels.' The man could not understand the words, but he shrank back at the tone in which they were delivered. 'Ask him if he knows that they have become enemies of Rome.'

I did.

He didn't.

'Sir!' a soldier of Varo's section then called out. 'Sir, over here!'

Justus moved. I followed.

The inquisitive soldier had been searching the grounds beyond the huts. Beneath the earth, hidden underneath turf-coated slats of wood, he had found a store of barrels. Varo prised them open. Grain. Salted meat. Wine.

'Planning a party?' Justus asked the elder.

There was no need for a translation. The man's eyes had grown fearful when the store was discovered. A punch from Justus was all that was needed to convince him that things were about to turn ugly.

'Please,' the elder said to me. 'We have to hide our stores. We need them to survive the winter!'

'Why would you hide them?' Justus spat back as I translated.

'Because the rebels will take them,' the man admitted.

Justus sneered with triumph. 'So you do know about the revolt?'

The old man was trapped, and he knew it.

'They came demanding our sons. They came demanding our supplies. Our boys had already left to go to war for Rome. The food we had hidden when they left.'

'Why?'

'Because we have no one to protect it.'

He was right about that.

'Those supplies belong to Rome.' Justus smirked, turning to find a runner. 'Call in the other sections. We're going to load up here, and return to base.'

The runner saluted, and took off.

Again the old man didn't recognize the words, but comprehended every one.

'Please,' he tried with me, 'we will starve.'

Justus asked me what he said. I told him. He asked that I translate his reply. As I did, an ugly smile played out over the centurion's face.

I didn't consider the words at the time. I didn't consider that I was delivering a sentence on the villagers' lives. I simply listened to my commander's words, and repeated them.

'You won't starve,' I said on behalf of a great empire. 'As you are all enemies of Rome, you will be taken as slaves.'

The man blinked several times before the dreadful word fell from his mouth. '*Slaves?*'

I nodded, feeling neither guilt nor pleasure in the fact.

'But . . . but we are subjects of Rome! Loyal subjects! Our sons serve Rome!'

Justus looked at me to translate. I shrugged. The centurion pushed me for an answer. I gave it.

'Loyal subjects?' he scoffed, turning to shout at the man. 'This province is in rebellion! Your sons turned on Rome! Everywhere there is burning, and looting, and rape, and killing, but your village sits pretty, when not even two miles from here a Roman farm and a Roman family burned!'

I had no idea if the farm I had discovered had been Roman, but Justus had made that decision for himself, and now it seemed he wanted vengeance for it. Before the elder could protest, Justus grabbed the man's white hair in one hand, and drove his blade into his stomach.

I thought the women and children had been screaming before.

I was wrong.

❧ 15 ❦

Justus killed the other men within moments of the first. Only one put up any resistance. He lost a few fingers trying to parry my centurion's blade; then his throat was nicked open and he bled into the soil of his village.

More accurately, what *had* been his village.

Justus ordered us to pull apart the homes, and to cast the rocks down the nearest slope. It was breathless work, and a welcome distraction from the pitiful wailing of the women.

'I wish they'd shut up,' Varo grumbled. 'Justus has said they're not to be raped. What more do they want?'

I said nothing, and bent to pick up another part of what had been a home. Behind me, the chorus of torment wore on.

I'd like to say that those screams broke my heart. I'd like to say that the deaths of the old men pained me.

But they didn't.

'You really think they're supporting the rebels, sir?' I'd asked my centurion as he wiped his blade clean.

'Saw it in the last war,' the man confirmed, as calm as if he'd just gutted a basket of fish. 'Half of my century was killed the last time these bastards rose up, Corvus. I was just a legionary, then. I couldn't do much about it except watch my friends die.'

He paused for a moment. I did not doubt that he was seeing those deaths played out before his eyes.

'Things are going to be different this time,' he finally continued, and I realized the words were as much for his own ears as mine. 'I'm going to keep my boys safe, no matter what it takes.' He patted me on the shoulder, and stepped over the bodies of the dead men in the dirt.

Alone, I looked at their faces. Drained of blood, their skin was as white as their hair. Kneeling beside the dead and rocking with grief, daughters and wives dripped tears and spoke breathless farewells.

So this was war.

Loaded with supplies and shepherding the slaves, it took us two days to make our way back to the fort.

'Money for the slaves will be split between the century,' Justus had promised.

'Better put it straight into our funeral funds,' Octavius joked darkly. He was referring to the trust that each soldier was required to pay into in order to cover the increasingly likely eventuality that he would die in the service of Rome. Then he smiled. 'If the whole legion gets wiped out,' he asked, 'who gets the pot?'

'Whoever kills us, you dickhead.' Varo snorted. 'It's a fucking joke we have to pay into it anyway. If we do die in the army, the least they should do is shoulder the bill.'

'Digging a hole big enough for your fat arse?' Octavius laughed. 'You'd bankrupt the Empire.'

Varo swung a friendly punch at Octavius. Despite the futility of our patrol into the mountains, we were in good spirits. We were alive, for one thing, and we had the prospect of forthcoming monies from the sale of the slaves. I did not consider that the wine the money bought would come at the price of someone else's misery. That mothers would be separated from their children. That the good-looking would be raped by the wealthy, and the ugly would be playthings for the ranks. Perhaps even by the end of that first day back in the fort they would be owned and on their backs. Brothels were always keen to acquire new attractions, and no one fucks harder or more often than a soldier who knows that his life is likely measured in days.

No, I did not consider it then. None of it. I suppose that I knew, but I did not want to *know*. Better for me to concentrate on my own loss.

'I wanted a fight,' I told my friends.

'For the gods' sake' – Priscus shook his head – 'please lose that attitude before we go to the inn. I'd actually like to finish a drink before getting another stool smashed over my back.'

'You're not disappointed?' I asked the veteran among us.

He laughed. There was some pity in there. The way a grandmother looks at an eight-year-old child who claims that he's heartbroken, and will never recover. 'I'm not disappointed.' Priscus spoke patiently. 'We went into the mountains. We came back.'

'The enemy are still out there.'

'Exactly. So let's be grateful. Personally, I want to enjoy my time with such esteemed gentlemen before we go back to sweating and staggering all over the mountains. Varo?'

'Well, *personally*, I'd like to go bury myself in something hot and wet.'

'You're a regular Virgil, you.' Octavius shook his head. 'But some female company would be nice. Corvus?'

I kept silent. Octavius laughed.

'Of course not. No wonder your section always look so scared.'

I was about to slap him around the head when a young soldier ran over to us, and halted nervously.

'What?' Varo growled.

'Section commanders, Centurion Justus wants you to report to him.'

'Why?' the big man asked, and the youngster half stepped back as if evading a sword's bite.

'Orders, section commander,' he said.

It was Varo's grimacing face that forced the extra words from the runner.

'The centurion . . . he doesn't look happy.'

Priscus rapped his knuckles on the wooden door of our centurion's quarters.

'Come in.'

We entered into the open space that served as Justus's office. Running a century required administration; skill in battle was not the only attribute needed to become a leader of men. I looked around, and saw that our century's optio and the four other section commanders were all present. Octavius and I were the youngest in the room. The older veterans were all pushing towards the end of their enlistments, faces hard, skin tanned and tight. I had as little to do with them as I did the men of my own section, but only because a man can only have so many friends. There was no bad blood in the century, just an underlying sense of respect.

I felt that towards Justus now. I had considered his words in the village, and found no fault with them. Better to kill a dozen strangers than to lose one of our own. Better to kill a thousand than to lose one of my closest friends. Centurion Justus had seen war – I hadn't – and in that moment I'd decided that I had to trust him. The odds were already stacked against us, I knew. We just didn't know how badly.

Justus sought to change that.

'I've been to see the cohort commander,' he began, his arms folded, eyes passing over each of us. 'He's filled me in on the situation with the . . . insurgency.'

I could see that the word didn't fit well with him. I soon understood why.

'The legion commander sent out a tribune to speak with the rebels, and to give them a chance to change their minds. He hasn't come back, so you can guess how that went.'

No one spoke. I imagine each man was doing the same thing I was – picturing the inevitable slow death of a brave man.

'The cavalry scouts have been busy,' Justus went on, 'and so we at least have an idea of what the bastards are up to.

'They've split their number into three forces. The first, with the bulk of their strength, seems content to sit around the marshalling grounds where all this started.'

That was something at least. The marshalling grounds were out of striking distance from our fort. If they were to move, we could expect fair warning.

'The second force is striking east,' Justus informed us, 'towards Macedonia.'

Macedonia had been a Roman province for 150 years. I doubted the people there would rise as the newly minted subjects of this region had done, and yet . . .

'That province will have been stripped for Tiberius's army, boss?' Priscus guessed, mirroring my own thoughts.

Justus nodded.

'The general's heading back here, boys. The invasion across the Danube's off, in case you hadn't seen that coming. We've made some kind of peace treaty with King Marabodus, so Tiberius and his forces are making best speed towards us.'

No one smiled at that news. With the way things were panning out, best speed would not be good enough, and everyone knew it.

Justus shrugged. 'What's left of the forces in Macedonia are going to have to look after themselves.'

'And the third column, sir?' one of the veteran section commanders asked, his jaw twitching.

'They're heading for Salona'

Justus let the words sink in. Salona was the capital of the region in which we stood. It was positioned centrally on the coast, and was home to thousands of Roman civilians.

'Salona's got good walls,' Priscus offered.

'And warning,' another man added.

Our centurion shrugged again. 'Last we heard, Salona was prepared.'

There was a defeatist edge in the words that I could not place. Priscus heard it too.

'Boss, is there something else . . .?'

Justus gave the old head an ironic smile. 'You know war, Priscus. Things can always get worse.'

We waited to hear how that could be so. Justus didn't drag out our pain.

'The Pannonian auxiliaries have decided to follow the Dalmatians' example, lads.' He breathed out heavily. 'Another hundred thousand troops just came into this war, and they're on the wrong side.'

The silence held for a long time. It was heavy, a thick grey cloud on the horizon. We all knew what was coming.

'Cunts,' Varo finally uttered.

'Cunts,' Justus agreed. 'They're not an immediate threat to us, as they've been gathering to the north-west of here. For now, we don't know of any force that's approaching this fort.'

The words should have given us solace, but they filled me with nothing but rage. All this war, and I was still on the outside looking in.

'Surely we have to march, sir?' I asked forcefully.

The old sweats looked my way. There was only a little contempt in their stares. They knew that I meant well. That I simply didn't *know*.

'The Governor of Moesia's marching out to meet this new threat,' Justus explained. 'The honour of defeating the Pannonian rebels will fall to him.'

If there were irony in the words, I didn't hear it. My second question was already coming out of my mouth. 'Then what do we do, sir?'

The centurion looked at me as if I were an impatient child. I suppose that I was.

'We wait, Corvus. We wait.'

❧ 16 ❧

We waited.

With the province overrun by enemies we were confined to camp, but we were not idle. Watches were doubled, and we spent many hours on the walls, our eyes on the surrounding hillsides, looking nervously for any approach of the enemy. Sweat-soaked riders and their steeds came crashing back and forth through the fort's gates, but what news they took and brought was kept within the headquarters building.

'That's bad,' Varo guessed. 'They'd be shouting it from the mountaintops if it was good news.'

When we were not on watch or sleeping, Centurion Justus took the chance to drill the century, and we practised the basics of close-quarter battle, the daily bread of the heavy infantry. We practised changing from one formation to another without allowing gaps to open in our ranks. We practised sword drill. We practised shield drill. We practised the advance. We practised holding in place. We practised retreat. We practised until we saw the moves when we closed our eyes. Saw the cut and parry as we slept.

'Justus is a good officer.' Priscus spoke fondly. 'He's not leaving anything to chance.'

Varo had smirked when he heard that. 'Few days' extra drill should even the odds a bit.' Then he chuckled to himself. 'What were they before? Hundred to one?'

It was a dark joke, and it masked a fear that many could not hide. For some in the ranks, however, the sheer staggering size of the forces ranged against us was almost beyond comprehension, and as such, held no terror. I noted that half of my section fidgeted, tossed and turned in their sleep. The others slept like babes. I would come to learn that ignorance is a potent form of courage.

Until then, we waited.

And on the fifth day, they came.

There were a dozen of them, I was told, mounted troopers who had ridden through the fort's gates with such speed that alert centurions had feared the worst, and turned their men out into the night to form up, and to prepare to receive the enemy.

No one had expected good news.

'The Governor of Moesia has beaten a rebel army!' Justus announced, his smiling face open and beaming in the torchlight.

What else would we do but cheer?

We should have waited until he finished.

'Governor Severus has won an important victory,' our centurion went on, 'but not annihilated the enemy.'

For a moment, I envied the men who had stood in the front ranks of that army and spilled blood in combat.

'There's more,' Justus went on. 'The column that marched on Salona has been halted at the city's walls, and the enemy have taken heavy casualties!'

Another cheer. Another moment too soon.

'One column halted and another force badly beaten,' Justus concluded. 'The odds are still in the enemy's favour, men. We still have a lot ahead of us.' He looked over the ranks. Whatever he saw, he liked. He smiled. 'As we're already up, we may as well drill.'

I too grinned in the darkness. In Justus, I recognized a man who was as hungry to face the enemy as I was. He reminded me in many ways of Marcus. A professional. A leader. He just lacked the good looks, and the shining need for glory.

He drilled us past dawn. Pace by pace, we practised the dance of death's machinery. So engaged, we were unaware of the second group of riders that arrived mere hours after the first. We were unaware that they brought news that Moesia was being raided by the Dacians and Sarmatians, and that Governor Severus had turned back his army to face this new threat. We were unaware that the Pannonian and Dalmatian generals had now seen their true opportunity. An opportunity not only to end a war, but an *empire*.

All we knew was that the garrison was hastily assembled at noon, and that the eyes of the staff officers were wide, their fidgeting manner that of startled horses.

They were panicked.

'This can't be good,' Varo warned again, using his height to look above the helmeted ranks around him, and at the assembled force of half a legion.

When the gaunt, hook-nosed figure of our legate arrived to speak, my stomach twisted into knots of dread, anticipation and excitement.

The stern man spoke simply. 'Twenty thousand of the enemy are marching on Italy. And we have to stop them.'

↬ 17 ↫

We were the two and a half thousand men of half a legion. *They* were twenty thousand Dalmatian auxiliaries trained and equipped for war by the very Empire they now threatened.

'Look on the bright side,' Octavius said to me as we trod heavily back to our barracks. 'We've gone from odds of a hundred to one, to twentyten, and we haven't even had to get dirty.'

I didn't laugh. I didn't smile.

I had what I wanted at last. Combat. Battle. I would lose myself in the clash. I would die in it.

I expected that we all would.

'What the fuck is he doing here?' Varo asked, his thick brow knotted.

I followed the lump's surprised eyes.

Brutus.

Dressed for war.

'I don't know why I'm shocked,' Priscus said, shaking his old comrade's good hand, and taking in the sight of Brutus once again in uniform, and under arms and armour.

'I don't remember you looking this fat.' Octavius grinned. 'You were hiding a few chins under that beard, eh?'

He was exaggerating, but Brutus was not the strong and vital man he had once been. His left arm was crippled, his shoulders no longer a thick slab of rock.

'Want to tell us what this is?' Varo asked. He tried to be gentle, but even so, I saw Brutus bridle a little at the words.

'What do you think, lump head?'

'It looks like you've forgotten you're a civvie,' Varo said. 'How the fuck did you hear about what's happening, anyway?'

'Who are you talking to, Varo?' Brutus shrugged, his useless arm making giving the motion a tragic quality. 'I have friends that tell me things.'

I don't know if those words were supposed to land a blow, but I saw them strike Varo nonetheless. Somehow, the man seemed to shrink a foot in height. I think we all did.

'Justus has been drilling us day and night...' Priscus tried. 'It's not that we wouldn't have told you.'

'I didn't mean it like that.'

'Still . . .'

There was silence for a moment. I looked at Brutus's useless shield arm. He looked at the others. They looked at the dirt.

Was I the one that had to say it?

You can't hold a shield, Brutus.

Because of me.

I held my silence.

Varo spat on the floor. 'Now's not the day to get yourself killed, mate.'

This time, Brutus grinned. There was a sign of his old self for a moment. A man tipped to one day carry an eagle.

'I think our choice in that matter's been taken away, comrades. They outnumber us soI think our choice in that matter's been taken away, comrades. They outnumber us something like eighttwenty to one, don't theythey?'

'The ones coming tomorrow do,' Octavius replied, acknowledging the fact that, should by some miracle we survive the coming rain of blood, then we were only one step into the storm.

Brutus knew it. 'So my choice is to die on the field, or to wait for them to come to my home, and die watching as Lulmire is raped in front of me? Maybe, if we're lucky, they'll get carried away and simply burn the town before they loot. That's what awaits us, boys. Are you really going to tell me that I can't die in battle?'

I could see that Priscus was trying not to look at Brutus's limp arm.

He failed.

'It's not up to us,' he tried gently.

'It's not,' Brutus agreed, turning towards Centurion Justus's quarters. 'But I thought you'd be glad to see me.'

'We are, you dickhead.' Varo grunted.

Brutus said nothing as he walked away.

'He's in a great mood,' Octavius said, folding his arms.

Varo clapped his friend on the shoulder. 'Why wouldn't he be? Nothing puts a smile on your face like being a dead man walking.'

'It's not that.' I spoke up, certain, yet surprising myself.

The eyes of my comrades turned towards me. 'It's Lulmire,' I said confidently. 'He knows that nothing he does can protect her – not even dying – and that's a fate worse than anything he'll find on the battlefield.'

I didn't tell my comrades how I knew that.

They didn't ask.

Instead, we took our leave of each other in silence, and went to ready our sections for battle.

That afternoon was spent preparing for combat. It just wasn't the kind of preparation I expected.

The century was spread inside and out of our barrack block, each man scrubbing at the metal of his armour using ash from a wood fire and wet rags.

'I didn't realize looking pretty was so important for fighting,' I grumbled.

'Got something better to do?' Varo asked me.

'Sleep.'

'You can sleep when you're dead.'

'Why wait? Tomorrow's going to be a long day. I want to be ready.'

'You *hope* it'll be a long day,' Varo corrected.

'Either way, I don't see why we're wasting our time scrubbing armour like we're about to march through Rome.'

'There's a couple of reasons,' Priscus explained, examining the gleaming greaves that would protect his shins, and which I had no doubt would be dull with dust and dirt as soon as our half-legion marched for the battlefield. 'First, we're professional soldiers.'

'So are they,' I butted in, but Priscus shook his head.

'They were raised to be auxiliaries, and they've had some training, but that doesn't make them professional. We've got people in this legion whose business has been killing for more than twenty years. Half the legion has served ten or more. There's only going to be one set of professionals on the battlefield, Corvus, and it will be us.'

I conceded the point with a grunt.

'Secondly,' the old sweat went on, 'the enemy *know* that they're the amateurs in this. When they take the field, and they see the packed ranks of two and a half thousand heavy infantry, the sun shining from our weapons and our armour, what do you think they'll see?'

I didn't answer, and so he did.

'They'll see the legions that beat their fathers and uncles in the last war. They'll see the soldiers of Augustus, Caesar and Scipio. They'll see the greatest killing machine the world has ever known, *and they'll fucking shit themselves.*'

I wasn't used to seeing Priscus so passionate. Neither were Varo and Octavius. We'd all stopped scrubbing, and were looking at the man.

'So,' Octavius ventured, 'you don't think they'll attack?'

'Oh, they'll attack.' Priscus smiled. 'They'll just do it with shit on their thighs.'

Even I laughed. Faced with the prospect of battle, and amongst friends, what else was there to do?

'I don't see why we can't just let them attack us here,' Octavius said, thinking of the fort and its walls.

This time, it was Varo who shook his head. 'Because they don't *need* to fight us. Their aim is Italy, and they can bypass us here. Do you want to stand on the walls safe and sound, and know that Roman towns are being sacked? Roman women raped?'

'Of course I don't,' Octavius agreed.

'Well, that's why we've got to march out.'

And as I caught sight of Brutus leaving our centurion's quarters, I knew that we would be doing it with one more man – he was smiling.

'Better get scrubbing.' Varo handed him a cloth. 'So Justus said yes?'

Brutus nodded. His friend smirked.

'I suppose that if you can wank him off that well with one hand, then you can fight with it too.'

Brutus laughed, and showed that his right fist was still good enough to deliver a solid punch into Varo's thick side.

'How *did* you talk him into it?' Octavius asked.

Brutus shrugged. 'Justus has known me since the day my draft arrived at the Eighth. He says that I've earned the right to decide how I die.'

There was an edge to that statement, as if challenging anyone to say different. No one did.

'I'm to follow behind,' Brutus went on. 'Obviously, I can't stand in the ranks, but by the time I can get my blade wet, I don't suppose that a lot of others will be able to either.'

'Fair point,' Varo acknowledged with a sly grin. 'I look forward to using you as a human shield.'

'My pleasure, big man.'

Conversation was easy then. My comrades spoke of old patrols, young women and drunken brawls. I drifted in and out of the discussion, thinking of what was to come. I didn't expect that I would live through it. I didn't expect that I cared.

I looked at my comrades. I loved them. They were worth dying for.

But Marcus . . . It pained me that I would never see my brother again. That I would never experience the energy of his being, or the bright comfort of his presence. I knew that he would relish the coming battle. I knew that in these moments he would deliver great oratory about how we had been blessed to die gloriously to protect Italy from barbaric invaders.

I didn't give a fuck about all that. I just wanted to kill, and I wanted to kill with Marcus.

'Wishing Marcus was here?' Brutus guessed. Even after years apart, my old section commander knew me well. Such things happened when you lived, ate, slept and shat with your section. At least, they did when you were a good commander like Brutus, and not one who simultaneously ignored and intimidated his troops as I did.

'I am,' I confessed. 'He'd love this. Death or glory for Rome.'

'You can have death *and* glory,' Octavius suggested.

Varo grinned. 'I'll ask you how you feel about that when there's a spear-shaft sticking out of your arse.'

'Oh, you big tease.'

We laughed; then Brutus looked back at me. I felt his scrutiny. It was uncomfortable, as if we were really meeting for the first time.

'You know, Corvus,' the older man began, 'I feel like I know you well, and yet I don't.'

I saw smiles play on the lips of my other comrades. We'd had this same conversation more than once.

'If it wasn't for Marcus,' Brutus went on, 'I wouldn't even know where you came from.'

'What's it matter?' I shrugged defensively. 'I'm here.'

Brutus turned to the others, and pointed at me. 'You see what I mean?'

Varo laughed. 'It's like trying to open a whore's legs with an empty purse.'

I bristled. 'If you want to play campfire stories, then tell some of your own.'

Brutus recognized the hostility in my tone. Older and wiser, he also recognized that it was not directed at him.

'All right, brother.' He smiled. 'I'll tell you a story. It's a story about a boy who became a soldier, who became a nobody, and who then became a soldier again.'

'I think I've heard this one,' Varo piped up. 'It's one of those Greek romances with the boys, yeah?'

The others laughed. I sulked.

Brutus clapped his friend on the shoulder. 'Ever since I was a child I've dreamed of what's coming tomorrow. I mean it, Varo. If I die – when I die – then it will be with a smile on my face, and a heart full of pride.'

'You forgot a head full of shit.'

This time, even I laughed a little. I knew that I should apologize for my earlier stubbornness.

'I don't mean to be an arsehole,' I said to Brutus. 'I just don't want to talk about the past. I don't know why it's important.'

Brutus met my pain-filled eyes, and spoke to me as a father to a son. A mentor to a student. A surgeon to a patient. He taught me something that I would see, hear and recognize for the rest of my war-filled life.

'Corvus,' he told me, 'no man should die amongst strangers.'

❧ 18 ❦

We formed up across the valley floor, spread between its steep sides in an ugly smile of steel. Our shields were flame red, our armour polished. In our hands we gripped javelins; by our sides hung sheathed swords. We were the greatest infantry in the world. The makers of an empire. Rome's blade. And now we stood, proud and waiting in the growing light of a spring dawn. We were a challenge. We were a threat. We were a vulgar display of power, every one of us trained, drilled and indoctrinated into the cult of the warrior.

To kill, or be killed.

I stood in the front rank of our century. Behind and beside me, the press of men and shield and weapons was as claustrophobic as it was comforting. Our files were one limb of the same creature. Above I could see a buzzard on the wind, and wondered at what it saw, picturing how the blocked forms of our centuries must look like the serrated shell of some armoured insect, a centipede that had crawled forth from its home inside the fort, and stretched with intent across the narrowest point of a fertile valley. A valley through which ran the road to Italy. A valley through which an army wished to pass to bring death and madness and sorrow to the places that many of us called home.

Not I.

This was my home.

I knew it with the same certainty I had felt when I first saw *her*.

I belonged here, surrounded by comrades and approached by death. The moment was drawing close where my mind would be given over to slaughter, and screams. If they were to be my own, then better they came from a spear-point than sleep. Better death than dreams.

I turned and looked over my shoulder. Octavius's section was in formation behind mine. He was the only one of my close comrades that I could see. Priscus and Varo were obscured by men and armour. Brutus was waiting behind the formation. I met Octavius's green eyes, and smiled. He didn't smile back. That made my own grow.

I was *happy*.

The day hadn't started that way. When I woke, my head had been throbbing. It still ached from the fall I had taken from the burning building, but wine had done the rest. Our armour polished as though we were about to take part in one of the Emperor's triumphs, we had found ourselves a set of benches close by the barracks, and done what comrades do when it is likely their last night on earth – we told stories, we made jokes and we made promises.

Brutus made us promise that we'd take care of Lulmire if he died.

Priscus asked that we send word to his brother in the First Legion, and to impress upon him that he had died happily, amongst comrades.

Octavius ask that he not be buried next to Varo.

Varo asked that Octavius be fed to pigs.

'And what about you?' Varo had asked me.

My answer was simple. 'Tell Marcus I said goodbye.'

We drank after that, and tried to pretend that should one of us die, then the others would be alive to see to the wish of their fallen comrade, but deep down, I think we all recognized the same – our small force would be overrun, and wiped out to the last man. We would all die fighting. Looking at my comrades, I was at peace with that prospect. No one cheats death. What better way to die than with these men? My brothers.

And so we had drank.

In the pre-dawn, goodbyes had been swift. A casual pat on the shoulder. A light-hearted remark. 'See you later.' 'Have fun.' 'Try not to get me killed.'

Beneath the light of a gloating moon we had formed up on the parade square. There was no oration save for the swearing of tired centurions. At times, when a soldier was too slow in his step, or sloppy in their drill, their vine canes did the talking.

'Get sharp, you fuckers,' Justus had growled after administering one such lick, 'this is the eve of glorious battle, not a back-alley abortion.'

Glorious battle.

I didn't reflect too much on those words as we waited for the order to march to the ground chosen for us to make our stand. Rather, I watched what was around me. I saw men laugh and joke. I saw chins jutted out with pride. I saw trembling hands. I saw prayer. We were dressed the same, armoured the same, and armed the same, but no one man was identical in his preparation for what was to come.

'Eighth Legion!' a voice had finally boomed from the head of the First Cohort. 'By the centre, in column of route, quick – march!'

And so we had stepped off to die.

It took less than two hours to reach the valley and to draw up across its narrow width. From my place in the front rank it was impossible for me to see the exact disposition of our force, but from my century's position, I could make an assumption. The First Cohort, double the strength of the others in the legion, held the position of highest honour and danger on the right flank. We were to their left, and by leaning forwards and risking a swipe of Justus's cane, I could make a guess that the Third and Fourth were to our left. The Fifth, I imagined, were held as a reserve.

I cursed myself then as I saw my centurion look in my direction. He was standing out in front of our formation – no reason yet for him to be within the ranks. I looked at the cane in his hand as he walked over to me. It seemed as though I was about to get my first action of the day.

Instead, Justus stopped within half a foot of me, and kept his voice low. So low, I doubt that even the men beside me could have heard him.

'If I and the optio go down, it's Priscus, then you.' Justus spoke simply, before half stepping back and looking into my eyes to see if I understood and acknowledged the order. I gave him a curt nod. I had no desire to lead, but then I supposed Justus knew as much. If the century was down to its fourth commander, then what better way to lead than to kill?

He was about to say something more, but suddenly a shudder of awed comment ran through the ranks like wind. The air was suddenly thick with an invisible presence, like the smell before a thunderstorm. Justus turned, and cleared my view of the hills beyond us.

The enemy had arrived.

They spilled into the end of the valley like tar, a writhing mass of twenty thousand light infantry and cavalry. Still too distant to make out individuals amongst the body, it appeared as some ghastly phenomenon almost incomprehensible to the mind.

I had never seen so many people in one place. If it weren't for the knowledge that we had the seemingly impossible task of killing them all, then perhaps I would have been driven by awe to my knees. Instead, my hand gripped my javelin so tightly that I worried the shaft would snap.

Justus turned to look over the faces of his century. He must have seen fear looking back at him, because he gave an over-casual shrug, turned his back on the enemy and began to clean the dirt from beneath his nails as though he didn't have a care in the world.

He was a good leader.

I felt the sudden need to piss, but was desperate not to be seen as weak by my comrades. I resolved to hold it until the enemy had been in our sight for some time. Already I could see that their approach to us would be that of a creeping tide, rather than a wave, at least until they were within striking distance. I turned my gaze up to the flanks of the valley's steep sides, and expected to see more of the enemy there, but there was nothing, and I thought back to what Justus had told us that morning: 'There's nothing but shepherd tracks on the high ground. They can bypass us in the valley, but they'll not get ahead of Tiberius and his army at that rate. Their one chance is to break through us, and to take the road. If we stand, Italy is safe.'

So all we had to do was to stand.

Looking back at the rolling mass of men approaching us, I fought back a shudder. I turned my eyes upwards and saw the sun at its zenith.

I knew in my guts that I would not see it set.

The enemy came up the valley like the dirty waters of a tidal river. I could see individuals now – not their faces, but the shape of their bodies. They carried oval shields and javelins. They wore light armour, or none at all. The metal of their mail, helmets and shield bosses were dull. I wondered what they saw looking at us? I wondered if Priscus's faith in spit and polish was proving true?

Then, as the enemy army drew to a halt, and four horsemen rode forwards from its body, I had the first indication that it was.

'They want to talk,' someone in our ranks commented.

'Keep your mouths shut,' another snapped.

The four riders closed half the distance to our force. Their horses were fine, their armour polished. Here was the enemy's leadership, or at least a section of it. They stopped and waited. I expected that at any moment a deputation of our own officers would ride forwards, but there was no movement from our own ranks except for the shrugging of nervous shoulders, or the quick swipe of the hand to clear sweat from a man's eyes – the day was becoming hot, and long. We had been in position since dawn. I wondered at how long and far the enemy had marched. A fair distance, I imagined. Little wonder they wanted to catch their breath. Had the odds been more even, I imagine we would have charged them immediately, but every moment we stood bought time for Tiberius to manoeuvre behind us and block the path to Italy. If the enemy were inclined to wait, I expected our commanders would have us stand until the end of days. They made no move to advance and parley, and so the four horsemen waited, their beasts chewing happily on the lush grass of the valley. The animals pricked up their ears as one of their commanders called to our army, his words lost to me. There was no reply. Then, a lone enemy rider began to walk his horse forwards. He had only gone ten paces when a javelin arced out from the ranks at our army's centre. It was beautifully thrown, and ploughed with clear and deadly intent into the ground before the rider.

The message was clear: there would be no talking.

As the rider trotted with his companions back towards his ranks, I wondered if the decision of our commander was wise. Talking took time, and we seemed to have little of that on our side.

The decision was born of pride, I realized. No matter the odds, no matter the situation, a Roman commander would act with dignity. To consort with rebels would be as unwelcome an outcome as the sacking of Italian towns.

Pride was Rome, and Rome was pride.

I shifted. The four horsemen had reached the swollen ranks of rebels that awaited their commands.

Within a moment, they got them.

The roar of the twenty thousand voices crashed through the valley like a ship run on to rocks, deafening and terrifying. It was like nothing I had ever experienced, and I did not know whether to feel awe, or dread. I suppose that, in the end, I felt both.

Not once did Justus ever turn to look at the enemy as they screamed and hollered. Not once did he break from the task of cleaning his nails. Then, when the enemy had finally cheered themselves hoarse and fallen silent, our centurion chanced to look up at the faces of his men.

'Did somebody fart?'

Laughter ripped through our century like a chariot. All of the tension the enemy had driven into us was expelled through that most natural answer to fear – laughter.

'Don't look behind you, boss,' one of the veterans in the front rank quipped, 'but I reckon those whores we short-changed have gone and fetched their brothers.'

We laughed some more, and men stamped their feet in anxious agitation, loosening muscles for what was soon to come.

Justus looked over his shoulder, then back to his men.

'Oh yeah.' He grinned wolfishly. 'Here they come.'

The enemy stepped forth with another roar of challenge, but that step was short, and their pace was slow.

They're scared, I realized, flexing my fingers against shield and javelin. *They're fucking scared.*

They came on at a child's pace, pushed no doubt by the ranks behind them. I reminded myself in that moment that these men had been conscripted into service only weeks before. They had never seen combat. They had hardly seen training. Priscus was right. There was only one set of professional killers on this battlefield, and it was us.

'Time to make widows and orphans, lads!' Justus shouted as he moved to take his place in the front rank. It was all the speech that he gave, and all that was needed. We knew that to run was to die. They had cavalry, and we had none worth speaking of. If we stood we had a chance. A chance, and not a good one.

But fuck it. Nobody lives forever, and this was what I had wanted since I ran to the legions: a javelin in my hand, a sword on my hip, and an enemy to kill.

I spat.

They charged.

Ten seconds from contact.

'Javelins!' Justus roared, and with every other man I repeated the order, and arched back to throw.

'Loose!'

I put all of my strength into the throw, and lost sight of my shaft as it merged in the sky with more than a thousand others, a steel-tipped storm of death that now slammed into the charging enemy like a raging wave against a harbour, tearing men down to die trampled beneath the charging mass that came behind them. Screams began to puncture the challenging roar, but still they came.

Seven seconds.

I judged that there was time for one more wave of javelins. I pulled my second from its place in the ground as Justus gave the order.

'Javelins! Loose!'

Another wave of killing, this time close enough for me to register the quickest of details in the rushing madness: men dropping to their knees with javelins in their guts; others struggling to pull the shafts free from their oval shields.

Three seconds.

'Draw swords!'

Mine scraped from its scabbard as I pulled my shield close to me like a lover. Above its rim, I saw a wall of death approaching – wild eyes, open mouths, terror. I don't know if Justus gave any further orders. I could hear nothing but the roar of the coming stampede.

One second.

As they rushed the last yards towards me, I realized I was screaming as loudly as they were.

Shit. So I *was* scared.

Contact.

The shock of the impact sent a spike of pain through my entire body, and almost knocked me from my feet. Only the shield of the soldier behind me kept me upright, and then I was pushing forwards against the resistance, ramming my sword back and forth. Into what I did not know, but I felt something hot and slippery on my hands, I felt breath on my face, spit in my eyes, and heard screams in my ears.

Then, in that moment, I got what I had wanted since the day my previous life had ended.

I ceased to think.

When a soldier tells you every intimate detail of combat in a battle of this size, he is lying. The crush of army against army is no work of art, but a mess of paint spilled in the dirt. It is screaming. It is cursing. It is crying. It is burning muscles, choked breath and sweat. It is blood, it is shit and it is murder. It is every sense heightened, bludgeoned and broken. Time is meaningless. There is no space, only a vision of wide eyes, spurting blood and gaping wounds. Only when the two forces pull apart do you realize that you're still alive. Only then do you realize what has been done. What you have inflicted.

What you have suffered.

How long it took for us to reach that moment I could not tell you. One moment there was an enemy in my face, and my sword was heavy with the weight of a falling body. The next, I was looking at the retreating backs of an army.

I fell to my knees, and puked.

19

A hand gripped me by the shoulder. 'Are you injured?'

Varo.

'I . . . I don't know,' I confessed.

Varo was. I thought I saw the white of bone on his forearm.

'The others?' I asked as Varo pulled me gruffly to my feet, and looked me over for wounds.

'Octavius and Priscus are all right,' he told me. 'Brutus too.'

For the first time, I began to take in the carnage around me. It was if hands were being removed from my eyes. A thick line of bodies ran like a tidemark of seaweed and debris on a beach. I almost stumbled as I recognized the damage wrought on my own century.

'We've lost over twenty,' Varo confirmed. 'You and a couple of others are about all that's left of the front rank.'

'Justus?' I forced myself to ask.

Varo pointed with his bloodied sword. The centurion lay on his back, throat torn open, his arms cut to ribbons. Our optio lay dead a few yards away from him, doubtless having rushed forwards to assume command.

'Priscus has the century,' my friend informed me, slapping me across the head to regain my attention. 'Come on, we're falling back. They're feeding other centuries up for the next attack.'

The next attack? Hadn't we beaten them?

I looked across the field, then. The enemy still clung to the valley like a curse. They had pulled out of javelin range, and as men dragged or carried their wounded and screaming from the field, others paced in front of their ranks, doubtless demanding courage and metal from their comrades.

'Help me with him.' Varo spoke sharply, seeing one of our own move in what I had assumed was a tangle of the dead.

Gums. A soldier from my section. Something had cut across his face. One eye looked at me in wild panic. The other dangled broken on his cheek.

'Section commander,' he pleaded, 'please, I don't want to die.'

'You're not going to die,' I said automatically.

'Come on. We've got to get back behind the other century and re-form,' Varo pressed me, and I realized that the army was giving ground so that the mounds of dead would become an obstacle for the enemy's next charge.

I looked down at Gums. His hands were pressed to where a bulge of intestine erupted from his stomach.

'I don't want to die,' he repeated weakly.

'Shut up and hold your guts in,' Varo growled. Then, putting one hand under the shoulder of his armour, and holding our shields in the other, we dragged the boy to safety. He cried out in pain, and I saw the men of the fresh century swallow their nerves as we passed through their ranks. Finally we were clear, and at the rear of the battle lines.

'I want my mother,' Gums pleaded.

He got Brutus instead. The old sweat looked at me with near pity before turning his attention to the boy I knew to be dying. 'Steady now, lad. It's just a flesh wound. You'll be fine.'

'Second of the Second!' Priscus began to call. 'Form up on me! Form up! Form up! Quickly!'

I did not look again at the devastation that was Gums's face. I could not stand the pleading in his one eye. I knew that he would see the truth on my face – that he would never see his mother again. That he would die on this blood-soaked field.

I looked at Brutus. A nod between us was all that we had, needed or wanted.

I ran to join Priscus.

I ran to await death.

I heard, rather than saw, the enemy's second assault. My view of it was restricted to the backs of the century that stood to our front. I watched their legs shake as they awaited the charge. I watched them loose javelins as well as their bowels. I watched their ranks spasm as a deafening crash of shield on shield rang across the valley.

I *smelt* it too. Open guts, open arses and the metallic stink of blood.

I looked to my left and right. Suddenly, I realized I had been in a daze since my own clash with the enemy. Where the fuck were my section? I knew that Gums was dying, maybe already dead. What of the others? I arched and craned. For the first time I saw Octavius. He was looking at the sky, as though he were wishing himself anywhere but this field.

'Three Section, report!' I shouted. 'Form on the left of me!'

I called again. I waited.

It was Priscus who came to me.

We grabbed the back of each other's helmets, and rested the steel of our brows against one another.

'Varo told me you lived,' he sighed.

'I need to find my section.'

For a moment there was silence between us. Ahead, there were screams of pain. Screams of challenge. The drum and thud of shield on shield. The ringing, torturous chime of metal on metal.

'Your section's gone, Corvus.'

I didn't know what to say. We broke our embrace.

'I need you to take the century if I go down,' Priscus told me.

I said nothing.

'Corvus,' Priscus spoke sharply. 'Now's not the time to think of the dead. I need you to take the century if I go down. Understood?'

'I understand,' I said.

But in that moment, as men bled and died by the dozen not a javelin's throw from me, I realized that I understood nothing at all.

I never had.

20

I thought that battle would bring me calm. Bring me a release.

All of my section were gone.

All seven of them.

I barely knew them apart from their names. I didn't think that mattered. I was just there to lead them. Protect them.

In that I had failed.

I spat blood. Why did I think it would be any different in the legions? I was destined to fail those who relied on me. I let my chin drop to my mailed chest. Movement at ground level caught my eyes.

The wounded.

They crawled through the rank and file of the century in front of us, mouths disfigured through pain, clamped tight against agony. They were bloodied, gashed, butchered. I felt my throat tighten and stomach rise as I saw one tortured wretch dragging a length of coiled, ropey guts behind him like a boatman at the pier.

My section . . . were their ends so hideous?

I didn't see the blow that sent me sideways. I staggered into another soldier, my head suddenly ringing as though it were inside a town's bell. The rim of my helmet was down over my eyes. I pushed it up, and expected to see the enemy on top of our ranks.

Instead I saw Varo.

'You looked like you needed it,' he grunted.

I checked the punch I was about to throw at him. He was right.

'What can you see?' I asked. Varo's height gave him an advantage. From the grimace on his face, I took that it was nothing good

'We're losing.'

'We are?'

'Line's bending.'

How was he so fucking calm?

I looked at the sky. The carrion birds had come, drawn by the scent of open stomachs, their circling silhouettes hideous in the sunlight that was soon to fade. *How long had we been fighting?*

'Long enough,' Varo grunted as I asked him. Faced with death, I had never seen my friend so stoic. 'Get ready,' he told me then. He had seen something down the line. Confirmation of it came moments later.

'Prepare to withdraw!' echoed down the ranks.

Withdraw?

I looked down at the wounded. I saw one veteran whose knee was a mash of bone and flesh. He would not be able to keep up with the withdrawal. 'Help me with him,' I said to Varo, but I felt his iron grip on my arm before I had even taken a step forwards.

His eyes were still ahead on the battlefield. 'Don't,' was all that he said.

'Varo . . .'

'Don't look down, Corvus. Keep your eyes looking over the century ahead of us. Don't look down.'

'Varo, we . . .' We what? We could carry all of our wounded in our arms? We could sprout wings and fly them from here?

What could we do?

I didn't know, and so I made a mistake. Despite Varo's words, I did look down. I looked down and all around, and I saw dozens of wounded. Men of my legion. Our brothers. Not all of them were dying. Some had wounds that were survivable. They could live.

If only they could walk.

'We need to form casualty parties,' I tried.

Varo shook his head. He was still looking to the front of the battle, where the enemy churned and smashed against our line like storm against seawall.

'We can't spare the men,' he told me when I said it again, and with bile in my throat, I knew that he was right. A withdrawal was the most dangerous manoeuvre an army on the field could attempt. With no way to watch your footing, men could slip or stumble, breaking the unified front of shields, into which the enemy would rush like a plague. And they *would* be coming. They *would* be following. There was no doubt of that, now. I could smell it in the air the same as every other man. I could feel it. Feel our ranks buckling as though we stood atop an earthquake. Centurions and their optios beat and harangued their men to keep tight, keep in line, but the gaps were coming. The formation of polished, professional soldiers was gone, and in their place stood blood-painted animals who just wanted to live long enough to see another sunrise.

And for that to happen, the wounded would have to be left behind.

'Second Cohort!' came the voice, repeated by two dozen other leaders. 'Second Cohort, at the half-step, withdraw!'

Terror, then. I should have listened to Varo. I should have kept my eyes up as we began the slow shuffle of shields. Instead I looked at the veteran with the ruined knee. He knew what was happening. I expected him to call out. To beg for mercy. To plead for help.

Instead I saw him smile.

Not a happy smile. Not a painful one.

A soldier's smile. It was the smile which said that bad things happen, and on this day, on this battlefield, they had happened to him. His voice was like gravel as I heard him shout: 'Die hard, boys! Die fucking hard!'

He pushed himself up on to his backside, and laid a sword across his lap. That was the last I saw of him. Like dozens of others who could not find their feet, he would be left to die by his own hand, or by the enemy that pressed against our front line, giving us no inch as we tried to pull away.

I took another half-pace backwards, feeling my heel hit against something of metal and flesh. It groaned. This time I did as Varo told me. I did not look down. I stepped over the obstacle – a brother of my legion – and I hoped that I could be forgiven. That he would not curse me for following my orders before the desires of my gut and heart.

I chanced a look to my side. Varo. I had always known him as a physical bastion, but today his presence was a bulwark for my mind. With him on my flank I was anchored. Steady. I could do what needed to be done.

My foot hit another wounded man. I stepped over. A few more paces. I heard whimpering. I heard someone beg for a clean end. I kept my eyes up. I saw a pair of javelins come in from the mass of the enemy. Watched them pluck a soldier I had known for three years off his feet, dead before he hit the ground. I saw a lot of things like that as we stepped back, my dry tongue stuck to the top of my mouth as though it had been nailed there. The broiling sea of the enemy gave our front lines no rest, but after some time the going became easier for those of us towards the rear – there were no more wounded to step over. Either they had walked to the rear of our force, or they were dead.

Varo: 'We're turning.'

I followed his eyes to the top of the steep mountain ridge on our right.

Except it was no longer on our right. It was coming ahead of us.

'We must be wheeling the legion,' he said.

Were we? It's not for the rank and file to know such things. Our battle is confined to hardly more than a few javelin lengths around us – less, in the front ranks – but the position of the ridge was an undeniable truth. We were turning, moving to almost a right angle from our original position, though further down the valley, beyond our initial contact. Why? Why would we give ground this way? Our lines held intact. If they did not, we would already be a broken rabble, chased down as we fled by the enemy cavalry. So why the manoeuvre? What the fuck was going on?

I got my first taste of the answer as I saw the front ranks ahead of us become still, as if they had broken out of a seizure.

'Enemy's backing off,' Varo said, though he seemed to doubt every word.

I expected to hear taunts follow them. Challenges. None came. Every man who had fought struggled to stay on his feet. I knew what was coming next.

'First Century!' I heard my friend Priscus bellow. 'In open order, quick march!' We opened up gaps in our ranks and files. Within moments, the men that had been fighting before us began to move back through us. Beneath the rims of their helmets there were hollow eyes, devoid of any spark of life. They were ghosts. Hollow vessels. They reacted to orders because they had been drilled and drilled, and that discipline kept their bodies obeying even when their minds had fled.

This time I did look down. I couldn't face them. When I looked up, it was not Roman soldiers that I saw, but a rebel army. The space between us was a canvas of bodies that moved as the wounded writhed and crawled. The enemy were barely a hundred yards away now, and they were moving. Moving fast.

But not towards us.

'We beat them?' I asked, incredulously.

Varo looked at me then. 'No, Corvus.' I think that I saw tears in his eyes. 'They're marching on Italy.'

We had lost.

❧ 21 ❧

I stood in the front ranks of a defeated legion and watched as our enemy marched by us towards Italy. Towards Roman lands that were ripe for sacking, and Roman citizens who were destined for rape and slavery. They marched onwards because we had failed. There were only a hundred yards between us and the rebels, the streaming procession of thousands, but for all the use we were now, they might as well have been on the other side of the Adriatic.

I looked about me as best I could. I could see treetops behind us. A small wood, maybe. Behind that was the menacing ridge where sheep and goat trails ran through the jagged stone. I wondered if some shepherd had watched on like a god as war played out beneath his gaze.

I turned back to my comrades, then. If it was possible to age a decade in a day, we had done so. There was little conversation – a few muttered curses here and there – but the atmosphere wasn't one of pity, but bitter shame.

I felt a presence pushing through the ranks to come to my side. Brutus. 'We lost,' I thought I heard him say.

I had a question for him. It took me a long time to ask it. 'The lad from my section. Gums. He lives?'

Brutus kept his grey eyes staring out at the rolling sea of the enemy, and said nothing.

The sun was touching the mountaintop to our front when Priscus returned with our orders.

'We haven't lost,' was the first thing he said, and then he explained how we had come to be in a position to watch the mass of enemy walk by as though they were on a summer stroll.

'The legate could see that we couldn't hold,' our veteran explained – though I supposed we were all veterans now. 'There was a river running through the valley over on the left flank. He used a wide bend to anchor us, and pivoted the cohorts back so that the valley was open to the enemy.'

The legate had been correct in assuming that the enemy would take an open road to Italy over a grinding battle. There was nothing to be gained by killing what remained of us, but in Italy they could shake an empire. Find riches and plunder. And for every moment they wasted in battle, Tiberius and his army in the north would be closing the gap to cut them off.

'What does any of that matter?' Varo growled. 'They're past us! They're on their way to Italy!'

He took no solace in the fact that he still lived. I don't think that any of us did. Shame is a powerful force, and its blade was in our guts as fiercely as any rebel sword could be. There was more, too. Pragmatically, we knew that there was no happy ending for a beleaguered force in a hostile country where the enemy numbered in the hundreds of thousands. Die today or die tomorrow seemed to be our choice. At least by giving our life on this field we could have achieved something.

'We still can,' Priscus said as Varo gave voice to that sentiment. There was no smile on his face, but there was life in his eyes. There was a force I could trust. That I

119

believed with every fibre of my body. Priscus had been there for me since the day I arrived at the legion. If he told me we could win, then we would win. I wanted to embrace him. Instead I asked him how we would beat an army ten times our size.

He put his hand on my shoulder as he told me. 'We're going to attack.'

At first I thought the words were bluster. Some attempt to drag our shattered morale from out of the bloodied dirt.

I was wrong.

The first evidence came after dark; after the sun had crept behind the ridge to our front, casting the valley into a pink haze. That morning, I had never thought to see a sunset again, and though shame at our defeat burned at me I was grateful to see its majesty. Now, it seemed as though it was the next sunrise I was unlikely to witness.

Because we were going on the attack.

It had struck us all as craven that our legion commander would spare our lives and allow the enemy to march on Italy – some men had even muttered that he should take his own life for his failure of command – but now it became clear that he had had a plan all along. Recognizing that his understrength legion could not hold the line forever, he had offered the enemy the open route that it craved. In doing so he had saved two-thirds of his force for an audacious roll of the dice – we would take to the goat trails of the mountain behind us, overhaul the enemy in the night, and fall on them in the dawn.

Simple.

Deadly.

And with almost no chance of success.

'At least it *is* a chance,' Varo offered, anxious to draw blood and rid himself of the sense of failure that clung to us all.

When darkness had claimed the valley we were pulled back into the small wood that had been at our back. Here, I discovered, the walking wounded would form a wall of shields at the front of the trees. The enemy would have scouts to watch our movements, and should they try and probe they needed to be met with challenge and javelin. The main body of the enemy, we were told, had advanced out of the valley, and encamped for the night. Our own scouts had brought this information, and these hard men would now be the ones to lead us along the mountain trails to outflank the rebels.

Octavius started laughing.

'Keep the noise down.' Brutus hissed.

He couldn't, and so Varo hit him across the back of the helmet. 'What's so funny, you dickhead?' he demanded, as quietly as it was possible for the big man to speak.

'Are we the bad ones?' Octavius asked back.

'What?'

'Are we the bad ones, here? You know, like in every story, there are good ones and bad ones. Are *we* the bad ones?'

Varo snorted. 'We're the good ones, you cock.'

'Just wondering,' Octavius replied, and though I could not see his smile, I could hear it, 'because this all reminds me of something.'

Priscus asked him what.

'Thermopylae,' my friend enlightened us, referring to the famed last stand of the Spartans, a tale that all aspiring warriors relished.

'There've been a lot of last stands,' Varo grunted, clearly unhappy with how ours had gone.

'I don't mean that,' Octavius told me. 'I mean how the Persians got led through the mountain pass to come out behind the Greeks, and then beat them.'

'Exactly,' Varo said. 'And we'll do the same.'

'That's what I'm asking. Are we the bad ones? Are we the Persians?' Octavius teased. 'I think you'd look good with a pointy beard and a couple of young boys in your harem, Varo.'

'We're the Eighth Legion, you dickhead,' the big man reminded him. 'And I'd save your breath. This climb is going to be a lick. There's a reason their army tried to fight its way through us instead of going over the mountains. There's no secret paths here, just fucking hard ones.'

No one spoke much after that. Water was brought to us from the river, and my tongue finally peeled itself off the roof of my mouth. From countless night duties I could recognize the silhouettes of my comrades even in their battle dress, and I was not surprised to see Brutus with us in the dark, despite Priscus and Varo begging him to stay with the walking wounded.

'Prepare to move,' a voice said finally, the words passed on quietly as a whisper from man to man. All about me then I heard the hushed sounds of soldiers getting to their feet, piss pattering the ground, chain mail and kit being tested for silence and 'comfort'. Then I heard the first sounds of our force moving away from the valley floor. Away from the ground we had soiled with blood and shit. Where the birds and beasts now feasted on friend and foe alike.

'I love this job,' I heard Octavius utter.

And then, in the black, we followed on as a snake of soldiers visible only in my mind. We followed on into the rock and the mountains.

We went on the attack.

❧ 22 ❧

One day, when I was barely a man, I had turned up bloodstained and breathless at Marcus's family home, and asked him to run with me. That day and night we scaled ridges, traversed mountains, and ran so hard and long that my toenails began to come off, and I saw blood in my piss. I thought it was the hardest physical test that I would ever face.

I was wrong.

The moon this night favoured the rebels of the land, the slim light it cast doing little to illuminate our path through the jagged mountains. The climb was steep, the footing loose. Men tried not to swear and groan as their feet went from beneath them. Equipment in their hands, their faces ate rock and dirt. More than once I heard a man go rolling back down the steepest parts of the trail, sometimes crashing into others and taking them with him on their descent. I don't know what happened to those men. If they broke bones, then they bit back their pain. I imagine that more than a few of them would be waking with bent limbs on a lonely mountainside.

If they lived.

For my own part, my chest fought a war against my chain mail as it heaved for every breath. My right knee throbbed from where I had slipped and driven it into a rock. I'd done it with such force, and ground my teeth so hard against the pain, that they too now ached. Already drained from combat, my limbs felt hollow, yet somehow as heavy as I had ever known them. The spot where I had hit my head in the town fire began to hurt once more, and the pain grew into a pounding that consumed my entire skull. I wanted to spit and curse fate, but there was not a single drop of moisture in my mouth, just the dirt of a dusty trail kicked up by a thousand pairs of feet. Never had my body felt more miserable. More wretched. I imagined that every man felt the same.

And yet we made it. We made the climb up a pass so steep that to fall was to die, and I am certain that some did. Shield tied off on my back, I used my javelin's butt to dig in the dirt as I clawed rock with my left hand. I could feel blood on my palms. I could taste it when I licked my lips. I felt it in my eyes. The blood on my face wasn't mine, and I knew in those moments that my life could be worse. That I could be the person who had bled on to me, now doubtless being pecked at by birds. Pulled apart by wolves. Yes, in my relatively short number of years, I had realized that life could always get worse.

But, as I reached the crest of the spine that ran between the valleys, I also knew that – in short moments at least – it could get better, too. When the ground became flat, I felt an exhilaration through my body that could only be matched by the joy of sex. I had left my smiles in another life, but I was content as I drew in deep lungfuls of cool air, and my muscles thanked me for the break in their punishment.

There was no talking at the top. A wind came over the ridge, not harsh, and against this backdrop could be heard the sound of the ragged breaths of the men who had climbed. The *soldiers* who had climbed, for surely this was the kind of feat that is only accomplished by the most desperate, or the most disciplined, and we were both.

We pushed on along the ridge. I could feel in the air that we wanted to drive forwards and close on the enemy, but this was no paved road, just a flatter goat trail, and so as the wind teased my face between my cheek-plates, and cooled the sweat that soaked my body, we stumbled on. We stumbled on, and then we began to stumble down. We were coming off the pass. Off the mountain. I looked into the night. Into the sky where I thought the horizon would be.

I saw a sliver of silver. A blade of the gods. And then, as we came out on to a plateau, I saw something else. It was below us, and as beautiful as it was frightening.

It was the campfires of an army.

Below us were the enemy. Above them, we waited like hungry eagles in the dark.

I looked back to the silver on the horizon. When dawn came, so would we. For many, darkness would quickly follow light.

No attempt was made to form centuries. We were on a narrow plateau on the mountainside, not a parade ground, and so the whispered orders that came around were simple: follow on to the low ground. Form up with whoever is near you. Wait for the order to advance, unless the enemy is alerted. If they wake, then attack. Kill for Rome. Kill for each other.

They were the kind of orders that I wanted.

Like the silhouettes of the men around me, I rested on my shield as we awaited the order to advance. It was an old soldier's trick taught to me by Brutus. In such a position you could close your eyes and, fatigued as we were, slip into a shallow sleep. I was too tired to think about my past. Too tired to think about my future. I just closed my eyes and waited.

It was the sound of shuffling feet that let me know my rest was over. I was alert in an instant. At least, as alert as I could be following a day of battle and a night of climbing. But I was ready to follow. I was ready to kill, and I was so tired that I was certainly ready to die.

Like an upright corpse, I trod the dirt and gravel trail behind the man in front of me. His silhouette was huge.

Varo. Good. No better man to die alongside than him.

The fires below us numbered in their hundreds. They were an invitation to the afterlife, and we hurried towards it without conversation, but not without noise. I could hear the bump of shield. I could hear the drawing of breath. I could hear sandals on the rough mountainside. Hundreds of pairs of them, growing louder as fear began to grip us, and the inevitable quickening of the pace came – we just wanted it over with. We wanted to be in there, amongst the enemy. Enough of a night full of dark, and a head full of what ifs? Give us battle! Give us victory, or defeat!

Suddenly I was moving downhill at a jog-trot. The fires were getting closer. Still there was no shouting. No voices. It all seemed to be going so fast. They'd looked so far away, but it was a trick of the night. I could smell them, now. Smell the wood smoke of a sleeping enemy. I felt the movement ahead of me slow, and realized that I was no longer walking on harsh rock and dirt, but on the flat and greeting embrace of the plain. We were forming up, and I felt Varo's shield hand grip me and pull me into a rank beside him.

I looked to my left and right. I *felt* the presence of the formed body of men around me. Somehow we had done it. Against nature, against the enemy, we had come through the night and now stood ranged in our ranks to visit death on his camp. There would be no withdrawal today. No more clever gambles of the legate's. We would wait for the sliver of dawn's light to become a spill. We would wait until we could see enough of our enemy to kill them, and then we would advance. By the time the sun slid over the horizon, I expected that we would all be dead, but maybe we would have won enough time for Tiberius to shut the door in the rebels' face, and bar their way into Italy.

Maybe. I had no one that I cared for in that land. Save Marcus, my family stood here in the ranks around me. The legion could fight to save Italy, but I would fight for the lives of my comrades, if only for a dawn.

I looked at the horizon. Black sky was now grey ash.

A voice rang through the night. It was the promise of death, of pain and bloody murder.

It was the promise of a reckoning.

The promise of battle.

'Eighth Legion! Advance!'

We stepped off in shadow.

Less than a day before we had faced this enemy on the open plain. As a brute barges open a closed door, they had used their mass to force us aside.

Not today.

Today we came for them in dawn's fading darkness, and if yesterday they had been brutes, then today we were assassins. We were dealers of death. We were nightmare made flesh. The enemy had carried the field, marched through the pass, and then they had rested. They were amateurs, and amateurs in victory forget that a win in war is but a fleeting moment. Survive one sword stroke, and the next might take off your head. That was as true at the strategic level of leadership as it was for the foot soldier, and the leadership of these men was lacking. Even our call to advance had drawn no response. Only when the tramp of a fifteen hundred pairs of feet was on their head did the enemy know that they were waking with a blade to their throat.

And those blades were thirsty.

'Eighth Legion! Charge!'

In rank and file, we came like demons from the shadows of their fires. The dark night gave birth to us, our arms and armour shining in the firelight, caked in the dry blood of our enemy's brothers. They were sleeping on the ground, exhausted, 'victorious'. For many, the first sign of their misconception was cold steel in their insides.

Gods, it was a slaughter.

Flame, and the exaltation of seeing a panicked enemy – that was my impression of our charge. I drove my blade downwards as often as up, and before I had chance to breathe, I had killed, and I had maimed.

'Please!' a rebel begged in Dalmatian.

I drove my sword into his chest. Then I was on to the next.

Flame and death. Amateur against professional.

We butchered them. Hundreds died in those first moments of terror. Maybe more than a thousand. The stink of blood and guts cut through the stench of sweat and the smoke of their fires.

I saw Varo take off a man's arm with a swipe of his sword. He finished the rebel by stamping on his face. He turned. Saw me.

He was smiling.

'Fear the Eighth!' he roared into the night. 'Fear the Eighth!'

Oh, there was fear. It was everywhere. In wails, and screams, and the fleeing backs of our enemy. Perhaps, if they had numbered only ten times our own force, we would have beaten them all before the sunrise.

But they were almost twenty thousand, and we were not much more than one.

Behind the bolting foe, in the depths of their camp, the enemy host rallied.

They rallied. And then they attacked.

'Hold the line!' someone was shouting. 'Hold the line!'

I looked to my left and right. Flame lit the fugitive figures of the enemy as they raced for life from our now halted soldiers. Behind them was a stirring black mass. A mass that was soon to charge against us.

Something bumped into my back. I turned, my sword up.

Priscus. He wore the helmet that had once belonged to Justus. He was my leader now, as well as my friend. 'Form up!' he urged me, then shouting to the others: 'Here! Form here! Three ranks! Three ranks! Form!'

A stranger came to each side of me. We touched our shields. Roman soldiers were replaceable parts, and we could fight as well with one comrade as another, though I hoped that my brothers were close. There was shouting in the night. Shouting in a language that I understood, and I knew that the guttural growls were no order to retreat.

'They're coming!' I shouted, the words hard in my scorched throat. 'They're coming!'

And they came. A black blizzard. A storm of flesh and steel.

'They're coming!'

I heard a laugh behind me. I'd recognize it anywhere. *Octavius.* 'Hey, Corvus? Do you think they're coming?'

I had no time to laugh even if I'd wanted to. The enemy were upon us, battering against my shield, dying on my blade.

'Fear the Eighth!' I heard Varo bellow from somewhere, and other men took up the call. I screamed it myself as I rammed my sword into flesh. Shoved my shield against shield. Spat in my enemy's face. 'Fear the Eighth! Fear the Eighth!'

The battle line was horror. Pure horror. But I was lost to it. No time to think. No time to do anything but gnash my teeth and fight for every second of life. I didn't even know that the battle was no longer being fought in the shadows of campfires but in the growing light of dawn. I didn't know that the skies were now the same slate grey as Brutus's eyes, and in that light, the enemy now found a reason to fight for something greater than defence, and survival.

They saw the eagle of the Eighth.

I felt a hand wrench me back. 'Rotate! Rotate!'

I stumbled back as Octavius took my place. Held above the heads of our men I saw the gilded standard of our legion, the enemy swarming towards it like ants on to a carcass. The eagle was a symbol of the Roman Empire that they had rebelled against, and they *wanted* it. They knew the pain that its loss would cause. The news would carry across the world. Even the Emperor himself would be struck a blow. The eagle had come from his divine hand, and now it was coming close to falling into the paws of the men who had told him '*no!*'

'Protect the eagle!' a centurion growled. 'Protect the—' His words cut off as a spear tore through his throat.

I looked wildly about me. Varo was doing the same.

Shit. He looked worried. 'They're rolling up our flanks!'

Our extended line was no match for the number of the enemy. They were outflanking us, their numbers allowing them to bypass our fighting front which was held engaged. Soon, they would fall on the unprotected backs of our legion. Then we would die.

'Form square!' came the order, our legion command having seen the same. 'Pull in the flanks! Form square! Form square!'

Thousands of hours of drill and discipline is what kept men obeying the orders, and moving as one unit – albeit a battered and scarred one. Centurion Justus – now dead on the plain – had pushed us in our every free hour at the fort, and in those actions he now saved the lives of others. As the flanks fell back under control the enemy were held at bay, though only just. The Eighth was reduced to a bloody square of embattled brotherhood, and against these four walls of flesh and iron the enemy seethed.

'Get the wounded in the centre!' Priscus yelled. 'Get the wounded back! Get them back!'

Some were dragged. Others crawled. Maybe it was one of these men that caused two beleaguered soldiers to trip backwards, opening a gap in the front rank. It was only there for a second, but in battle a second is enough, and into this cavity now poured the elite of the enemy's troops. The professionals. One look at their hard faces was enough to know that these were the bastards who had lived a life of violence long before Rome had tried and failed to bring them to her standard. Now here they came, shouting and killing, tearing into our ranks like a serrated blade.

Our unified front was broken.

The enemy were everywhere.

It was over.

❧ 24 ❧

Chaos.

Pure bloody chaos.

The enemy had broken through one side of the square, and this put them at the backs of the other walls of flesh. Some of those men turned, others didn't, but any hope at cohesion was now lost. Walls of shield and battered ranks began to fall apart into knots of desperate soldiers and individual melees. This was a legion on its knees – we were just awaiting the killing blow.

I looked for my friends. I wanted to die with them. I wanted them to know that I had been with them until the end. A true comrade. A true brother.

Instead I saw the eagle. The standard-bearer was long dead. A soldier streaked in blood, arm ruined from combat, stood holding the totem in his place.

'Brutus!'

I tried to run to him. I tried, but this was battle. Instead I had to cut my way towards him like a man clearing thick brush, my swings wicked and evil. So single-minded was I that only the shield drill of a fellow legionary kept my blade from his throat.

Chaos.

And in the middle of the screams and the stink, my friend with his hand on the eagle. He couldn't even defend himself, the idiot. He was at the centre of a feeble last stand of about a dozen men, about which the enemy snapped and lunged like angry wolves. One firm rush and

134

they would carry the standard away. They would lose men to do it, and they knew that, but once they overcame that fear then the eagle would be gone. I couldn't have given two shits about that if it didn't spell death for my friend. Something had to be done.

It was Priscus who did it.

'With me! With me!' He saw his oldest comrade in danger. He saw our personal tragedy, and our legion's disaster. He saw the end, and he charged towards it without a backwards step.

I followed. I was on his shoulder. That was how I saw the spear push out of his back. That was how I saw my friend – my teacher, my brother – spitted like game.

I screamed. I roared. I had no time to mourn him, then. The enemy were in my face, and so I killed for him instead. Like wildfire I danced amongst them spreading death, hacking with my sword, biting with my teeth. My fury bought me inches, and in this space I turned to find my brothers. Priscus was on his back, the shaft of the spear held upright in his lifeless body. There was a man beside him on his knees. It was Brutus. The eagle was in his hand. I knocked a young rebel aside with my shield, and covered my comrade with it.

'Fear the Eighth!' I heard a voice boom, and I felt the presence around us as soldiers fought to buy the eagle's salvation. There was nothing to be done for Priscus.

'He's dead!' Brutus shouted in my face, his grey eyes wild.

'Come on!' I yelled back. 'We need to move!'

'I can't!'

'He's dead! We have to move!'

135

Brutus shook his head, and looked down. He was on his knees because a blade had torn open the front of his thigh. Muscle and sinew smiled back at me through the gaping wound.

I wasted no time in dropping my sword and shield, hauling my friend on to my shoulder like an unruly child. 'I'll carry you!' I promised.

'The eagle!' Brutus pleaded.

Fuck the eagle. His life was my concern, and so I took my first step.

My knees almost buckled. I had a man more than my own size on my shoulder, and my body had been continually punished for almost an entire day and night.

I stumbled again. 'Fuck!' On instinct I reached out to steady myself. My hand bumped against wood, and I grabbed at it. For a horrible second, I thought that I was bracing myself against the spear lodged into Priscus.

I wasn't.

I was holding the eagle of the Eighth. The famed totem. A symbol of Rome's glory.

And now my walking stick.

Holding Brutus over my left shoulder, I used the eagle to brace with my right hand. My head was forced down by the bulk of my comrade, but I saw enough of a red blur ahead of us to recognize our lines – or what was left of them. In my ear, I heard the scream of men and steel as someone fought a rearguard to protect us. I don't know how far I stumbled – twice almost dropping Brutus as a dying man grasped at my feet – but at some point he was pulled from my shoulders, and my knees finally gave way.

'Protect the eagle!' someone shouted.

'Fear the Eighth!' another roared.

I was trying to push myself up from the bloody ground – trying to die on my feet – when darkness took me.

PART TWO

❧◆❧

I awoke in a field of bones. Tens of thousands of them. White, and gleaming.

I walked. I saw the shattered skulls of children. The smashed ribs of men. I saw piles. I saw patterns.

I saw death.

I walked for hours. Maybe days. I walked from the field of bones to a mountain. I climbed its steep trails. Scrambled up its slopes. At its summit I expected to find clarity. Reason.

Instead I found Priscus.

He was smiling. I couldn't understand why, or how. There was a gaping hole in his chest. 'Hello, friend.'

'Priscus?' That smile. 'Where are we?' So patient and paternal.

So calm.

I wanted to punch him. '*Where are we?*'

My friend looked at me as though I were simple. 'We're dead.' He laughed. 'We're dead, Corvus.'

I shook my head. If this was the afterlife, then why was I talking to him? Why not *her*? 'I'm looking for—'

'Beatha? You won't find her here.'

I took a sharp step backwards. How did he know about her? How the fuck did he know her name? I'd never spoken of her to my comrades.

My old friend saw my ill-ease. Put a hand on my shoulder. 'Do you trust me?'

'Of course . . .'

'Then trust me. She's not here.'

I bit back my angry words. Instead I looked down the mountainside at the field of bones. 'Where's Brutus?'

'Brutus?'

My patience snapped. 'Brutus, you fucking idiot! *Brutus!* Where is he?'

A shrug. 'Not here.'

I looked for something that I could kick instead of my comrade, but the mountain was bare. 'So who is dead?' I demanded. 'Tell me that!'

A smile. 'I am.'

I snorted at my friend's tolerance. 'You and me then, is it, Priscus? You and me and a field of bones.'

Priscus shook his head. 'Not you, comrade,' he said. 'Not now.'

Then the old soldier smiled goodbye, and closed his eyes.

I woke to the stink of blood and wounds. I heard moans. I heard prayers.

I opened my eyes.

A hospital.

I was lying on the floor. I looked to my left. The soldier was so close to me that I could see the pores of his grey skin. Hear the shallow rasp of his breath. His eyes were closed. He looked like he was going to die. I turned to my right. This one already had.

Shit. I'd been put in with the 'expectant'. Those who had fallen foul of triage.

Those who weren't going to live.

The legion had only a small number of surgeons, and before blacking out, I had been standing on a field strewn with wounded. At some point the saw-men would be busy taking limbs, but first they would patch up the soldiers that could get back into the fight – there was a war to win after all, and the ceiling above me was evidence that I had survived one of the first battles of it.

For now, at least. I looked back to my left. Grey-skin's raspy breaths had stopped. I tried to speak. I tried to stand. But the pain in my head told me that I should lie down. Lie down, be still, and wait for my own turn to die.

And so that's what I did.

A soldier needs more than friends. More than comrades.

He needs *brothers*.

It was my brothers who found me on the floor, packed amongst the dead and those soon to join them. It was my brothers who took me from the legion's hospital 'for burial', and instead carried me into the town beside our fort, and put me on to the table of a civilian doctor.

'How much can you pay?' I was told the local man had asked.

'What are your children's lives worth?' Varo had growled back.

I wasn't the only one that they'd taken there; Brutus lay on a bed beside me, his leg thick with bandages, eyes heavy with sorrow. I swallowed back my fear.

His skin had the same grey complexion as the man who'd expired beside me on the hospital floor. 'I'm getting better at dying,' Brutus croaked.

The pain in my head was receding. The pain in my heart was growing. I tried to swing my legs from my bed so that I could stand by my comrade's side. Instead, weak as a newborn foal, I collapsed heavily on to the floor, taking a jug of water with me. '*Shit!*'

I heard a door opening. Rough hands gripped me by the shoulders and legs, placing me on the edge of the bed like a child.

'You're alive,' I said when I saw their faces.

Varo and Octavius. 'We're alive,' said the big man.

'But not Priscus . . .'

They looked solemn. Varo spoke. 'Not Priscus.' He didn't give voice to the other truth in the room – that Brutus seemed likely to join him soon.

Octavius looked uncomfortable, and ran a hand over his head. I noticed the fresh scars where blades had nipped his flesh. Then he said what all soldiers say when they need to find their courage: 'I'll go get us something to drink.'

'What happened?' I asked Varo.

He told me. He told me of how he had found me amongst the hundreds of casualties. He told me about his threats. How he had held one of the doctor's children hostage until he had cleaned and sewn the deep wound on Brutus's thigh. 'There wasn't much he could do for you,' Varo explained. 'You've just been flat out. He said you'd either wake up, or you wouldn't. Even if you did, he said you'd probably be an idiot. More of one, anyway. How's your head?'

It hurt, but I could live with hurt, rather than singing pain. 'Better.'

143

'You must have got knocked out,' Varo guessed. 'A swinging arm. Flat of a blade. Who knows? I lost sight of you in the fighting, and the stretcher parties put you in with the worst cases. Those that didn't die on the field.'

I had a question. 'Why aren't we *all* dead?'

It was Brutus who answered me. His smile was a bright line in his ashen face. '*Tiberius came.*'

Or more accurately, Varo explained, Tiberius and his army had come close enough so that the rebels knew their entry to Italy would be blocked, and that by continuing to engage our force they risked a bigger army falling on their rear. Instead they had chosen flight, and retreated back through the same plain where we had first faced them.

'We did enough,' Varo said proudly. 'We did enough to hold them, and keep them from Italy.'

But at what cost?

My friend looked at the floor. Of the two and a half thousand men who had taken the field in the plain, little over twelve hundred remained alive, and of them, hundreds were injured. He went on to list the men known to us personally who had perished, most revered amongst them Priscus and Centurion Justus. 'I wish he'd hurry up with that fucking wine,' Varo simmered.

Octavius arrived moments later. Varo grabbed a cup and drank as though he'd just wandered out of the desert.

'Here,' Octavius said to me, passing me my own. I motioned that he should give it to Brutus.

'You first,' the old soldier insisted. 'You saved my life, Corvus. *Again.*'

144

I needed that drink, then. Like Varo, I threw it back in one. It was clear from his skin that if I had saved Brutus, then it was only for a matter of days. 'How long since the battle?'

'Two days,' Octavius said. 'You were out a long time. Do you even remember what happened?'

'You saved my life,' Brutus said sharply. 'And you saved the eagle!'

I'd forgotten about that fucking stick.

I snorted. I had never been one for the customs of the legion – save for the tradition of violence – and they knew as much. 'I needed something to brace myself,' I told them honestly.

Varo believed me and laughed, but Brutus shook his head.

'You saved the eagle.'

'It was a walking stick, Brutus,' I insisted, more harshly than I should have done, but despite my words the dying man kept smiling. I knew then that in his mind I had risked death to protect the standard, and that meant more to him than having his own life saved.

'I held it for a while,' he said proudly, his pale face shining with the honour. 'I held the fucking eagle, boys. I held an eagle in battle!'

My comrades smiled. Varo patted his old friend on his good leg. 'Yes you did, mate.'

'Was it everything you thought it would be?' I heard myself ask. There was acid there. Why?

Because Priscus had died, of course. He had died charging to save a piece of metal and wood. Yes, Brutus was the one holding the bastard thing, but I knew my comrades, and there wasn't anything they wouldn't give to uphold the nobility of the legion. The loss of the standard would have been a worse fate for them than their own ends.

'It was everything I thought it would be,' Brutus confirmed, and I could see the smile in his eyes.

'But you're dying.' I said it bluntly, but it still cut me.

Brutus recognized my pain, and I don't know if I ever saw him look more honest, or happy. '*I held an eagle in battle, Corvus,*' he explained. 'What would I have been in life after that? I love Lulmire, but life after battle? Life after comrades? I carried an eagle against an enemy of Rome! I was always going to die after that, one way or another, don't you see? This way, it just gets done a little quicker.'

I had nothing to say back to him. My friend was choked on honour and glory. If Marcus were here, I expect he would have cried tears of pure pride. Not I. I saw only that Brutus was leaving this world.

There was a long moment of silence that weighed heavy with my sorrow.

'Well, you know how to light a room . . .' Octavius smirked. 'Can we just get pissed now?'

There were coughs of laughter. 'Let's do that,' Varo agreed heartily. He poured wine into the cups; then he tipped more on to the room's tiles. 'Fuck the doctor.' He smiled. 'This is for our comrades.'

Brutus held up his cup. 'To Priscus.'

We drank to our friend. We drank to our comrades. Twice Octavius left to bring us more jugs. He was quick.

'Lulmire's here,' Brutus told us. 'But she knows I need some time with the lads.' We all knew what that meant. Time to say goodbyes. Brutus sniffed at his wine. 'Just do me a favour, will you, boys? When I do my final fall-out, toast me with something better than this goat's piss, will you?'

Varo snorted. 'We're just waiting for you to hurry up and die before we break out the good stuff.'

We laughed. Hard not to with that much wine in the belly. Hard not to when so many of your force was killed, and you still draw breath – for the moment, at least. Brutus was soon for the afterlife, but I did not doubt that we would see him there before too long. Even with the arrival of Tiberius and his army, there were still two hundred thousand rebels to kill.

Octavius said as much.

'You're going to be busy boys,' Brutus agreed.

There was a hushed knock on the door. 'If it's that doctor I'm gonna throw his kids on a fire,' Varo growled, but it was Lulmire.

Brutus smiled to see his wife. She had fresh dressings in her hand. 'I think this means our time's at an end, boys.'

Varo looked at me. 'Can you walk?'

The wine in my head told me yes. The wine in my limbs told me no. I stumbled.

My comrades caught me. 'We can carry you between the two of us,' Octavius assured me with the can-do attitude of a drunk.

I turned to Brutus. I didn't want to say goodbye, and so I didn't.

'I will see you again,' I told him. He went to speak, but I silenced him with a look. 'You told me once that you wouldn't die without saying goodbye,' I insisted. 'That still stands, Brutus. It still stands.'

Then, before he could speak, I turned my back on grief.

❧ 26 ❧

As promised, my brothers carried me from the town to camp. They set me down in my bed, and when I woke in the morning, I wished that I hadn't.

I was alone. A few days ago, this room had been home to seven other soldiers. Seven young men under my command. All gone now. All dead. I thought of Gums. How he had pleaded for life. How his eyeball had dangled on his cheek.

I took a deep breath. The air was warm but my skin was cold and bumped. I stood. My body held. No ache in my skull. No more than I would expect after drinking, anyway.

I looked at the seven empty beds. Where were those boys now? Buried, or gnawed at by animals where they had fallen? Were they with the gods? Their families?

Something caught my eye. It rested at the head of one of the bunks. I picked it up. Held the dainty thing in my calloused hands. It was a horse carved from wood. It was worn. Ancient-looking. Instinct told me that it was the childhood toy of one of the boys who had died under my command, left in the safety of the barracks to await his return, too precious to be risked on a battlefield.

I looked into the creature's carved eyes. 'He's not coming back.'

I wanted to be heartless, then. To show indifference. I thought about hurling the thing out of the window, or throwing it into the hearth of our stove, ready for winter.

I wanted to show myself that the deaths of the seven young men I was supposed to lead had not affected me. That I was an island amidst the flow of misery that was washing over our legion.

But I could not. Instead I placed the toy at the head of my own bunk.

I had been looking at it for a long time when the call for assembly was sounded.

In armour polished by my comrades, I stood outside the barrack block with what was left of our century. Where there had been eighty, there were now thirty-five. Another dozen of our comrades were in the hospital. Some were expected to return. Others had lost limbs to the bone-saw.

Varo stood at the front of the formation in the place that Centurion Justus had held, and Priscus after him. Both men had died for their leadership. To the rear of our thinned ranks Octavius stood in the position of optio. I begrudged neither man their rank. Station was not something that I sought. They had stepped up as others fell, and I simply wanted to fight. That desire was as strong in me as ever, I realized. There was too much to think of, otherwise.

'Century!' Varo boomed in his deep bass. 'Atten-*shun*!'

Our sandals stamped down in unison. Something about having been in battle – having fought and bled as the Eighth – had pushed us further into becoming one mind and body.

I had no idea why the parade had been called, and there had been no time to ask my brothers, but now the reason for it marched across the front of our formation and returned the salute of my friend. It was our cohort commander, his left arm bandaged, and with him was a man I would never have expected to see at such a pathetic assembly of soldiers.

He was our legion commander, known to us as Hook-nose – it stood as sharp as a reaping scythe beneath his scarred brow.

The legate turned to look over the bedraggled century. Was that sorrow that I saw in his narrow eyes? Love?

Maybe. It was certainly pride. 'Men' – his chest swelled as he began – 'yesterday, I spoke with you as a legion' – so I had missed that, thank the gods – 'but today I wanted to see you like this. I wanted to see the family that bore such heroes.

'We have faced dark days, but from darkness come the greatest shining glories.'

I had no idea what Hook-nose was talking about. I let my eyes flick to Varo. His soldier's mask was in place. Impassive. Stoic. It looked over the heads of the men in front of him. He had done so on the battlefield, while I'd let my own eyes drop to the horrors at my feet.

'You are Legionary Varo?' the legate asked of my brother.

'Yes, sir!'

'It's a severe offence to lie to an officer ...' The aristocrat smiled as he delivered the well-worn line. '. . . *Centurion*.' Varo's promotion was confirmed. 'Well deserved!'

'Thank you, sir!'

'I hear you're the man who began the battle cry?' the officer went on. '*Fear the Eighth*.'

151

For a second, Varo's mask slipped. 'I . . . I don't remember, sir.'

'He was, sir!' someone shouted from the ranks, and the legate smiled.

'They fear us all right, Centurion Varo,' the officer told him, his tone earnest. 'After that battle, they *fear* us, and I think that your cry is a fitting challenge for this legion. When we face our enemy, "Fear the Eighth" will be our call.'

'Thank you, sir!'

The cohort commander stepped in to avoid further embarrassment to his newest centurion. 'Legionary Octavius?' he asked of the parade. 'Report.'

'Yes, sir!' Octavius answered, marching to the front of the formation.

The legate returned his salute. 'I confirm your appointment to optio.' The officer smiled proudly.

'Thank you, sir!'

As Octavius marched back to the rear of the formation, I expected that the officers would leave. Maybe speak some words about glory, first.

I didn't expect that they'd both look straight at me.

'Legionary Corvus!' the cohort commander ordered. 'March out!'

Shit.

Stiff as a rock and red from the attention, I marched out to the front of the parade and saluted the legate.

'Legionary Corvus reporting as ordered, sir!'

The commander of a butchered legion looked at me as though I were his firstborn son. 'Legionary Corvus, your actions on the battlefield are in keeping with the highest traditions of this legion, and for your part in preventing our eagle from falling into enemy hands, I give you this.'

I followed his eyes. There was something in the cohort commander's hands – a gold disc, engraved with the face of Jupiter. The legate took it from him and affixed it to my armour.

I was a decorated soldier.

'Thank you, sir,' I mumbled. *What will Marcus think?* I asked myself as I threw up a salute and prepared to fall back into the ranks.

'Not yet,' my cohort commander said quietly.

I stood rigid. What now? The legate had that look again: pride. Buckets of the bloody stuff.

'Legionary Corvus, you saved our eagle in battle.' Hook-nose spoke loudly enough so that everyone could hear. 'You saved the eagle of the Eighth,' he said with conviction, 'and for that, it gives me great pleasure to honour you with this appointment: as the legion's standard-bearer!'

Shit.

The cohort commander began the applause. It gave me moments to form a stumbling denial. 'Sir,' I began as it died away, 'I . . . I just want to kill the enemy, sir.'

'You'll have plenty of chances to do that, standard-bearer.' Hook-nose grinned like a hungry shark. 'The rebels have had their turn. Now *we* go on the offensive.'

❧ 27 ❧

I looked at the bird on a stick. The sacred totem. The symbol of our legion. The only thing it stirred in me was memory. The feel of Brutus on my shoulder as I'd carried him from the pile of dead and dying, and back to the ranks of what seemed like our last stand.

Maybe that was the point, I realized. Maybe that was the idea behind the eagles. That a veteran would see, hear and feel those moments where he had fought and bled beside his brothers. With their sacrifice in mind, surely he would be more likely to offer his own in the glory of Rome, for what was that glory when it was broken down? It was brother fighting for brother. Comrade dying for comrade. The Empire's borders would grow as a result of it, but on the battlefield, it was the kingdom of one's friends that was a soldier's concern.

'Well, maybe not if you're Marcus,' I muttered to myself, thinking of how he'd probably be on his knees before the eagle now, and I wished that he was with me. Not so that I could see the pride on his face that his oldest friend carried one of the few eagles in the world, but so that I could make lewd jokes about his admiration, and cast accusations about where that bird would be nesting if he were left alone with it.

I folded my arms and let out a sigh of self-pity and boredom. Gods, I was bored. I was bored, and I was lonely. I wanted to be with my friends, but the role of standard-bearer was a solitary one. I'd already kept myself busy by

154

shining the bloody bird until it blazed. Now I wanted to play dice. I wanted to drink. I wanted to fight.

I had tried to impress that later point on the legate to the point where my – now former – cohort commander's scowl had threatened to grow its own fists. The appointment was not an offer for me to consider. I was being volun-told that I was to take this position, and that was that. I supposed that I wouldn't be the last soldier to be handed a rank or task that he had neither asked for nor wanted, but that was scant consolation as I was left with nothing to do but *think*.

Brutus was on my mind often in the days that followed the battle and the regaining of my consciousness. Lulmire had brought no word, and so I assumed that the hard old bastard was clinging to life, or that his death had broken her so completely that she couldn't bring herself to tell us. Of course, I could have investigated myself, but . . . but while there was no news, there was hope. Why seek out misery when it is so good at finding us?

Varo and Octavius had their hands full. Because of the heavy casualties suffered, the Fourth and Fifth Cohorts were being disbanded to bring the First and Second to full strength – the Third would remain at half – and so my friends were busy drilling their men in preparation for the coming battle. Where that would be, and when, I could only guess. What I did know was that there were two hundred thousand or more of the enemy under arms. Fearing that the intended target of the Danube invasion, King Marabodus, would break the treaty, turn the table, and invade across that river, Tiberius had been forced to leave a strong army in the north of the region. Even with his arrival in Pannonia, we would still be outnumbered.

'Will they fight?' was the question I heard when I was fortunate enough to be in the company of other soldiers. Will they fight, or will they take to the hills? The legions wanted a pitched battle on the plains. Something grand and glorious that could decide this war – sorry, *domestic uprising* – in a day.

I didn't see such a thing as being likely. Brutus and Priscus had talked about the early campaigns in this region that had – supposedly – brought the Pannonians and Dalmatians to heel. Once the men of the region realized that they could not stand in open battle against Roman legions with anything less than a huge advantage in numbers, they took to harassing attacks. Brutus had told me that he had friends sent to clear the enemy from their mountain strongholds. He hadn't seen many of them again.

Yes, 'Will they fight?' was the talk of the legion, but no one seemed to be asking *why* the enemy were fighting in the first place. Weeks ago, these men had been raised to fight for Rome. Why then had they turned their blades towards the Empire's throat?

Some word of it came through the rumour mill. Seeing the strength of the region's warriors assembled on the marshalling grounds, Bato – a local chieftain – had been moved to give the assembly a simple choice. 'That we fight a war is inevitable,' he was reported to have said to the mass of soldiery. 'Either we die to expand Rome's borders, or we fight to build our own! What would you have it be?'

Hard to argue with such a choice. Hard to argue with fighting against the men that had enslaved or killed your fathers, uncles, cousins and brothers, rather than serving them.

I was near alone in that opinion, of course. The few times I had ventured it I had been beaten down with pompous assertions about the glory of Rome, and the brazen cheek of the rebels for not appreciating what they were being given. I did not blame my comrades for this. Many of them were from Italy. I was not. I had been born and raised in Iader, on the Dalmatian coast. Yes, it was a Roman settlement, but no island is immune from the sea that washes around it. Many native Dalmatians had come from the hills and coastal villages to take advantage of what the town had to offer – a bustling forum and market. A harbour. Security, and order. I had many friends there, and had been raised speaking both Latin and the local tongue. There was no doubt in my mind now that the boys I had grown up playing soldiers with were now my enemy. They were my age, and so would have been the most likely to be pressed or volunteered into service. Then, at the marshalling grounds, willing or not, they would have been informed that their enemy was now Rome. The rumour was that Bato had offered the Dalmatians a choice, but in reality, I doubt the men holding spear and shield had any more say in the decision-making of their leaders than we did with ours. It was the lot of most men to obey and die. Very few got to make the choice over what those deaths would stand for.

I looked at the eagle again. Those hooded eyes. How many deaths had it witnessed? How many battles? How many triumphs? How many failures? Little of the latter, I supposed, or else she would be adorning a king's hall now, and not my solitary companion.

'I should give you a name,' I thought out loud. 'How about Gallus?'

Chicken.

The eagle looked back sternly but said nothing. I took that as approval.

I turned to my other companion, then. Hee held my left flank – the small wooden horse that had belonged to one of my section. I tried not to think about how its former owner had died, and instead wondered at what happiness this child's toy had given him. It was a joyful mystery to me.

'You can be Xanthus.' One of the horses that drew the chariot of Achilles, a story that Marcus had repeated to me as a child until it was pouring out of my ears. So vivid was the memory that, for a moment, I thought I heard him speak.

'Corvus!' he shouted, running to me. 'Corvus!'

No dream! My friend. My oldest, greatest friend. I sprang to my feet to embrace him, but I was too slow . . .

His face wide with awe, Marcus dropped to his knees in front of the eagle.

Before I could help myself, I began to laugh.

❧ 28 ❧

It was a long time before I was done suggesting the crude acts that Marcus could perform with the staff of Gallus, the legion's eagle. As a child and a young man I was always trying to be a comedian, but those days had died when I had tramped on my father's skull. Only Marcus could pull the jokes from me now. He was a window to my past. The parts that I wanted to remember, even with the pain that they caused me.

I hugged him so tightly that I thought his back would snap. 'Gods, I have missed you.'

Marcus stood back from me. There were tears in his eyes. Tears on his cheeks. 'I'm so proud of you, Corvus. *Standard-bearer? Corvus*, I'm so proud!'

'Did you bring wine?' I asked, uncomfortable with the adulation, even from him.

'Forget the wine, brother, give me the stories!'

'Wine,' I insisted.

'I'm taking a walk,' I called to the sentries who were posted nearby – I wasn't the only one charged with her protection. After all, I could hardly turn up in the latrines with the legion's standard in my hand, could I?

'These men are your friends?' Marcus asked me as we walked away.

I shook my head. 'I get different ones every day depending on which cohort has the camp guard, and I can't talk to them. Legate would have their heads if they seemed distracted.'

'But he'll be all right with you drinking?' Marcus smirked.

'He loves me,' I said honestly. 'Calls me the hero of the Eighth.'

Marcus grinned. '*Fear the Eighth.*'

'You heard about that?'

'The whole army's heard about that! The battle is growing famous, brother.'

'What are they calling it?'

When Marcus smiled with pride, I could tell that the name was going to be a pompous one. 'The battle of the night and day,' he said with adulation in his tone.

Gods. Worse than I thought. 'It was day, then night,' I corrected.

'Well, that's what they're calling it.'

'Great.'

My friend looked at me sideways. 'Shouldn't you be wearing your bearskin?' he asked, referring to the thick fur that draped from helmet over shoulders, a symbol of my rank.

'Slaves are still cleaning it,' I said. The previous man in my position had left his mark with pints of blood.

'There's nothing more important than the appearance of a soldier,' Marcus replied. 'It's the four Ds, Corvus. Dress. Discipline. *And dealing death.*'

I rolled my eyes. 'I missed you, brother.'

I found a quiet inn with Marcus. After a few drinks, I relented under his barrage of questions about the battle, and began to answer. The memories were not pleasant for me, but neither were they painful. I suppose I was numb. I don't know how much of that had to do with the wine. It certainly became easier to talk once the first jug was empty.

Marcus hung on every word. At times there was pride on his face, at other times, envy. Never was there disgust or fear that he would likely face such horrors, and soon. 'I can't wait for battle,' he told me honestly.

I didn't hold his naivety against him. The truth was that I had been eager to spill blood, and now it seemed I was still anxious to spill more. 'You lose yourself in it,' I explained. 'There's no past or future, brother, there's just that breath. That stab, or parry.'

'You loved it?'

I shook my head. 'No.'

Marcus frowned. 'But you want more?'

I did.

'I don't understand.'

Neither did I.

'Tell me about the eagle.'

I told him about Priscus instead. Marcus took a deep breath of pride. 'He died for Rome.'

No. 'He died for Brutus.' I'm not sure if that was true. At times, Priscus had displayed flashes of the same devotion to a faraway city as my oldest friend.

Marcus shrugged his shoulders. 'Brutus is a soldier of Rome, and so if Priscus died for Brutus, then he died for Rome.'

There was no getting away from it, and so I drank. 'Well, here's to Rome then.' Here's to the city neither of us has ever seen. Here's to the city that controls our lives, and our deaths.

Marcus grinned. The toast had probably got him hard. 'To Rome!' He saluted.

The next day, he'd get his chance to die for her.

❧ 29 ❧

By virtue of my new position I attended the fort's headquarters building to hear the legate's orders for the coming campaign against the rebels. As well as Hook-nose, the briefing was attended by the legion's tribunes, cohort commanders and senior centurions. My friend Varo was not amongst the mass, which was just as well – the courtyard at the centre of the building was tightly packed, and Varo would have likely crushed someone with his bulk. I had been required to bring Gallus with me, and I stood with the eagle at the front of the assembly. In such a position, I could see the faces of the men whose orders breathed disciplined life into the legion. Their faces were hard, and eager. They wanted after the enemy. They wanted blood.

Hook-nose promised it to them, but not before he had pointed me out as an example of what made our legion the finest in all of the army – nay, the world. I was glad that I was wearing the bearskin, then. The slaves hadn't been able to rid it of the stink of blood and guts, but at least the hooded peak formed by the bear's maw did something to hide my face.

'Men,' the legate went on, 'our legion has been tasked by the noble Tiberius with clearing out the enemy from between Siscia and Salona.' These were the main camp of Tiberius's army, and the regional capital on the coast – a walled city that had withstood the early attacks of the rebels. This enemy had now retreated into the mountains. 'It's our job to dig them out!' the legate explained.

162

I watched the faces of the gathered officers. I saw some grit their teeth. Another snarled. They wanted open battle but, to get at the enemy, they'd take whatever they were given.

'Halfway between the cities is the River Titius, and we'll use that as our axis of advance. It's no good for river transport, and so the baggage train will be needed for supplies. Eighth Cohort, you'll provide its security. Don't think that you'll be in for an easy time, though. We expect the rebels to target you to try and gain supplies for themselves. They'll be getting hungry in the mountains.'

'We'll feed them some steel, sir,' a voice promised.

Hook-nose grinned. 'I'm sure you will.

'Now, the two tribes between the cities are the Colopani and Sardeates, and both are expected to be hostile. First and Second Cohort, as you have both had the honour of being recently blooded, you will advance along the river plain, so much as there is one. We don't expect that the enemy will stand and fight, if they are even there at all. Recent scouting reports suggest that the fighters from those tribes are up in the mountains.

'Number Seven Cohort will clear the mountains to the east of the river. Number Six, the west.' *Marcus*. 'The Ninth will follow on behind the baggage train to catch any rebels emerging from their holes, while the Third and Tenth will remain here to hold the fort, and to act as a reserve force. Prince Arminius's cavalry will be split between the reserve and the valley floor.'

I followed Hook-nose's gaze to a tall, muscled man of royal blood and bearing. He had the blond and vital look of a German, with an honest and noble face that was shaved in the Roman way. A simple inclination of his head was all that he gave to acknowledge the legate's order. Like all well-born, the man seemed perfectly at ease with power and command.

'Now,' Hook-nose asked of his assembly, 'are there any questions?'

I watched as a number of hands went into the air, but I didn't listen to the enquiries, or their answers. Instead I thought of Marcus, and how his cohort would be going into the mountains. I thought of him, and remembered what Brutus had said of his own comrades who had carried out that task in the last war.

I never saw most of them again.

Marcus's cohort held the fort's guard duty, and so, after the briefing had broken up, I sought out Varo and Octavius.

'I like your new hat,' the slighter man greeted me, poking at the bear on my head. 'Stinks though.'

We were in the spacious centurion's quarters that had once belonged to Centurion Justus, but were now home to Varo. I looked at my friend, and saw worry in the lines of his face. Not worry for himself, I was certain, but from the burden of command – he was about to lead eighty men on a combat operation for the first time.

'I only ever wanted to soldier,' he told me with a sigh. 'The extra money's nice though.'

'Got to live until payday first.' Octavius smirked. There were only two pay parades held a year, and our second was still some time away. 'Isn't that your job now?' he asked me.

164

I nodded. As standard-bearer, the legion's coffers would come under my watch. Like the eagle's security, I would not be expected to carry out such tasks single-handedly, but it was yet another burden that I wished to be rid of.

'I want to come with you,' I told my comrades. 'I don't want to be carrying a fucking stick around with the headquarters staff while you're fighting.'

'Fighting?' Octavius laughed. 'Didn't you hear? There're no rebels where we're going, Corvus. This is just a pleasant stroll in the country.'

'Be quiet, you dickhead,' Varo rumbled, in no mood for jokes. 'Corvus, I'm not going to say no to having you close by when things get ugly.'

'You think they will?'

He shrugged his thick shoulders as though the answer was obvious. I suppose that it was. 'It's war.'

'Domestic uprising,' Octavius corrected.

'Shut up. Now listen, Corvus. The legate likes you, right?'

'Loves me.'

'So use that. Tell him that you want to keep going up the ranks. Tell him that you want to learn all about leading, and war. Maybe that way you won't be stuck in the rear. It's not like there's going to be a battle line for you to stand in with the eagle.'

'More than that,' Octavius added, latching on to the idea, 'tell him that with all these narrow mountain passes and stuff, what's the point in risking the eagle? We all know there's no big battle coming. Why risk it falling into enemy hands in some skirmish?'

I could see that Varo liked that notion. So did I. 'I'll try.'

And I did.

'You're a fiery bastard, standard-bearer,' Hook-nose told me. 'I knew that I'd made the right choice with you. I think those are all excellent ideas. No point imperilling the eagle unnecessarily, is there? We'll leave her under the watch of the Tenth Cohort.'

I tried not to show my relief.

'Some people have a nose for battle,' the legate went on, evidently believing I was one of them. 'You go where you see fit. This will be the first action for most of the men in the legion. They need leadership, and they need inspiration.' His eyes burned into mine. Evidently, I was the latter. 'Move around my legion, Corvus. Find the fight, and inspire my men. Show them what it means to be a hero of Rome.'

I didn't feel much like a hero when I sought out Marcus that night. Rather, I felt like a child.

'What's on your mind?' my friend asked me. 'Brutus?' he asked insightfully.

I nodded. No word had come. No question had been sent. 'I should go and see him.' But I knew that I wouldn't. Twice I'd been too slow to save his life.

I didn't have long with Marcus. As second in command of his century, he needed to be checking and double-checking his troops before we marched out with the dawn.

'I can't wait for this,' he told me. It wasn't the great battle that would have been the invasion across the Danube, but it was something at least. Something my friend had wanted all his life.

The goodbye was no easier the second time. 'At least this time I can come and find you,' I promised.

His smile threatened to light up the night. 'Imagine that, brother. You and I side by side, shield by shield, and with an enemy to our front.'

What can I say? That *did* sound good. The only thing that could be better would be returning to a time when war was a child's game to me, and nothing more. A time when I had dreamed of Rome, and her, and nothing else.

But those days were gone.

Blood, then. War. 'It does sound good,' I told my brother, and I embraced him. 'I'll see you in the mountains.'

❧ 30 ❦

I walked beside Varo. In my hand was the bridle of a dark, thick-set, good-tempered pony. I called the creature Balius, the second of Achilles' horses. Xanthus rested inside my pack. I wondered what my friend would say if he knew I was carrying a child's toy on the clearance operation.

'This is shit,' he muttered instead.

This was our sweep south to flush out and kill any rebels between Tiberius's main base inland, and the coast. We were five days in, and so far, the only enemies confronted had been the scorching heat and the hateful terrain. I was with my old cohort, and we were in the low land, so much as it was, an abandoned valley running beneath the peaks of scarred mountainsides. On those peaks and reaches moved the Sixth and Seventh Cohorts. Somewhere to the west of me, Marcus would be sweating and panting for Rome.

'This is shit,' Varo insisted again, his words low enough so that only I could hear, though I knew the words were intended for himself. At times a soldier needs a battle cry. At others, he simply needs to voice his frustration. Varo was far from the only one doing so.

The Roman soldier is trained to be able to cover twenty miles a day in full kit. Therefore, five days into our operation, we should have covered a hundred miles, and be halfway to the coast.

We'd made less than twenty.

The reason was the terrain, of course. There were no paved roads, but even so, in the valley, we could have pushed

168

on at an aggressive pace. The problem was that in doing so, we would outstrip our comrades in the mountains. If there were rebels ahead of us, then we would be placing our head in the noose. For those of us in the low ground, much of the day was spent static as the hard-pressed scouts and messengers raced between the limbs of the legion to maintain as much cohesion as possible.

'Here we go again,' Varo said to me. Up ahead, the soldiers of the century ahead were beginning to stop. The action rippled down the line. The newly minted centurion turned to his men. 'One Section, push out sentries on the left flank. Two Section on the right. The rest of you, get on your arses and take your helmets off.' Varo turned to me. 'No point having the lads' heads cooking.' He was a good leader.

'Hotter than Sol's balls,' I agreed, thinking of the sun god, and happy with my decision to let my horse carry my helmet and bearskin.

I looked at the mountains either side of us. They were brutes, their lower slopes a carpet of sharp-looking trees. Everything in this region looked tough. No wonder Hooknose was proceeding with caution.

'Do you think we'll see one?' Varo asked as he wiped a layer of sweat and dust from his face, hundreds of pairs of feet having kicked up the dirt trail. 'A rebel?'

'I don't know,' I answered honestly. The few villages we had come across had been abandoned some time ago. Even if the enemy did not have a force ahead of us, it was hard to believe that the huge number of rebels would not have dispatched spies and scouts to watch the movements of one of Tiberius's legions.

'Everyone's going to know we're coming,' Varo grumbled.

Maybe, but I knew that this land was not a unified region like Roman Italy. It was a place of tribes and chiefs who looked to themselves first. 'If a chief at one end of the valley has a feud with the chief at the other end, he'd probably be happy to let us at them,' I explained to my friend. 'They know we won't be staying in the valley, and once we go, and his competition's dead, then who's to stop him taking the new grazing lands?'

Varo snorted. 'No honour.'

'It's the game, I suppose,' I said, thinking of how Tiberius had been threatening to destroy the Marcomanni across the Danube before rebellion had brought him back. Now, that German tribe had been paid handsomely to behave. 'The chiefs here, they just play it at a smaller level.'

'No honour,' Varo said again.

Ahead of us, movement was rippling down the line. Men were getting to their feet. The sentries were returning to the column. Varo pulled on his helmet. 'Prepare to move,' he said to his soldiers.

We inched onwards.

I stayed with my old century that night. In the darkness we heard wolves. On one mountain we saw flame. Not a lot of it. A single dwelling was the guess.

'You should check in with Hook-nose,' Octavius warned me. 'I know he loves you, but he'll be forgetting your face. Officers have short memories.'

Varo chewed through a mouth of biscuit. 'He's right.'

And so the next morning I pulled myself into the saddle, and rode Balius to the headquarters group that was placed between my old cohort and the First. I had ridden as a child but I was long out of practice, and so our pace was a gentle meander beside the long line of sullen troops, each man fighting his own battle with boredom. I saw a few look at me. I saw a few talk. Some even waved. I was known now, I realized. Known as the man who had saved the legion's eagle.

The headquarters group was easy enough to find. Recognizing that the progress of his legion would need to be painstaking, Hook-nose had taken to setting up in a tented position twice a day, rather than being constantly on the move. It made him easier to find for his dispatch riders, and I saw one of these wiry men rein in his beast now, before throwing himself nimbly from its back. A slave came forward to take the reins, and the man ran in the direction of our legion command.

I pressed my heels into Balius's flank – such haste could only mean the enemy.

I brought my horse to a stop next to the dispatch rider's own. I wanted his news, but I did not want to face the legate and risk being held in headquarters or sent on some other task. Sure enough, the rider soon reappeared – he would be taking orders back in the direction that he'd come.

'Comrade, what's happening?' I asked.

There was white foam on his lips, and dirt on his face – he'd had a hard ride. 'Sixth Cohort came across a fortified village.'

Marcus. 'Did they attack?'

'They were preparing to when I left.'

Without thinking, I offered a prayer for my friend. 'You're going back?'

The man nodded.

'I'll come with you.'

The cavalryman looked at me, and didn't see a horseman. 'It's a tough ride . . .'

It didn't matter. 'Lead the way,' I said evenly. 'My brother's up there.'

Poor Balius. He suffered on that climb. On the narrow paths of dirt and rock. The trail was steep and angry, but there was no time for me to see to my horse. Instead I had to look to my own survival. We were but two men, and the rocky outcrops that littered the heights begged for ambushes to be laid. I could only pray that the Sixth had been diligent in sweeping the heights. I tried not to think about how easy it would be for the enemy to slip back in; these mountains were their homes.

I didn't need the dispatch rider to tell me that we were getting close. Three black smudges over the ridge did that. I took confidence from the sight. If buildings were burning, it meant that our men had made it inside the fortified village. Still, there would be a butcher's bill to pay for that accomplishment. What would I do if Marcus were among the dead? I had always known that my greatest friend could become a casualty of war, but until the dispatch rider had confirmed that Marcus's cohort was going into a fight I hadn't *known*. It had just been a rumour of fear before. Now its talons were deep in my guts.

What would I do if he were dead? Maybe just ride on into the mountains until I found a rebel polite enough to kill me, too. I didn't want to leave Varo, Octavius and, if he still lived, Brutus, but life without Marcus seemed so . . . pointless.

'There they are!' the dispatch rider announced.

We came over the lip of the ridge. There was a century of the cohort here; sentries had been posted as the other men rested on the ground, their faces haggard from almost a week of crossing such terrain. 'The fight's over?' I asked, knowing that the men would be kitted up and prepared to move as a reserve if it wasn't.

'Yeah,' one of the sentries answered me. 'Was over pretty quick. You going up there?'

'I am.'

'We haven't had word on the casualties, yet. Do you mind sending word back? We've all got mates up there.'

I promised that I would; then I rode onwards. I passed another century. Then another. Neither was the unit of my friend. Two centuries had made the attack, I was told. Marcus must be among them.

The fortified village loomed ahead. It sat on a summit, man-made walls of stone filling the spaces where nature had provided bastions of rock. It would have been formidable to bandits and brigands, but to Roman soldiers it had fallen quickly, and now three of the six buildings inside were ablaze.

My heart stuck in my throat. Before the wall, I saw that seven bodies had been lined up beside each other. Roman soldiers. The butcher's bill.

Balius was exhausted, but I pushed him on. In my haste to get from the saddle I half fell, and then I was over to the bodies, scanning them, moving from face to face. Some were young. Some were old.

None were Marcus.

'Oi,' a comrade of the dead accosted me. 'What the fuck are you doing?' There was a spade in his hand. Part of the burial party. I had no doubt he'd use the tool on me if I gave the wrong answer.

'I'm looking for my friend.'

He softened. 'Name?'

'Marcus. He's an optio.'

'Not dead,' the man confirmed, and I felt a weight rise from my shoulders. 'This is everyone.'

I looked at the fallen. Most had wounds to their faces, necks and shoulders. Killed as they had stormed the wall. 'A hard fight?'

The soldier scraped his spade along the dirt, and looked at the dead. 'Hard enough.'

I went in search of Marcus.

I found my friend. His arms were red with blood.

'Corvus?' There was no surprise in his tone. He was numb. Numb from combat. I had experienced it myself, and now I bore witness to it in my brother.

'I came as soon as I heard. I'm sorry, Marcus. I wanted to fight with you.'

He smiled, then. 'I finally got blooded. It was a long wait.'

'You killed?'

'Two, I think.'

I looked around me. The enemy dead lay out in the dirt. Two dozen of them. Maybe more.

They weren't all men.

'Any survivors?'

'Of theirs?' Marcus shook his head. 'A couple. We told them what would happen if they tried to stand. Did they think they could hold back a cohort?'

I wondered at that. What would have happened if they had surrendered? Likely they would have been accused of supporting the rebels. Maybe the men would have been killed, and their women and children enslaved, or worse.

I heard evidence of that now. Screams from one of the huts that was not ablaze. A woman's screams. Then a second voice. She sounded younger.

Marcus saw me looking. 'This is war, I suppose. The men are entitled to the spoils.'

I nodded. What Marcus said was a law as old as time. Still, the screams scratched at the inside of my skull. I was glad of the distraction when a centurion walked over to us, his face almost totally swathed in bandage. 'I've got to go back to the rear and get this fucking thing sewn up,' he swore. 'I'm taking the walking wounded with me, and two sections as stretcher-bearers and escort. The rest of the century is yours until I get back, Marcus. All right?'

Marcus delivered a salute as though he was talking to the Emperor himself. 'Yes, sir.'

'Look after my men,' the centurion said, and I could see that it pained him to be leaving. 'Who's this?' he then asked.

'My brother from Iader, sir. Corvus.'

'Corvus?' His one visible eye opened wider. 'The man who saved the eagle? It's an honour to meet you, standard-bearer.'

He put out his hand. I took it. I saw him look about me, and realized that he was seeking the legion's standard.

'Under the guard of the Tenth, in camp,' I explained.

'Ah, well, a hero of the legion like yourself is welcome in my century anytime. Especially if he's a friend to Marcus.'

'He's my brother, sir,' Marcus corrected with a smile.

It was a proud moment for him, and I loved my friend for it. I almost smiled myself, but then another scream of a raped woman cut through the mountain air.

The centurion shook his head. 'I told the lads to gag her.'

He took his leave then. I shadowed Marcus as he took control of his men. He was a natural leader. There were work parties to be organized. Roman dead needed to be buried. The enemy were rolled down the steep mountainside. The stone of their wall followed them. The position would not be left for the rebels to reoccupy.

I heard the sound of hoofbeats, and turned. The man in the saddle was squat and stern: cohort commander of the Sixth. 'Marcus. You're commanding the century now?'

'Yes, sir!'

The officer surveyed the industry of my friend, and nodded in satisfaction. 'Scouts say there's another village a few miles ahead. We need to keep the pressure up, so I'm moving the cohort out now while we still have daylight.

Finish your work, stay here for the night, then at first light, move out to meet us. We're going straight along the ridgeback, but I'll send you runners at dawn. They'll meet you on the trail.'

'Yes, sir!'

The cohort commander returned the salute. 'Good job today, Marcus.'

When the old soldier was out of sight I crossed the two steps to my friend and embraced him. I knew how much this meant to him. 'I'm so proud of you, brother.' His first action. His first kills. I yearned for the days when we had been children, and innocent of life's cruelty, but Marcus had dreamed of this day since he had come marching out of the womb. 'I'm so fucking proud of you.'

He was my brother.

❧ 31 ❦

The night did not pass quietly.

There were four women. I learned that from their screams. Each had their own melody of pain. Each had their own words that begged for mercy. I doubted the Italians raping them understood any of it.

I did.

'Please!'

'Stop!'

'Not her. Not my daughter . . .'

I stood a lonely vigil. Marcus and his men had been slogging hard through the mountains. Most chose sleep over rape. Sentries were rotated. A double guard was standard practice at night, but I stood alone, with only the screams for company. I did not enjoy the sound of such misery, but . . .

But they were far easier to bear than the death of Marcus would be. The women had been on the wrong side yesterday – the losing side – and this was war. It was as simple as that.

Wasn't it?

I tried to clear such questions from my head, but where to take my mind? Should I think about Priscus with a spear through his chest? Should I think about Brutus, decaying if not already dead? By his own admission, his life had run its course once he could no longer serve in war. Perhaps I should think about the death that had sent me running to become an instrument of such violence in the first place? A party to rape.

Another scream. It was shrill.

A child's.

I spat on the ground. The girl's screams were her *own*. Damn it, Corvus, the girls screams are her *own*.

The wheel of death spun in my mind, but where else could I take it? I would not voice my concerns out loud. Who did such a thing? And even if I could find some kindly soul to listen – some soft touch amongst the hard steel of the legion – then perhaps that someone would take pity on me, thinking me full of sorrow and timid mourning.

They would be wrong.

I was full of anger. Brimming with it like a boiling cauldron. The thought of the dead didn't make me want to curl up and join them. It made me want to punch, bite, strike and kill.

'Brother?' Marcus. Quiet, but awake.

'Over here.'

He joined me in my place amongst the rocks. The night was as black as pitch. No moon. 'They could march their army by our noses and we'd never see them.'

'Smell them though. Hear them.'

My brother knew what it meant when I was terse. He stayed quiet.

'You should go back to sleep,' I said.

'I'll keep you company.'

We stood in silence until the black night bled to grey, and death and dawn came to the mountains.

The cloud hung like grey wool about the peak. Visibility was low. Dawn had yet to grow to day. It was time to move out.

For the first time I saw the four women. They were kicked out of the hut. None had clothing. None made any protest. Their spirit had fled in the night. They were empty vessels, now. Ghost ships adrift in the current of war.

'We can't take them with us,' Marcus told his men. 'You've had your fun, lads.'

I couldn't see the features of the men as they heard those words. I don't know if they mistook the order, or proceeded on their own initiative. I just saw four shapes shoved on to their knees. Heard the sound of blades sawing into flesh. The crunch as the steel grazed against spine. I heard the gags as the women writhed on the floor, and the curse of a soldier as pumping blood shot over his feet. 'Give me some bastard warning next time!' he growled at his comrades.

Unburdened, the century fell into loose ranks on the trail. The mountain was no parade square, but there was safety in formation, and Marcus would hold to one as much as was possible.

'Prepare to move . . .' he told his men, the order passed from mouth to mouth, muted by tactics and tiredness.

'I'll catch up with you,' I told him.

Concerned with command, he didn't question my decision.

The century moved off. My mount Balius had been taken back to legion HQ by the dispatch rider. I stayed behind alone. I shouldn't have. If there were rebels waiting in the shadows, drawn by the screams, then I would not be able to outpace them. Not weighed down in a legionary's war gear.

But instead of leaving, I stood alone in the silence. There were no sounds of choking, now. The women had leaked their lives away before the last pair of sandals had marched by their heads.

When the light of dawn was long enough, I looked at them. Three were face down in the stained dirt. The fourth was on her back, her hands on her neck. Between her legs was as bloody as her opened throat. Her rape had been violent. Her death, more so.

All about me on the peak was silent stillness. There was a finality in the air. A judgement on the value of life. The mountain didn't cry for its children. Not a single stir, or accusation. Not even so much as a breeze.

I looked down. The dirt was dark red beside the child.

The sun had risen before I walked away.

'What's wrong?' Marcus asked. I had caught up with the group before the sun had burned the haze from the mountains. Now, it felt as though a torch was being held in our faces as the century took a pause for breath and water. 'The heat?' It wasn't the heat. 'Corvus. Speak to me. *I'm your brother.*'

I could see that my silence was causing him pain. It was the only reason I opened my mouth. 'Those women today,' I shared begrudgingly, 'every time I see something like that, it just . . .' I wanted to hit something, then. *Kill* someone. I forced myself to finish. 'It just reminds me.'

My greatest friend. As he had done so many times before, Marcus put a hand on my shoulder. His patient look righted my ship. A ship that was heading for the rocks of self-destruction. He was the only one who knew exactly *what* I was being reminded of. 'You'll want to hit me for what I'm about to say,' he promised. 'You've hit me when I've said it before.'

Maybe I would, but I could see that he'd take that punch without complaint. He'd still be there for me. Like all brothers, we had bloodied each other's noses before. 'Just fucking say it,' I growled. Did I want to hear it?

'You have to let her go.'

Yes.

But how? Better to ask the sun to rise in the west and set in the east than to ask a man to forgive, and forget.

'Fuck off, Marcus,' I growled, though my words were weaker than my anger.

Did he just fucking smile?

'Brother, listen. *Look*, and *listen*. We have what we always wanted!' he said, gesturing at his century. 'We're soldiers, brother! Soldiers at war!'

I snorted, and shook my head. I loved this bastard, but he was wrong. So wrong. I wanted to embrace him for that foolishness, but I couldn't do such a thing in front of his command. Instead I tapped the sword on my hip. 'This is what *you* always wanted, Marcus,' I told him. '*You.*'

I had wanted her. Nothing but her.

Maybe I would have told him that again, if I hadn't heard the sentry's call: 'Runners coming in!'

The two lithe men were soaked in sweat. One spoke, bringing breathless word from the main body of the cohort: 'You're ordered to clear a ravine that runs to the west, sir. The scouts saw movement there. I'm to show you the way, and he'll take word back to the cohort commander that you got the order, sir.'

Marcus looked the two men over. 'What century are you?'

'Fourth.'

'Anyone know these two?' he asked of his own command. Only when a handful confirmed that they did was Marcus satisfied as to their identity. He would not be drawn into a trap by the enemy posing as our own runners.

'You're a cunning bastard,' I told him as the scouts led off.

'You can go back to the main cohort if you want?' he offered, ignoring the compliment. 'The runner can lead you. This is likely to be a wild goose chase, brother. I've lost count of how many times we've done this kind of thing since we started in Siscia, and we've never found a thing.'

I shook my head. 'If you do find something, then I want to be beside you when it happens.'

Marcus smiled. He knew that I wanted to protect him.

I smiled back. *I wanted to kill.*

The floor of the ravine was a narrow, malicious bastard that caused a man to stumble over half-buried rock as soon as he raised his eyes from the dirt. The sides of the pass were no more than a hundred yards apart, and rose sharply upwards from the rock-strewn ground. Here and there, copses of hardy trees had grown in tight fists, and it was in such an area that one of the cohort's scouts had seen movement. 'Sun shining off metal,' he'd said.

'Which copse was it?' Marcus had asked the runner.

'They didn't tell me, sir.'

And so we searched them all, at least at first. A few footprints were found in the dust, and a keen-eyed soldier spotted the hind leg bone of a hare which had been exposed to flame, though we saw nothing of a fire, or the men who had lit it. Instead we found steeper ravine walls, and slow progress.

Marcus called a break for his men to take some shade in the lee of a rocky outcrop. After posting sentries on the track, he joined me and shook his head. 'We can't clear every copse,' he'd decided. 'I hate not being thorough, brother, but the cohort could be waiting on us. Look down there.' He pointed – the ravine was beginning to twist through the mountain towards the west, an ugly scar. 'We'll make that turn, see what we have in front and then—'

My friend's words cut off and his eyes went wide as an arrow pierced the air between us, slashing by with angry hiss. 'Get down!' Marcus shouted, pushing me. 'Cover! Cover!' he yelled at his men. A second arrow found its target before they could obey. Somebody screamed in pain. 'Shields!' Marcus barked. 'Shields!'

His men scrambled to follow the order. They were mostly young, this century of my friend's. Very few out of their twenties. Their eyes were wild and searching.

Thwack. A third arrow dug into a shield. *Crack.* A fourth hit a rock.

There was no fifth.

Marcus was looking at the trees. 'They're in there,' he told me through gritted teeth.

I put my hand on my friend's shoulder, and shook my head. 'They're gone,' I said. I don't know how I knew that. I just knew, and so I stood up. Maybe I just wanted to be wrong.

No arrows came at me.

Marcus stood quickly beside me, and in that moment I was hit by remorse. I had endangered my friend, I realized. How could a centurion – even an acting one – take cover while another man stood exposed?

I felt terrible, but if Marcus was angry with me, he showed no sign. '*Cowards.*' My brother swore, staring at the hiding place of the enemy with such heat that I thought the trees might burst into flame; then he called, 'Section commanders! Report!'

One casualty – an arrow in the shoulder. No way to send him back to the rear. Not from here. 'Bring in the sentries,' Marcus ordered.

Those men came gratefully back to their comrades. No one wanted to face an attack alone.

'Sir,' a section commander called to Marcus, nerves tickling at his eyes, 'we're one short.'

'Where the fuck is he?' Marcus demanded. 'This is not the time to be sneaking off for a quiet place to shit.'

'I'll find him sir.' And the sentry's section commander took his other men to look.

They came back empty-handed.

I looked at Marcus, and saw the realization settle in my friend's stomach. It was a hard thing to watch, as though part of the soul I had known as a child was cut away and discarded as offal. When Marcus uttered his next words, I

185

knew that he had hardened as a man. 'We can't spend any more time looking for him. Prepare to move out. Double sentries day and night from this point.'

Thinking of the missing man, something grabbed at my guts. I had thought that we were professional killers. Now, I realized, we were like the baker, or butcher. While each worked with food, neither could do the other's job. War amongst the slopes and rocks was a different occupation than the one that we'd been trained for.

Up here in the mountains, *we* were the amateurs.

We came across the missing sentry later that day.

We found his head first. Then his feet. They'd been placed on the track, lonely but for the flies.

'They took his sandals,' Marcus noted.

We pushed along the track. Body parts of what had been a soldier decorated the route. Goading. Taunting. After the feet came the lower legs, then the upper. His cock and balls lay on a hot slab of rock. His naked torso was propped invitingly on an outcrop.

'No,' Marcus told his men when they begged permission to retrieve the pieces of their comrade – he could smell a trap.

Inside the ravine, our bodies began to cook along with our tempers. The heat was fierce. The outside of my body was soaked, while the inside of my mouth as dry as a desert. I wanted to complain, but I would not shame Marcus in front of his men.

Yet I already carried shame that day. I would admit it to none but myself, but the toil of heat and armour caused me more distress than the gruesome adornment of the trail – I had not known the man. Never even looked him in the eyes. What I saw of him was in pieces, and though I pitied the soldier, I pitied myself more – I was miserable, angry and had no one to fight.

Twice more the arrows came. Both times we saw nothing but the shafts in our shields, and a dead soldier on his back.

'Carry him.' Marcus ordered – he would not hand the enemy more ornaments.

A stretcher was formed from a blanket and javelins. Our progress had already been slow; now we were moving like thick lava. I felt men looking at me. I wanted to punch them. When I thought that I wouldn't be overheard, I told this to Marcus.

On any other day, he would have laughed. 'You're the hero of the Eighth, Corvus. They're watching to see how you behave. They're looking to take their lead from you.'

It was late into the afternoon when our luck finally turned. The arm of the missing soldier had bled into the dirt, and in that blood, a rebel had trodden. 'They went up there, sir,' our lead man said. There wasn't much of a trail, but it was enough. They were ahead of us.

Marcus looked across the ravine – its side was cloaked in trees. I knew what he was thinking, but the day was growing short, and our progress had been shorter. 'Keep following the trail,' he told the lead man, and we began to work our way upwards into the mountain, towards the higher ground, the path ahead of us a winding goat trail that led between grey, ominous rocks.

I didn't like it. Neither did Marcus. 'Shields up at the front.'

We were prepared. This ground ahead of us was perfect for an ambush, and our eyes burned into those rocks as we sought out the first sign of our enemy. We were ready. If the rebels were to our front, then we would take their arrows on shield, and storm their positions with sword.

They knew that.

That's why they hit us in the rear.

Screams overlapped. 'Enemy rear!' Panic in every note. 'Enemy – shit! I'm hit!'

'All-round defence!' Marcus shouted as he took off running down the trail and towards the point of the attack. I followed as men turned their shields outwards, overlapping where they could, crouching behind their individual bastions to avoid sniping arrows.

I saw quickly that the two rear men of the column were down. They had been placed further back to warn of such attacks. In their deaths, they had done so. That was a soldier's sacrifice.

'Sir,' a handsome soldier pointed out to Marcus, 'he's not dead! He's still alive, sir! I can get him!'

Marcus didn't have chance to tell the man to stand fast – he was already on his feet and moving. The enemy let him reach his dying comrade before putting a shaft into his lower back.

The scream shook the mountains.

The brave soldier fell across the body of the man he had tried to save, struck down by a hidden killer amongst the rocks.

'You fucking cowards!' someone cried with desperate fury.

'Sir, he's still alive!' said another – the same words as the man who now writhed with an arrow in his kidneys. I realized then the enemy's game. They wanted to suck the men out of formation. Out from the cover of our shields.

Marcus saw it too. Dozens of nervous eyes were looking to my brother for his leadership.

He was not found wanting. 'Hold! Hold. No man moves unless I order it. We'll form testudo and move as one to get them. Century, form testudo!'

Shield banged against shield as the infantrymen established the famed formation. Now there was protection to all flanks, and above.

At least, there should have been.

Beneath the shields, I saw fury flash over my friend's face. The formation was ragged and gapped, and through no fault of his men. The trail had seen to it. Still, there was no better way. 'At the half-step, march!'

It only took a half-dozen paces to recognize that movements created on the parade square – and used to victory on plain and in siege – would not work on a mountainside. 'Man down!' a voice called quickly. 'He's dead, sir!'

Holes in the formation opened as rock twisted and turned the shields on the narrow trail. Another man cried out.

'Halt!' Marcus shouted. 'Halt! Down on your knees and hold formation!' An arrow thumped into a shield. Like this, we were safe. Beneath our protection the air was stifling. Heat. Dust. Dread for a comrade – his moans continued. The soldier with the shaft in his back lived on, and lived in pain.

'He's trying to crawl to us, sir!' a man in the lead file shouted. 'He's not far, sir!'

But he was far enough. Marcus's face was dark as he gave the order. 'We hold formation here. If we move, they'll keep picking us off.'

A long pause. The discipline of the legion told the men to shut their mouths, and obey. Their hearts told them to save their friend. Marcus knew as much. 'If you want to live to bring vengeance for our brothers, then hold! We can't avenge them if we're dead!'

The wounded soldier kept crawling. His closest friends began to shout encouragement. Urging him on. Begging him to reach the shields. He was close enough for us to see the agony in his eyes when the enemy put a shaft between his shoulder blades. His handsome face dropped into the dirt. Curses flew at the rocks. Shields shook.

We stayed in formation.

'Marcus,' I whispered in my brother's ear, 'what are we waiting for?'

His answer was numb, and yet, full of violence. 'Night.'

Darkness takes the valley. The ravine becomes a grave, filled with the black dirt of night.

'I'm going out,' Marcus tells me.

'Where?'

Where else? To find the bowmen that killed his men.

'I'll come with you.'

'No.' No? 'I'm not ordering you, brother,' he explains. 'You're not under my command, but these men are, and if I don't come back, then I need you to lead them back to the cohort.'

I know he's saying this because he loves me. I hate it all the same. 'Let me go instead.'

His hand squeezes my arm. 'Those are my men lying out there.'

I think of what he's saying. I think of Priscus. Then of Varo and Octavius. If they fell, would I let another take my place in the hunt to find their killers?

'Just come back,' I tell him.

Marcus asks for volunteers. Every man in the century begs for the chance to spill blood. He picks three of the best, and then they are gone: a whisper in the darkness; the promise of death. Like the men kneeling in the dirt beside me, my part in the play is reduced to praying that the blood runs from my enemy, and not from my brother.

We keep a 50 per cent watch. Half of the century awake, half asleep. No one actually sleeps. Long into the night we hear a scream. No way to know who. There is no accent to raw pain.

In the dawn, four shapes come out of the grey. They are carrying something in their hands. They throw them on to the rock and dirt.

Three heads.

I look into the face of my oldest friend. I look for the signs of the child who wore a smile from ear to ear. Instead, I see the cold eyes of a killer.

'Collect our dead,' he tells his men. 'We're moving out.'

There are no more attacks. Marcus was ordered to clear the ravine, and he has done so. Three enemy dead. The cost: six Roman dead, and two wounded.

'This is no way to fight a war,' my brother tells me.

We find the Sixth Cohort at the site of another fortified village. For a moment, I wonder if maybe the last two nights and a day were a nightmare, the scene is so familiar. Huts burn. The screams of the raped cry out. A half-dozen legionaries wait with eternal patience to fill holes in the dirt – or, more accurately, be buried beneath stones. The mountain soil is too hard to dig.

Marcus leaves the century outside the village. He tells them to see to their arms and armour. He sends some men to find water. I walk beside him as he looks for the cohort commander to make his report. Though I wished he had been spared it, I am proud of my brother. I can see the way that his men look at him now. They trust him. He is a true leader. A true soldier. What I always knew him to be.

We find the cohort commander in the middle of the village. A handful of soldiers are with him. On their knees in front of him are 'the enemy'. Two dozen. Children and old men. The only males of fighting edge are butchered meat on their walls. The women are being raped.

'They could never stand,' I say to Marcus. 'Why did they fight?'

I assume that they had a choice.

He doesn't answer. Instead he makes his report. The cohort commander looks over the gore on my friend, but makes no further comment. No one has clean hands up here.

The commander of five hundred turns his attention to me. I see his expression, and despair of it. He's looking at 'the hero of the Eighth'.

'Standard-bearer. We've been talking to these supporters of the rebels.' He gestures to the old men. Black eyes. Thick lips. I think he'll want my help, then. Through Marcus, maybe he knows that we both speak Dalmatian.

The commander does want my help, but not like that. He grabs a village elder by the hair, and drags him towards me. 'If I'd known you were coming I would have waited for you before attacking, standard-bearer. It would have been an honour. As it is, well, at least you can have a chance to spill enemy blood.'

I look from him to the trembling white-haired man on his knees. Perhaps I am mistaken?

I am not.

'The miserable bastards aren't talking. If they were to help me catch the cowards who are killing my men in the dark, then maybe I would be inclined to show mercy.' I could see in his eyes that any such clemency had since fled. 'Open the throat of one,' he tells me, 'and maybe the others will open their mouths.'

I hear the sound of steel as a blade is drawn from its scabbard.

My own.

I look down at the man who has been condemned. Even his eyes are shaking. His old, red eyes. 'Talk,' I tell him in Dalmatian. 'Where are the rebels hiding? Where do they get their supplies? Who is supporting them? *Talk!*'

No talk. Just a plaintive whimper. His spirit has fled. He is already broken by the threat of what is to come.

'You see what I mean?' the cohort commander says. 'No reasoning with these mountain cretins. Open him up, standard-bearer.'

I look about me. The scent of death has drawn dozens of hard faces. Do they see my doubt? Is that why they look at me? Have they come to see the mettle of the hero of the Eighth? I can feel the man's shaking through his hair. I move the blade to his throat. I feel something hot against my feet, but it is not blood. He is pissing himself. Nobody laughs. The mountain has drained them of their appreciation of comedy. Here, their only entertainment is death. I should look to Marcus. I just need a sign. A single look. An acknowledgement that what I am about to do is pointless, and savage, and wrong. I don't know why I feel this way – I have never shied from killing man or beast – but the old man's fear is even more pitiful than the most idiot sheep.

I turn to face my friend. There is no emotion on his face. He simply nods.

With that simple motion, he decides both the old man's fate, and my own.

I cut.

The old man bled to death at my feet. He left the world in spasms, the screams of his kin making a symphony of his death. I thought of Centurion Justus. How he had told me that such barbarity against the enemy was a necessity to see our own men through alive. As I looked around the assembly of soldiers' faces, I saw no condemnation in their eyes. I had butchered an animal, and nothing more.

'Will you talk now?' the cohort commander asked the others.

They would not, and so they screamed instead.

'Maybe they had nothing to say?' I asked Marcus.

'What does it matter?'

Maybe it didn't.

We sought out wood ash. Marcus wanted to clean his armour. I wondered if he was doing it to be rid of the memory of the people who had painted it. I was wrong, of course. 'I feel like a soldier again,' he told me once he was the cleanest legionary on the mountainside.

We didn't speak much after that. We were too tired for words, and among true friends – brothers – words are decoration. Simply being in each other's presence is enough.

But I had other friends. Other brothers. 'I need to go and see them,' I told Marcus, though it broke my heart.

He nodded. He tried to make it easier. 'We'll be held in reserve for a while. No more clearances like that.'

I wasn't easily fooled. 'You told me you do them all the time.'

A week ago, he would have smiled. 'There's cavalry coming.'

A dozen mounts. We walked to them. 'Why so many?' we asked a trooper.

'Too many dispatch riders going missing.'

'Can he get a ride down with you?' Marcus asked. 'He's the standard-bearer.'

'Of course.'

I turned to look at my friend. I wanted to know why he wanted rid of me.

But I saw the answer behind him. His century. The burden of command was heavy enough. He did not need the weight of carrying his friend into danger, too.

'I should get back to my men,' he said, and I saw the pain that the words caused him.

'You should.' I wanted to say more, but as every soldier learns, goodbyes are only tolerable when they're short. 'Keep your shield up,' I said, 'and move fast.'

'The same to you, brother.'

I pulled my friend close. After the ravine, I knew that his men would understand. 'Don't fucking die, Marcus,' I threatened into his ear. 'Don't you dare fucking die.'

I stood back, and watched as my brother walked away to his soldiers.

I never saw that man again.

PART THREE

❧ 33 ❧

I found Varo and Octavius in the valley. They were bored by their own mission. Worried by my absence. They asked me questions, and I told them lies.

'See much action?'

'No.'

'Kill anyone?'

'No.'

Varo looked at my feet. I'd tried to scrub them in the river, but the material was still stained by the old man's piss and blood. He knew that I was full of shit. 'Rumour mill says the Sixth cleared a couple of fortified villages?'

I was caught in a truth, and so I told him about stone walls, dead soldiers and raped women.

The big man shrugged. 'That's war.'

Now that I had opened my mouth, I realized that I was troubled, and that his simple answer was not enough. 'I grew up a hundred miles from here,' I explained to myself as much as to my comrades, 'and if my father wasn't a Roman citizen, then I wouldn't be either. I'd have been drafted into the auxiliary cohorts, I'd have been told we were rebelling against Rome, and now I'd be your enemy.'

'Be thankful that you're not then.' Octavius smiled, ripping off a fart.

'It doesn't bother you?' I asked with irritation at my friend's breezy attitude. 'Those men in the villages, maybe they had family with our enemy, but *they* weren't the enemy.

They weren't picking up a shield and a sword.'

Octavius raised his hands. 'So? What are you getting at, Corvus?'

'*So?* So why did they have to die? They weren't a threat to Rome.'

Varo shook his thick head. 'Doesn't matter.'

'Why doesn't it?' I demanded, hoping to understand it all. Hoping to sit with the same certain peace as my comrades. 'Tell me why, Varo. Tell me why we're killing the same people that we were protecting a few weeks ago. Tell me why the dead that I'm seeing are old men, women and children. Tell me why the people that I grew up with are now my enemy. Please. I need to know. Fucking tell me.'

The lump looked at me as though I was an idiot. I suppose that I was.

'Because that's war.'

It was *our* war, and after two weeks of it, we were still only halfway between the cities of Siscia and Salona, trapped in the mountains like stale air. As we inched further south the mountains were becoming more angry, appearing as shark's teeth turned up to the sky. Deadly, and vicious.

Hook-nose rotated his troops. My old cohort climbed to the east to replace the Seventh. The Sixth, and my brother, were similarly replaced. The change came after the legate had visited his troops in the heights. He wanted to know why progress was so slow, and so he went to see for himself. I expect that he went thinking he would find excuses and dragged feet. Instead he found heat, and ambush, and soldiers dragging the bodies of their friends as arrows from an unseen enemy tasted flesh.

Relief rolled over me when I'd discovered that my old ccohort would be taking to the heights in the east, and not the west. The Seventh had come under attack, but they'd suffered far less than Marcus's cohort. For whatever reason, the enemy presence was stronger in that part of the region. Tribunes on the staff had concluded, because of the coordinated nature of attacks, that there was one enemy band operating there under a single command. Sometimes, in the night, assaults fell on different outposts or units at almost the same time. Often these attacks would last for no more than a few seconds – a couple of sentries killed; some supplies set ablaze – and then the enemy were gone, swallowed by night and the land that they called home.

I sat back against a slab of rock, Varo and Octavius either side of me. We had climbed all day. Balius had been returned to me, but I had turned down the saddle so that I could share the same hardship as my comrades. How could it be any other way? We were soldiers.

'I feel like my lungs are still halfway down the hill,' Octavius wheezed. 'If these mountains are what we're fighting for, then they can have them back. What use are they to us?'

There was no answer for him. Not a real one, anyway. 'If we don't control the mountains,' Varo began, 'then the officers back in Rome don't get to colour in this part of the world on their maps.'

The time to worry about a soldier is when he is not complaining, and I knew that there was more to my friends' grumbling. There were nerves in it. An edge of fear. These rocky slopes were death's domain. Before the battle on the plain, we had stood in ranks of shining steel and watched and waited as our enemy advanced. There had been time for goodbyes. There had been time to prepare for the end. Here, a soldier could drop dead before his comrades' eyes with an arrow in his throat as they sat down to share biscuits. A sentry duty could be a death sentence, the butchered soldier found days later, or never at all.

'We were born fifty years too late,' Octavius told us. 'Imagine being in the battle lines of the civil war? None of this fucking around like goats in the mountains. Line against line, lads. Legion on legion.'

Varo didn't look so certain. 'You'd be all right killing Romans?'

Octavius shrugged. 'They're not my mates. And look. They rebelled against the Empire, didn't they? How's that any different to us fighting the auxiliaries?'

The big man was not convinced. 'The auxiliaries aren't citizens.'

'The Emperor pays their bills.'

'No. It's not the same.'

'Well, either way,' the shorter man insisted, 'if you turn against the Empire, you get what's coming to you. They lost their citizenship when they sided with Pompey, Marc Anthony and all those other cunts.'

'So you'd have fought for Caesar?' Varo asked.

'Of course.'

I break my silence. 'You'd have fought for whoever your legion did,' I told him. 'Whoever the senator was that your legate decided to follow. Do you think you'd have had a say in that?'

'I'd like to think so.'

'And I'd like these mountains to be a beach, but it's not going to happen, is it? We don't get to make decisions, Octavius. Not the ones that change the world, anyway. When was the last time you chose something for yourself?'

My friend spat. 'I'm choosing not to listen to you, you miserable twat.'

Varo laughed. It was the first time I'd heard him make that rumbling sound in days. I missed it. But then, I missed a lot of things.

'I'm going to check on the sentries,' he told us, getting to his feet and looking down from that great height as though he were our father; had he stepped into that paternal role when Priscus had fallen? 'Cheer up, you two. We may not be able to choose much in life, Corvus, I'll give you that, but we can choose our mates.'

Despite my stubbornness, I nodded at his words.

In that part of my life at least, I had chosen wisely.

Three days later I was told by a dispatch rider that I was to accompany him back to the legion's headquarters on the plain – or rather the narrow strip of land that ran beside the snaking river. 'What's it about?' I asked, but the soldier was no more privy to Hook-nose's mind than I was.

I sought out my brothers. We were stained in sweat, but free of blood. The enemy had not discovered us, nor we them. I found Varo and Octavius at the head of the century. Behind their armoured figures, drawn in jagged lines of misery, stretched the peaks of the mountain range.

Varo saw me first. 'Quite a view, isn't it?'

Octavius wiped sweat from his eyes. 'Pretty, from a distance. Talking of which, what's up with you, Corvus? You look like Balius just took advantage of you.'

'Hook-nose wants to see me.'

'Smile then, you dickhead,' Varo said, taking his own advice. 'Get yourself some decent scoff at headquarters. Go and see Marcus.'

Marcus. When his cohort had been relieved and moved to the lower ground, I had told myself that I should be with my comrades in the mountains, and the place of most danger. Maybe that was the truth. Or maybe . . . maybe I hadn't wanted to see the changes in my oldest friend. The smiling boy becoming the hollow-eyed killer.

Varo asked, 'What's wrong?'

'Nothing.'

He laughed. How could he be happy in this? He saw the question in my eyes. 'I've got a sword on my hip and comrades by my side. Look at this view, Corvus. Look at it! Life is good, you dickhead. Life is good.'

I squinted. 'You truly believe that?'

He put one of those thick arms over my shoulder. 'We're not lying on sofas getting wine poured down our throats by slaves, and I don't suppose that we ever will be, but life could be worse. A lot worse.'

It could. And if I hadn't already seen enough evidence of that in my life, then the legate would prove it to me.

'Standard-bearer! Come.' Hook-nose greeted me with a wave once I reached his headquarters on the valley floor. 'I've had the eagle brought up from the rear.'

I felt my pulse quicken. 'Battle, sir?' I asked hastily, but the commander of the legion shook his head.

'It's time to visit the wounded.'

❧ 34 ❧

I walked with the eagle in my hand. To me the standard was Gallus, famed chicken of the Eighth. To others, it was a symbol of divine inspiration.

Men snapped to attention as they saw us come: a decorated soldier and a legion's eagle, a potent combination to inspire pride in any legionary's heart. I felt none myself – the gilded lump of metal on a stick just meant that I had my hands full, and that I couldn't wipe the dripping sweat off my face – but while I might not have shared the emotions, I supposed that I understood them: the men's pride in the eagle came from a desire to belong to something greater than themselves. It came from a desire to be proved worthy. To bring light to a dark world. Order to chaos. To walk amongst heroes. To be one yourself.

And how to do that?

By sacrificing all for the glory of Rome.

I smelt the results of such thinking long before I saw the hospital. It was the stench of conflict. Blood. Piss. Puke. Shit. Here on the valley floor, the reek of open wounds hung between the mountains like a curse. Up on the peaks, violent death waited, but down here, amongst the tents of the legion's reserve, death lingered, toying with its victims through the suffering of others.

I walked with Hook-nose. The legate wanted to pay a visit to the steady trickle of wounded that were being sent back as a result of the enemy's ambushes. There were sick men in the legion too, but we'd be giving their dwellings

205

a wide berth. 'You can't catch an amputation,' Hook-nose had said, wise enough to know that even the fittest legionary could fall down without so much as a touch. 'Many of these men will be invalided out of the service now, if they survive,' he'd then explained. 'They need to know why.'

'Yes, sir.'

'It won't be easy for them, standard-bearer, but they'll take strength knowing that their suffering is for Rome.'

'Yes, sir.'

We weren't alone. A half-dozen officers and a section of guards walked with us through the heat; the valley's air was as still as a tomb. That it was becoming one for so many soldiers was evidenced by the rows of graves freshly scratched into the dirt. The valley floor was hard here; the resting places of the dead were shallow. A fox or a dog had got at one of the fallen, a half-eaten hand protruding from the earth in friendly greeting.

'Give that man some decency!' Hook-nose growled at one of his officers. I looked behind me, and saw that the section of troops in our wake were amused by the macabre sight. One waved back to the corpse. He did so discreetly and behind his officers' backs, a clandestine skill developed quickly by those in the ranks.

I didn't blame the man for the act, nor feel any ill will towards him for it. I knew why these young soldiers were cracking whispered jokes and hiding sick smiles – they were scared. The stench of decay was becoming stronger, and with it came the moans of men who had found steel in their flesh. At some point in this campaign, the section of troops behind me would be ordered to tramp their way towards the sky, and to put their heads into the rebels' noose in the mountains. They would face ambush. Disappearing sentries. The whisper of death in the night. I could see from the lack of lines on their faces that it was not something they'd already experienced. Here now was nervous fear. After the mountains, they would be painted with the look of those who had been driven beyond fatigue and emotion. I had seen it in the men of the Sixth Cohort when I had left Varo and Octavius and returned to the valley floor. Their eyes were hollow, as though they were seeing through me, and into the next life. Perhaps, when I made my discovery, I looked the same way.

Marcus was not with them.

'*Where is he?*'

Nobody spoke.

'*Where's his century?*'

Nobody talked.

The legate's runners had found me before I could ask any more – I was to collect the legion's eagle, and accompany Hook-nose on his mission to inspire the cut and the stabbed and the ripped and the beaten.

A surgeon met us at the tents. He was a stranger to sleep. His clothes were wet where he had made an effort to have them cleaned before this visit. It hadn't worked. The toga was as stained as his hands. Hook-nose shook one.

'Show me to my men.'

I lowered Gallus and ducked under the tent flap. The tent's sides had been rolled up where possible to allow for some breeze, but even so, the humid heat beneath the canvas was like a wet slap in the face.

'As you were, men,' Hook-nose told the wounded men who were trying to either stand or sit to attention.

I cast my eye over them. A dozen. All young. At least, I assumed they were – one had his face swathed entirely in bandages. It was to him that the legate spoke first, after placing a hand on the man's shoulder. 'This is your legion commander. What cohort are you from, soldier?'

The words were muffled by material, but there was no doubting the pride in them. 'The Fighting First, sir.'

I saw Hook-nose smile at soldier's pluck. 'So you fought in the battle of the night and day?'

'I did, sir.' The bandages nodded. 'I was front rank, for a while.'

'Did you cut the bastards down?'

'I did, sir. I don't know how many, sir, but it was a lot, sir. Sir, do you think I can get back to my century soon, sir? I'd really like to get back to them!'

I saw pride wash over Hook-nose with such power that his face twitched. The legate turned, and looked at the surgeon.

The man shook his head, pointed at his own eyes, and then shook his head a second time.

'We'll see what we can do,' Hook-nose promised the blind man. He gestured to me then. Guessing what was on the legate's mind, I lowered Gallus so that the eagle was within the man's grasp. Hook-nose guided the soldier's hand until it rested on the precious metal.

'Touched by the Emperor's own hand, and now your own, soldier.' Hook-nose spoke with reverence. 'You may not be with your cohort today, but so long as this eagle is carried you will always be with the Eighth. Our fallen, our wounded, from this war, the past, and the next. You don't need to worry about getting back to your comrades, soldier. You are already with them.'

We moved on to the next man.

Hook-nose spoke to all of them. Every one. Almost without fail, the soldier asked the legion commander when he could rejoin his unit. On two occasions, I saw battle-scarred veterans weep – not because of their injuries, but because they knew that their wounds would prevent them from ever standing beside their brothers again.

'There are no malingerers here,' the head surgeon promised Hook-nose. 'These men are true heroes of Rome, sir. They just want to fight.'

As an aristocrat, the legate had been trained in oration since childhood, but words failed him as his heart beat with pride at the valour of his men.

'How did I come to deserve such lions?' I heard him mutter to a tribune as we walked free of the tents, and that same pride had gripped me as we had moved from man to man – soldiers who were willing to rip out their own stitches if it meant being able to fight alongside their friends.

But there was only one lion in the valley that I called brother.

Marcus.

I had to find him.

❧ 35 ❧

I walked into one of the tents that made up the legion's headquarters while on the campaign trail, the canvas trapping the smell of hot air and unwashed bodies.

I laid eyes on a clerk. He shrank a little when he saw me. There was fear on his face, but it was the ink on his fingers that interested me – in front of him was a long list of names. Before the clerk could object, I snatched it up.

Casualties. Lots of them. A dispatch to Rome of statistics. Numbers that would multiply in grief. Tears would be shed. Orations would be given. Libations would be offered. It was the way of Roman war. First blood on the field, then ink on the page. A chain of misery written into parchment that would claw its way across the Empire. At its end, families would feel the same sorrow in their hearts as did the fallen soldier's brothers. Tragedy from the mountains delivered to cities, villages and farmsteads.

'I can read it for you, if you like?' It was a kind offer from the clerk, and didn't deserve the harshness of my reply.

'Shut your mouth,' I growled. My father had insisted that I learn my letters. One of the many lessons he had taught me. My possessed eyes darted across the lists, searching for something I was desperate not to find.

I reached the end of the names. There were a lot of them.

But no Marcus.

I fixed the clerk with a stare. I noticed a slight tremble in his hand. His was a war of words, not warriors. He knew who I was. My temper had been a topic of conversation through the rumour mill long before my stand with the eagle.

'I'm looking for my friend,' I said, trying and failing to appear amicable. 'Are these up to date?'

'As much as they can be, standard-bearer,' he offered. 'These names here' – he pointed to the bottom of the list – 'came in this morning with the dispatch riders.' He was trying to be helpful. 'May I ask the name of who you're looking for? Maybe I—'

I snapped Marcus's details out of my mouth. Name, rank, unit. After a moment, I saw the stylus-scribbler's eyebrows raise. Then he began to quickly leaf through dispatches. 'Here,' he said triumphantly, as though he were handing me the head of the enemy general.

I looked at it. 'A promotion list?'

'From General Tiberius, standard-bearer. Your friend's promotion to centurion has been confirmed.'

I handed the paper back. Marcus, now the centurion he had always wanted to be.

I thought then of the man that he had replaced. The grizzled soldier had been injured in the face on the day that Marcus had first drawn blood. How long ago?

I asked about the officer who had entrusted Marcus with his men. His wards. His sons, and brothers.

The clerk's face paled. 'He died of his wounds, standard-bearer. Infection.'

'You remember him?' I asked impressed, yet suspicious.

The ink-stained man nodded gravely. 'Every one,' he said after a moment.

The clerk's squinted eyes told me that it was the truth. Like all of us, the mountains ensured that this man had a burden to bear.

I put a hand on his shoulder. It was the kind of thing Marcus would do, but what I said came from my own heart.

'Good.'

I sought out the Sixth Cohort, and found their commander washing in the shallow river. He was naked, and his tanned arms and shins looked as though they were attached to the wrong torso, so white was his skin.

'Standard-bearer,' he greeted me. 'Not the baths, but it'll do.'

I exchanged the minimum of pleasantries, and then asked after my brother. Despite the absence of Marcus's name from the list of casualties, I still felt my stomach knot. It would hardly be the first time a bureaucrat had made a mistake.

'Marcus? Alive and well,' his commander informed me, and I felt relief wash out of me like a flood. That cavity was, however, soon filled with guilt – I hadn't seen my friend for weeks, and I needed only to look at the scarred and bruised flesh of the bathing men to know that those weeks had been a tale of breaking backs and broken blades.

'Is he here?' I asked the officer, meaning the valley floor.

He scooped water on to his lined face before he answered me. 'Seconded to the First Cohort. They needed an additional century. They asked for my best, so I gave them Marcus.'

Pride is no small thing, even in the face of danger – *especially* in the face of danger – and I felt it well in me now. Marcus, my brother, requested from amongst his peers. I had to see him. How had I let it go so long? Damn my fear. He was closer to me than blood. War could not change that. *War would not change that.*

I bent down to the stream and scooped a handful of the blissful water into my mouth. I knew that I was about to be thirsty for a long time.

'Where is he?'

I went into the mountains in search of 'the Barbers'. That's what Marcus's century were calling themselves now, my guide informed me. He was of the same cohort.

'This boss said that every century needed a name along with its number,' the soldier informed me, referring to the cohort commander whom I'd talked to at the river.

'A name?'

'That's right, standard-bearer. The boss's only rule was that it had to be something aggressive and warlike.'

I pulled a face. 'What's aggressive and warlike about the Barbers?'

The soldier grinned at me – I recognized it as an expression that one gives to a man who is not a party to an inside joke.

We joined a resupply column forming up in the lowest reaches of the slopes. Pack animals and burdened men. Slaves. Both were the property of the legions. Where had they come from? A dozen shades of skin, a dozen tones of hair, all united by the same expression in their eyes: hopelessness. I looked at the men who now ordered them into a ramshackle column – tidy ranks would not survive the first hundred yards of track. The armour of these soldiers had been scrubbed in the valley, but there was no getting the dirt from their lined faces. Even after a short respite, their eyes were grey and lifeless. Gone were the songs. Gone were the jokes. The mountain had leached humour away, breaking the spirit of the soldiers as certainly as their slaves had been broken to the whim of their owners. The mountains were our masters. Slaves of Rome, slaves of war, slaves to the sharp-toothed leviathan that seemed intent on devouring us all, piece by piece.

'Lovely day for it, isn't it?' a toothless soldier asked me, his spirit endowed with greater strength than most.

'Lovely day,' I made myself reply. I was the fucking standard-bearer after all.

A rippling order. 'Prepare to move.'

A rippling movement. 'Move.'

Like a wounded caterpillar, the column lurched forwards, and upwards.

One foot in front of the other. Feel the loose stone give. Feel the creak in your knee. The stab in your ankle. Feel the hot sweat that stings your eyeballs, those empty orbs scratched by dust and drained by stress. Try and keep your head on a swivel. Try and scan the rocks. Try and think about how you will react if you get attacked from that position. Try and think about how you will cover and withdraw the casualties if you get hit from there.

Try not to think about why you are here.

Try not to think about when, and how you will leave it.

Try not to think about how you came to be here in the first place.

'Standard-bearer?' The toothless soldier. 'We're gonna catch our breath here, if that's all right with you?'

Here was a collection of half-torn-down hovels. I could smell goat shit, and rot.

'Bit on the stinky side, isn't it?' the old soldier asked me as he sucked on a dry biscuit.

'Here.' I offered him some wine. It was good. Very good. The legate had given it to me himself.

The man's eyes lit up as he drank it. 'Take another pull,' I offered, but the soldier handed it back.

'Can't deprive a man of his luxuries up here, standard-bearer, but thank you. I'll get this lot moving again just as soon as everyone's had time to put something down their necks, and drop their arses.'

Following his own advice, the man moved away and dropped to his haunches; the biscuit was still in his mouth. I thought of the rigorous standards enforced upon me as a child – eating and the use of the toilet as regimented as any other part of my schooling – and I almost smiled. Only the stench of death kept my lips tight.

I found them in the closest hovel. Their skin was black, and bloated. In parts it moved. Creatures smaller than my

215

thumbnail were the masters of death's domain, and here was a feast worthy of whatever hellish gods had spawned them. There were four bodies. All naked. All rotting.

None with their heads.

The answer to that mystery was found as we passed through the gate out of what had been a village. The heads sat atop a wall, eyeless and maggot-ridden. Some joker had arranged them so that each pair were kissing.

Maybe it was this distraction that kept us looking in, and not out. By the time the men up front had heard it, and called a warning, a loaded cart was plunging towards our ranks from the track ahead. It was loaded with rock, and turned the slave that it hit into a bloody smear on the mountainside. The man hadn't moved. Was he dumbstruck, or tired of life?

What did it matter?

'That cunt was carrying the fucking biscuits,' the veteran raged, poking his javelin into the stew of slave and oat. 'Someone's going to go hungry.'

Not the slave.

'Prepare to move!'

My feet moved doggedly up the mountain track, but my mind wandered carelessly into my past.

There it was met by an ambush of misery.

I landed hard at the bottom of the wall, the blood on my hands smearing the hot tile. There were shouts behind me, more plaintive than angry. I didn't think that I needed to fear pursuit – not immediately, at least – as the first priority of the slaves would be to save the life of my father. I had tried to kill him, but I knew in the next breath that I had failed.

'Corvus!' A voice thick with blood and broken teeth. 'Corvus, get back here!'

Instead I ran.

First to the beach, to wash off the blood in the waters of my childhood. My adolescence. My innocence. As I scrubbed torn knuckles I knew that I was washing myself of family. Of security. Of love. Everything I had known had changed in an instant.

No. Not everything.

Marcus. Through blood and betrayal he would stand by me, I knew it.

I looked at my tunic, marked by the stains of my act. I looked at the sun, now at its zenith. My father had use of his tongue, and I had no doubt that he would be sending slaves to summon the town's watch. That he lived for now did not mean that he would survive his injuries – if he died and I was caught, it would be the most hideous end for me. If he lived and I was trapped? I did not expect mercy. Rome was an empire built on patriarchy, and I had viciously turned on my father. He was the emperor, I was the rebel, and in such a conflict there could be but one resolution – death.

And so I ran.

It was three miles to the villa that was Marcus's home. It sat atop a small hill amid the orchards of our childhood. The trees were heavy with fruit now, the shadows welcoming, and I used them to creep unseen to the lowest point of the outer wall, hauling myself over as we had done whenever we were up to mischief.

'Marcus?' I whispered outside his room. 'Marcus?'

My heart was in my throat. My brother was home on leave from his beloved Eighth Legion. If he had gone into town, dare I wait? A better question: dare I run without him?

My lungs began to move again as I heard a hand on the door. It opened inwards.

My brother, so noble, so perfect. I, a wretched creature of stains and torn skin.

I embraced him. I wanted to weep. I wanted to tell him everything, but the words choked in my mouth. Too much to say.

'What can I do?' he asked me.

'Run with me, brother.'

We ran.

I woke with weak sun on my face.

Dawn.

I lifted my head from the helmet that was my pillow, and looked about me. My sleep had been deep, if not troubled. The First Cohort, whom we had joined in the night, had already stirred. In the dark I had asked for Marcus, but my friend had been dispatched to clear a village further west with two other centuries.

I tried to work up enough moisture in my mouth to spit. It felt as though our legion had become caught in a cruel circle that continued to feed itself. Where was the battle? Where was the enemy? Nowhere. Instead there was nothing but the seemingly endless loop of climb, search, descend, and the gods grant that each grinding turn of that wheel was free of ambush and dead friends.

A soldier had been watching me. His face was young, but his eyes belonged to a man at the end of his life. I nodded assent for him to approach.

He knew me. Knew of me. 'Standard-bearer?'

'Yes?'

A flicker of something passed over his face. Pride? 'I saw you at the battle of the night and day,' he told me. 'I saw you save the eagle.'

I rubbed at my face. Thick stubble there. I needed to shave. 'They need to come up with a better name for that fucking battle,' I told the lad.

'I'll think of one,' the soldier promised.

I looked him up and down. His tunic and armour hung off his slight frame. 'How old are you?'

'Sixteen, standard-bearer.'

I noticed blood on his tunic. He saw. 'The enemy's, standard-bearer.'

I searched for something that sounded like the kind of thing the inspirational standard-bearer would say. 'A good kill?'

He hesitated. 'No, sir.' Licked his teeth. 'A woman.'

'Women can be enemies too,' I offered.

'Yes.' But I could see in his face that the death at his hand was born of butchery, not battle – if there was even a difference there. Whether under the gaze of generals and eagles, or that of a sixteen-year-old boy soldier shitting his pants, the result was the same. Blood in the soil. Blood on the hands.

'You should shave,' I told him with a smile. There wasn't a hair on his childlike face.

Something twitched at the corner of his lips, then. I could see that he wanted to say the same to me. 'I know,' I told him, feeling at the dark stubble on my gaunt cheeks. I took out my razor. It was dull. Every hair clung as stubbornly to my throat as we did to the mountains.

The young lad was still watching me.

'What's your name?'

He hesitated. I lowered the razor.

'. . . Scipio.'

Named for one of Rome's greatest generals. I smiled as I wiped the blade against my tunic. 'Do you intend to follow in his footsteps?'

Scipio shrugged, and looked around us at the savage peaks. 'At least the enemy can't bring elephants up here, sir.'

'That's what they said about the Alps,' I replied, teasing him. I scraped my throat again. 'You should get back to your century, Scipio. I expect we'll be moving out soon.'

But he didn't leave. He needed to know. Some life had come into his tired eyes. Some purpose. With a look, I gave him permission to give voice to his question.

'What was it like?' the boy asked. 'Carrying the eagle in battle, sir?'

There it was. The question in every young man's heart. The thirst for glory, honour and meaning.

There was already enough desolation in this campaign. I couldn't bring myself to trample on the fire that burned in the boy's heart.

'Glorious,' I told him, allying myself with the emperor, the senators, the recruiters, and the old and bold soldiery who saw out their active service far from any battlefield. 'It was glorious,' I told him, perpetuating a myth as old as time.

He left then, smiling, and behind him I saw the price of lies.

There was a column coming into the makeshift camp, and there was a killer at its head. His face was as hard as the stone at his feet, a baleful grimace stretching skin baked almost black. Amongst his company of soldiers his armour burned brightest, but it was the killer's eyes that seared like the open maw of a volcano. He was a terrifying sight to behold, hate encased in chain mail.

It broke my heart to see him, because this man was my brother.

'Marcus.' I greeted him hesitantly, having watched the officer fall out the hard, gaunt men of his command – the Barbers, who were growing infamous in the legion for their ruthlessness.

'Corvus,' he replied.

There was no embrace. No more words. It was as though I was talking to a corpse, and my heart wrenched to see such a change in a man who had been so quick to emotion.

Two soldiers approached. They dumped stained sacking at my brother's feet.

'Help me with these,' Marcus said.

I hoisted one. It wasn't heavy, but the smell was rank and oppressive. I knew what I was carrying.

We walked in silence, I a half-pace behind him. So many questions in my mind, but I found my lips sewn shut. Did I really want the answers?

'Hard patrol?' I finally asked. Stupid question.

'Yes.'

'I spoke to your cohort commander in the valley,' I tried. 'He's very proud of you.'

Nothing.

'As am I.'

Nothing.

'Sir!' Marcus called.

The commander of the First Cohort. Eyes rimmed with dark bags. A skeleton in armour.

'Centurion. How many have you brought me?'

Marcus dropped his bag, then bid that I do the same. I took a step back to save my feet from what I knew was coming. Marcus emptied the sacks, and nine heads rolled into the hard dirt.

The cohort commander trapped one with his foot. 'Good work,' he told his man.

I looked at that good work. Three young men, one old man, three women, two children.

'Rest up,' the commander told his man, kicking one of the heads down the slope as he walked away.

Maybe Marcus felt my eyes, then. Maybe he felt my doubt.

'What would you like me to say, Corvus?' He spoke in a tone I had never heard from him before, slow moving but as deadly as lava. 'We're at war.'

I said nothing. Marcus turned to the collection of trophies at our feet. His words were for me, but he stared into dead eyes as he spoke.

'Do you think I'm enjoying it? I'm doing this to keep my men alive.' He looked at me, then. 'I'm doing this for Rome.'

There was savagery in his eyes. I wanted to step back. Instead I told him, 'I know.'

Marcus laughed. A laugh so full of anger and misery that it sounded like a mortal wound. 'What do you know about war, Corvus?' he chided me. 'Where have you been? How is it down in the valley?'

My pride bristled at the words. Before I knew it my mouth was open, and I was growling. 'I stood in battle lines before you, brother. You've had a hard time, I know' – I pointed at the skulls – 'but do not mistake this for war.'

Marcus's smile was a grimace. He folded his arms, those limbs scraped bloody by the rock of the mountain. 'No, Corvus,' he lectured me, 'it is you who are mistaken.

'This is war.' He kicked one of the heads. 'Not the battles. Not the glory. It is the willingness to do what is necessary. It is attrition. It is evil against evil, where only the most wicked will survive.' He stepped closer to me then. His hostility was such that I almost went for my sword. 'I will not see my men die.'

His eyes were ablaze. His message was emphatic. Marcus would become the immoral man in the mountains, and he would do it for the love of his comrades.

I couldn't let him.

I put a hand on his shoulder. He looked at it as though he'd bite it from my arm.

'Marcus, listen to me.' I tried. 'What if these mountains were Iader? What if we were sent into our home town, with the same orders as we have here? Our old friends. Our old neighbours. Are they truly an enemy because one day someone writes a command, and orders it so?'

His eyes drove into my own like a blade. 'This region has revolted against its lawful master. Against Rome.'

Rome. The city he had never seen. The idea for whom he would kill, and die.

'No, Marcus.' I had to try. 'A leader and his men have revolted, not the region,' I near pleaded in desperation. 'Think, Marcus. The people we grew up with. They were good people, and loyal to Rome, were they not? Would you kill them without mercy? Would you condemn them for the actions of other men that they have never met? Never seen?'

I was asking the wrong man.

'Yes,' he told me simply. 'Every one.'

A long breath escaped him, then. His eyes fell to the distant mountains. Somewhere, the ghost of my closest friend stirred. 'I will not do it, brother,' he almost whispered. 'I will not see another of them fall. I will not have another slip away in my arms. For my men, I will kill every rebel, woman and child in this province and beyond, if that's what it takes. I will do it for my men, I will do it for you, and I will not stop until I am sent to join those I have already failed.'

'You haven't failed anyone,' I begged.

But the mask was back. A mask of iron, and hate. When he looked back at me, I saw pity. Pity that I couldn't understand. Pity that I couldn't be the man that Rome needed me to be.

'You're just tired, standard-bearer,' my brother told me as though speaking to a stranger. 'You should head back down to the valley, and get some rest.'

I felt as though he had driven his sword into my heart. 'Marcus, don't.'

He broke away from my hand on his shoulder. 'I have to see to my men.'

He walked away. I wanted to follow, but my legs were concrete from grief. 'Marcus!' I called after the best part of myself. 'Marcus! Talk to your commander. We can find a better way. There has to be a better way!'

He stopped, and turned. When he looked at me, I saw only disgust in his eyes. Shame at my weakness.

'Leaders don't talk,' Marcus snorted. 'They lead.'

He turned his back, and grief ran through every fibre of my being.

I had lost my brother to the mountains.

❧ 37 ❧

I took Marcus's advice, and returned to the valley with the resupply column that same day, arriving late in the afternoon.

I soon wished that I hadn't.

'What's going on?' I asked a bloodied soldier who was helping a comrade to the aid station. Their faces were familiar to me.

'Second Cohort got ambushed,' the soldier told me, confirming my fears – these were men that I knew.

'Which centuries?' I asked quickly.

The man delivered the words I dreaded to hear. 'First and Second.'

I ran towards the hospital. Dozens of wounded were being helped or carried there. I looked among them for Varo and Octavius. Instead I saw Iulius, a weathered soldier who had taken over Octavius's section when my old friend had been promoted to optio.

There was a red slice across his upper arm.

'An arrow,' he told me, but I saw more pain in his face than such a weapon could have caused.

'What?' I asked. 'Tell me!'

He didn't answer at once, and dread climbed with hooks from the pit of my stomach.

I shook him. 'Tell me!'

The soldier met my eyes. I saw tears in his.

'Octavius is dead.'

I looked down at the body of my comrade.

Octavius lay on his back, an arrow through his throat. Eyes that had been bright with mirth now gazed at a blue sky as empty as the vessel that had carried my friend's indomitable spirit.

'You weren't supposed to die,' I told him, closing his eyes and brushing away the flies that sought to take treasure from tragedy.

I took my friend's dead hand in my own. His sword, unbloodied, had fallen beside him.

'You were a great brother,' I told the man who had been with me since my first day as a recruit. 'Do you remember when we first met? You complained I was taking too long in the latrine, and when I came out I tried to put you in it. The training staff caught us fighting and ordered us on to shit duty for a month.' I laughed then. It was a choke, but it was happy.

'I miss you already, you fucking bastard,' I cursed, squeezing his dead flesh. '*You weren't supposed to die.*'

And my comrade hadn't died alone. With tears blurring my vision, I looked about me now. Amongst the rocks of a narrow defile, a dozen other soldiers were going through the same ritual that I was, saying goodbye to men that they knew better than their own families.

I realized then that Octavius was the furthest forward of them all. As an optio, his place was at the rear of the century, chaperoning the troops into formation, but his position was no mystery to me; it only made me more sad – Octavius must have stepped up when Varo had gone ahead with a section of men to scout the dangerous terrain ahead, and had not returned.

I looked over my shoulder. Iulius, arm yet to be bandaged, leaned back against a slab of rock. He had brought me to this place of stone, safe enough now that other centuries had pushed ahead so that we might give honour to the dead.

It took me two attempts to break the man from his trance. No doubt he was replaying the catastrophic moments. The screams. The chaos.

'Standard-bearer?'

'Tell me again what happened?' I asked, looking back to the face of my fallen friend. I would not let go of his hand. I couldn't.

'We got sent on a patrol from the valley to investigate some smoke,' Iulius began. 'Us and the First Century in two columns—'

He stopped because I waved my free hand at him. 'I don't care about that. What happened to Octavius and Varo?'

The wounded man nodded. 'Varo didn't like the look of this route, so he went ahead with a section to try and find us a better way. We were a bit further back down the trail, then. There wasn't much sign of them going back, so Octavius was just getting us going when the arrows started coming in.'

I looked at the arrow in his throat. 'He died first?'

Iulius shook his head, and almost smiled. He had pride in the man who had once been his section commander. 'Look at his shield.'

I did. Four arrows were embedded in the livery of our legion.

'He stormed forwards to get us moving again. He knew we had to charge them to break the ambush.'

'And did you?'

'We did,' Iulius confirmed. 'Lost men doing it, and I think Octavius was one of the first, but if he hadn't started that charge, there'd be more of us on the ground here. I tell you that as a fact.'

I looked at his dead face. 'Leaders don't talk,' I said quietly. 'They lead.'

'What was that?'

I made no reply. Instead, with a silent plea of forgiveness, I let go of my friend's hand, and got to my feet. 'We need to find Varo and the others.'

Iulius grimaced, and looked at the sun – it was low in the sky. 'It's going to be getting dark soon,' he informed me gently. 'And . . .'

'Spit it out.'

'Shouldn't we bury the dead? There's a shallow over there we could dig out.'

Frustration gripped me. I looked at the mountains and ridges that ranged all about us. Varo was out there, but Octavius was at my feet. How could I leave him unburied for wolf, and vermin?

'I need to find Varo and the others.' I was speaking almost to myself.

'Don't hit me for saying this, but no one's following you into these hills at night, Corvus. If you want to do right by your friends, see to Octavius. It's what Varo would want, isn't it?'

It was, and I knew with angry certainty that I would not survive hunting blindly in the mountains at night.

'Fuck this place,' I snarled, hurling a stone. '*Fuck it.*'

And then I buried my friend.

We started digging out the shallow depression that Iulius had pointed out. Before we were even a half-foot down, our tools struck sparks against solid rock.

'This is no country worth fighting for,' an Italian soldier growled.

Darkness was closing fast, and with it our flanking troops would be withdrawn to the main body of the legion along the snaking form of the valley's river. We would have to bury our friends beneath stones.

'I'm sorry,' I told Octavius as I placed the final one over his face, his features mercifully hidden in the twilight. I don't know how long I knelt there, until a friendly hand shook my shoulder.

Iulius. 'We should go.'

He was right. Darkness had come. This land belonged to the enemy now, if it hadn't always.

We stumbled our way back to the camp, and found wine.

Somewhere in the black, a man screamed.

38

They bring me before them in chains. I have climbed the mountain in such bondage. My wrists are red welts. My bare feet are cut to ribbons from the sharp stone.

I am on my knees. There are four of them before me.

I do not ask why I am here.

I know.

I knew it from the first moment that I looked into their dead eyes: Priscus. Octavius. Varo – yes, he is here. The screams in the night . . . how can I hope for the impossible?

And . . .

'Beatha?'

Her stare cuts through me, a blade of ice. Where once there had been love and radiance, now there is only cold death.

'Beatha . . .'

I look at my friends on the mountaintop. They have gone from the world that they knew. Failed by the one that they loved. The one that they gave themselves to. The one who failed them.

'I'm sorry.'

My trial is silent. Their judgement is final.

My three comrades turn their backs, and walk away.

I have lost them to the mountains.

Only Beatha remains. With painful steel wrapped upon my limbs and grief wrapped about my heart, I stagger to my feet. My lips are silent, but my eyes beg. With bloody hands, I try to hold her.

She falls to ash in my hands.

When the mountain crumbles below me, I make not a sound.

I woke in silence. Felt as though I had run a marathon. The dream had drained me of every drop of strength, every ounce of meaning.

'Varo is dead . . .' I said to myself with quiet finality.

How can he not be?

My eyes adjusted to the darkness. My lonely campaign tent, weak moonlight shading the canvas.

I look for wine, but the skin is as empty as my hope. I wiped my eyes. They were dry. My tears have gone. I am numb. A carcass with a heartbeat.

I could change that.

I pushed myself up on to my knees. Pick up my sword from where it lies beside me. My actions smooth and unhurried. No ceremony, just the deliberate motions of one who wishes to see a job done properly.

The edge of the blade catches the moonlight that leaks inside the canvas. I took the pommel in my hands, and turn the blade towards my naked chest. I feel it prick the flesh. The first drop of blood.

I know what I can do. I know what I must do. I am here before them on my knees, and now I prepare to pass judgement on myself – what other sentence can I receive but death? I have only to fall. Hit the hard ground, then bleed into it. Nourish the dead soil. The same soil that has swallowed my comrades.

I breathe deeply.

I hesitate.

Why?

I am afraid. I am afraid, yes.

Of death? No.

I am afraid of what they will say to me when I see them. I am afraid that I will only reveal myself to be a coward. I don't deserve life, I am certain of this, but do I deserve the peace of death? Do I deserve their presence in the afterlife? Would they even look at me? Talk to me? I failed them. How can I face them as . . . this?

Beatha. How can I go to her when I have a blade in my hand, and strength in my body? What would she tell me to do? What would she counsel, guided by her great capacity for love, which was not reserved for me, but given freely to all people? She would not want me to abandon Marcus, despite what he is becoming in this war. With certainty, I realize that it is for precisely this reason that she would want me to remain – who else can turn Marcus back from darkness but his oldest friend? His brother? Who else will even try?

And then there are the innocent. The women. The children. The elderly. I am one man, not a god, and I can never change the face of war, but perhaps I can at least shield some from its deadly gaze? While I am alive, I can counsel restraint. Defend with my words those that I cannot guard with my shield. Beatha would love me for it. The others would understand. I am not turning on my legion. My empire. I am simply trying to be the best instrument of it that I can be.

I breathe out harshly. A warm breeze comes through the tent, and I think of Beatha's kiss on my cheek. She is smiling, and I love her. She has given me purpose.

I lower my sword.

'Up on your feet, you lazy tarts!'

He is Gripper, a squat centurion known for his tendency to grip his men by the throat. He is the man the legate has given me to search for Varo and the missing section.

'You have a day,' Hook-nose had told me, his eyes patient in his severe face.

'Ready when you are, standard-bearer,' Gripper tells me.

A nod is all I give him. Sunlight is fighting its battle for the horizon. I do not want to waste a breath.

We move out.

In the furnace heat of the valley floor we searched for the missing. We prayed for comrades. Expected bodies. Found nothing.

'Not a fucking blood trail or anything,' Gripper growled, looking as though he wanted to strangle the mountain. 'It's getting dark, standard-bearer.'

The night was coming, and hope was fleeing. The signs our best amateur scouts could find were muddled, and misleading. Three times we had come back to the same point. I had the feeling that we were being watched. Gripper thought it was more than that.

'They're fucking laughing at us.'

Maybe, but I couldn't hear the humour, just the hammering of blood in my ears as a voice in my head told me Varo was gone. That voice was calm and reasonable. The voice that screamed at it to shut up was angry and heartbroken.

'We need to go back, standard-bearer.' Then the hard man apologized, and I could see that it wasn't an action he relished. 'I'm sorry. I wish we could keep looking, but . . .'

But men die in war, go missing in war, and a century couldn't be put at risk to find nine men, not even when they were commanded by a soul like Varo.

'Move your men out, centurion.' I told him, and with those words, I felt as though *I* was the one to drop the axe on my comrade's neck.

The officer hesitated. He sensed something in my demeanour. 'And what will you do?' he asked me.

'I will find my brother,' I promised.

The only one that I had left.

39

At dawn I left to find Marcus.

The legion had reached a break in the mountains, and on this plateau between the peaks stood a village of some three dozen hovels behind stone walls. Marcus's cohort and one other had been drawn up in front of this bastion to intimidate the occupants into abandoning their stronghold, and to surrender.

From my vantage on the opposite ridge, I saw that none of 'the enemy' were stirring. I wondered if they had heard the stories. Why give up your arms when it will mean your head coming off your shoulders?

I wanted to be down there. I needed to be down there, not to fight, but to restrain. I wanted to be by Marcus's side not to kill with him, but to be his conscience, as he had so often been mine.

I wanted that badly, but I knew that I had to pick my battles. I was waging a war for decency now, and I knew that my words would only fall on deaf, hot ears if I tried to speak to them at this moment. I needed to fight my battles when men were calm. Their blood cold. Or, at least, so far as that was possible on campaign.

And so I watched as the cohorts stepped forwards, and the rippling ranks passed over the stone defences as though they were manned by children. It was no battle. The legionaries had faced greater challenges on the parade ground, and now here they echoed the orders to dig out the enemy hiding in their homes. To burn out the rebels. To take no prisoners.

'Can I join you?'

The strong voice came from behind me. It was a voice used to command. To leadership. It held force, but promised comradeship. There was an accent to the proud Latin.

I turned.

His uniform was that of a cavalry officer, though there was no sight of his mount. His handsome face was open and whimsical, as if the screams of rape and murder emerging below us were a prelude to a joke. I had seen him before. He looked older than he had when he had marched out to join Tiberius's army on the Danube. Older than when the Eighth and his auxiliary cavalry had been tasked with the operation to clear down to the coast.

He now looked with discomfort at what was happening in the town. After a shake of his head, the German turned to face me.

'Corvus, sir,' I greeted him.

'Arminius.' He offered me his hand, man to man. His rank and bearing spoke of noble birth, but he didn't show concern for it. I accepted the gesture, and in that moment I saw confirmation in his eyes that he felt the same loathing for this campaign as I did. A loathing of an empire's order that relied on butchery to survive.

'Those are our own citizens we're killing,' Arminius observed, his tone low. In the closest street, a man was being hacked apart by inexperienced boy soldiers. It was a bad death. A long one.

I turned my eyes from the sight, not in disgust, but because I wanted to take the measure of this man. My fatalism had not vanished, and I yearned to say out loud words that could condemn me to the cross should he betray my trust.

I do not know how he gained my confidence, but it was given to him as easily as a babe loves its mother. Perhaps it was because I had developed such contempt for my own life that I no longer cared for its preservation. I simply needed to unburden my soul. To make something of my life. To go to the next one with something that I could show Beatha. My friends were gone. Marcus too, in spirit. I couldn't talk up the ranks. I couldn't talk down. I needed someone outside of my legion, and here was such a leader, with his feelings of distaste plain to see.

And so I spoke.

'We're going to lose this war,' I said.

The words hung in the air. Defeatism was not welcomed in the ranks, and yet . . .

'Why do you say so?' The words gentle, and even.

I pointed to the town. 'We are supposed to be the shepherds, but we pushed the flock towards the wolves of war, and they panicked. Instead of guiding them back to the fold, we are slaughtering them where we find them.'

'What else could we do?'

'Talk to them?' It seemed so obvious, yet even as I said the words, I realized how ridiculous they would sound to soldier and senator.

'Do you think they would listen?'

I let out a frustrated breath. 'Now that there's been battles? Sisters and mothers raped? Family killed and enslaved?' I shook my head with bitter anger. 'No. No. Too many want blood, now.'

The prince nodded at the words. He watched the butchery in the village. 'Today is revenge for men who have lost brothers on this campaign,' he said. 'The next rebel ambush will be revenge for those who lose friends and family to our blades today. And so it will go on.' He turned to face me. His eyes were heavy with grief. 'I fear this province is destined to drown in blood, my friend.'

My province. Home to all those I had called friend, and teacher, and family, and lover.

'I can't . . . I can't let that happen.' I shook my head, picturing them all as gleaming piles of bone, the next words out of me before I considered their true danger. 'I can't serve an empire that does this.'

There. It was in the open. I had put a blade to my throat with my treasonous words. Arminius need only push, and my life was forfeit.

Instead, with a slight narrowing of his eyes, the noble considered my words. He did so until the man in the street had ceased his screaming. Other citizens, found cowering in their hiding places, were beginning theirs.

When he spoke, his words were heavy with responsibility.

'I look to my own people,' he said, and gestured to the death in the town. 'The tribes in Germania. When they feel as though they deserve a voice in the running of the

Empire that they are told they are a part of, will this be their reward? Will I be asked to carry my sword against those of my own blood?'

We both knew the answer. 'Yes, for Rome.'

'Rome *is* a light in the world.' As Arminius spoke, I could feel his love for that place, and its principles. 'But the torch is carried by the wrong people.'

My fingers were trembling with fear from speaking with such open disloyalty, but like the first hole in a dam, the pressure was building, and there was no holding back my torrent of seditious thoughts now.

'How do we change that?' I asked suddenly, needing to know the answer, certain that this man possessed it, and anxious to play my part.

Arminius turned to look at me. His blue eyes burned into mine. 'What are you willing to do?'

I could find no words, and so I placed my hand on the pommel of my sword.

Slowly, the German nodded; then he placed his hand on my arm. 'You are a brave man, Corvus,' he told me, and in that instant I feared I had been betrayed, and that he would kill me, or condemn me so that others could carry out the sentence.

Instead, as the screams of Roman justice echoed beneath us, Arminius told me how we would defeat an empire.

40

In the wake of the small town's falling and my conspiracy with Arminius, I did not seek out Marcus. He would have blood on his hands and fire in his eyes, so instead I rode to the valley.

My target was the legion commander.

I found him in his campaign tent. He was alone, and surprised to see me.

He was more surprised still when I drew my sword.

'Standard-bearer?'

I took a step forwards. The legate was defenceless, and I made my move.

I placed the blade on a campaign chest.

'We can't win with the sword, sir,' I told him simply. I had come here to save blood, not to shed it.

The legate looked back at me over his curved nose, his eyes narrowed in question.

'Sir,' I began the argument that I had rehearsed with Arminius, 'how are we going to pacify this region by killing everyone we come across? It's like trying to calm a bull by whipping it, sir.'

The aristocrat considered me for a moment, and then folded his arms. 'We put a ring in a bull's nose for good reason, standard-bearer.'

'A ring so that we can *lead it*, sir, not butcher it,' I replied, conveniently forgetting that often the animal was being led to slaughter. 'What use is the province if it is just an empty husk, sir?'

I saw distaste pass over his gaunt features. Rome's patriarchy was as much a part of him as his liver. 'That's no concern of mine, and it's certainly no concern of yours, standard-bearer. We are the instruments of Rome's will. The Emperor and the Senate decree, and we execute.'

I had seen the literal evidence of that all too clearly. 'But we can achieve Rome's aims without prolonging the suffering of this war, sir. If we get the locals on our side then the enemy will have nowhere to hide. They will have nowhere to draw stores. They will have —'

'Enough!' the legate shouted, slamming his hand down on to a table. 'Enough, standard-bearer! You forget your place!' He glowered. 'You forget *mine*!'

He looked at me as though I was an unruly child. I had been used to that look from my own father.

At last, a long breath escaped him. 'Our orders come from General Tiberius, heir to the Emperor himself.' He was trying to drill his words into my skull. 'Who are we to question him?'

'We are his soldiers, sir. We—'

'Exactly!' Hook-nose cut me off, but not viciously. 'We are his *soldiers*, Corvus. Not his diplomats, not his tax collectors, and certainly not his wet-nurses. We are here to kill and conquer, not hold hands with those who would shelter our enemies. 'Tell me. have you lost friends to this uprising?'

He knew that I had. Who hadn't?

'Yes, sir.'

'The closest of friends? Brothers?'

'Yes, sir.'

'Then it astounds me that you have an ounce of compassion for these criminals and savages, standard-bearer. They are our enemy, nothing more, nothing less.'

They were my enemy, yes, but the headless children? The raped women? Was I to believe that they had overpowered Varo? That they were the ones who had driven a spear into Priscus? I wanted to say that – to say it *all* – but one look into the commander's eyes told me that I had lost this battle. My tongue had failed me. It had seemed so simple when Arminius had suggested I counsel the legate on strategy, but why would a Roman-born aristocrat ever listen to a soldier like me? I had been prized for my bravery, not my intellect, and even that was a fallacy. Regardless, the only insight I was supposed to offer was that of my enemy's spilled guts.

'I'm sorry for speaking out of turn, sir,' I said, recognizing that I needed to retreat, and conserve my energy for another assault, some other day. 'I just want victory, and for this campaign to be over.' A half-truth.

Hook-nose didn't deny it. He looked at me with affection. 'We are being slow-bled here,' he acknowledged. 'It's not the glory you deservr, standard-bearer. You and all of my legion. But it's what we have, and it is our duty to see it through.'

'Yes, sir.'

He smiled, then. He really liked me, this senator. This aristocrat. He thought he saw in me the noble merits of Rome. Not even my outburst could tarnish the virtue of saving an eagle.

243

'I have some good news for you,' he said, the skin wrinkling about his hooded eyes.

'Sir?' Good news was a forgotten visitor.

'There are supplies coming in from Italy. I need you to go to the port and meet them. Account for it all, and then pass back through the areas we've cleared, and take it to Siscia.'

I was surprised by his order. 'Isn't that a task for the quartermaster, sir?'

The legate shook his head. 'The pay chests are coming.' He smiled, knowing how such a revelation usually buoyed up the men under his command. 'And those chests are your responsibility, standard-bearer.'

It was true. There was no escaping this duty, and in that moment, realization crept up on me like an assassin . . .

'You said they were coming into a port, sir?' I asked numbly.

The officer nodded. I knew the name of the place before he said it.

'Iader.'

I was going home.

❧ 41 ❧

I walked out of the tent in a daze. All about me was the bustle of a legion on campaign, but I saw none of it. I staggered through the industry like a drunk, not even breaking to snarl at the occasional soldier I bumped into with my unguided shoulders.

Iader?

I hadn't returned to that place since I had beaten my father, and run with Marcus. My closest friend had returned there on leave several years later, and he'd told me that my father yet lived, though he was sickly. Likely now he was dead. Had my crime died with him?

Perhaps it didn't matter. Who would identify me? I was not the bright-eyed, good-looking boy who had run away. Now my nose was crooked, my skin was near black, and my eyes were darker still. For every ounce of innocence that I'd lost I had gained corded muscle. The boy who'd run was unrecognizable from the one who would return.

And if I *was* identified? It would take someone with great gall to level a charge at the honoured Standard-Bearer of the Eighth Legion. Even if my father did so himself, what was one more death in the night when the whole region was ablaze? His was the first blood I had ever had on my angry hands. I had soaked the soil with much since. That I did not want to see other families butchered did not mean that I would not gut my own. His life had become forfeit many years ago, when he found me on the pier, ache in my heart and loss in my eyes.

I reached Balius, and swung myself into my horse's saddle. I would go to Iader. I had run away a boy, and I would return a soldier. A killer.

But first I would say goodbye to a friend.

Alone and unafraid, I trotted Balius out to the shallow depression where I had buried Octavius beneath the stones.

They were gone.

So was he.

I dropped from Balius's back and tied him to the skeleton of the tree. Then, blade in hand, I searched for my dead comrade.

I found him on a scree-slope. His decaying body had been hacked into pieces, and spread across the stone. Fat crows looked at me with lazy disdain.

I expected grief, then, but anger came in a charge of fire that consumed my entire being. I knew that the trick was a ruse of the enemy. That the need for decency would draw me into their trap. I didn't care. I simply ran up the loose stones, screaming challenge.

'Bastards! Bastards! Come and kill me, you bastards! Come and kill me! Come on, kill me!' I raged at the mountains. I howled at the war. '*Come on!*'

But none came. The world around me was impassive. When the echoes of my fury died, the mountains mocked me with their silence.

Fire fled out of me, my spirit doused. I sank to my knees beside the butchered remains of one of my closest comrades. I wanted an arrow from the rocks. Instead I heard nothing but the flapping of a crow's wings.

I waited a long time for the enemy to come, and then I began to pick up the pieces of my friend.

My cavalry escort met me at the edge of the camp. I sat astride Balius. My horse was loaded heavily but my eyes were empty.

'I pulled some strings so that my men and I will escort you,' Arminius informed me. 'I thought that we should talk.'

But he didn't say a lot after that. Nothing about my demeanour said that my encounter with the legate had gone well. Arminius could feel violence in me, too. All soldiers could. Not one had come within a javelin's length of me since I had returned to the main body of the legion. They could smell danger, or maybe what Balius carried on his back.

We rode out. My mouth stayed shut. Arminius listened to the reports of his nimble scouts, and his eyes searched the valley around us like a hawk's, but my own were picturing what lay ahead.

'I spoke to the legate,' he finally told me, trying to break our silence. That surprised me enough that I inclined my head to look at him. 'I do not believe he's someone who can be brought to our way of thinking.'

I gave a derisive snort. 'No shit.'

The German was taken aback by my tone. The last time we had talked I had been deferential, but here was open hostility. I think he sensed that it was against the world, rather than himself.

'How well do you know this port?' he asked of our destination.

'Well.'

'Could we find allies there?'

I felt my grip tighten on Balius's reins. 'Allies for what, Prince Arminius?' I asked him. 'We're two soldiers with madness in our minds. We are two men. Rome is Rome.'

The handsome bastard smiled. 'Rome was built by two men, was it not? It can be rebuilt that way, too.'

I shook my head. 'We've spent too much time in the mountains,' I told him, fighting the infection of his smile. 'The thin air's ruined our brains.'

He winked. 'Or has the elevation given us a clarity to see beyond the horizon?'

I snorted again. 'This is going to be a long ride. Why don't you save your charm, prince,' I said carelessly, for what use was decorum when you had admitted to a desire to betray your orders? Your empire? 'Tell me something about Germany.' *Tell me something to make me forget, if only for a moment.*

Arminius grew in the saddle. Here was pride. 'It's the most beautiful place in the world, Corvus,' he told me with certainty. 'Wide rivers, good soil and forest as far as the eye can see.'

'Forests?' I asked him, pulling a face. I was a stranger to such things. Woods, certainly, but forests? The kind where darkness ruled, and wicked things preyed on those fools that ventured into their depths?

Arminius saw my discomfort, and laughed. 'I have nothing to fear in forests. The gods of my people reside there. The spirits would greet me.'

'And what about the bears?'

He shrugged his armoured shoulders. 'I could make you a new hat.'

I laughed, the sound as coarse as the stone on the slopes about us. My own bearskin was bundled behind my saddle, but it wasn't the hide that drew the flies, and kept all but the German officer from my side.

'How did you come to be here?' I asked him, not wanting to think of my own path.

'My father is a chieftain. We pay homage to Rome, and he wanted me to learn Roman ways.'

'So you're not a Roman?'

Arminius scratched at his face where an insect had bitten him. 'They bestowed citizenship on the nobles of my tribe.' Then he gestured to his tall, formidable-looking troopers. 'But these men? No. As auxiliaries, citizenship will be bestowed on them when they finish their service.'

I looked at the faces of his soldiers. They were grim and warlike, but there was a spark in their movement that was absent from Marcus's comrades in the mountains. Was that inspiration Arminius?

'These men don't fight for Rome,' I guessed. 'They follow you.'

He was humble enough not to agree. Proud enough not to argue.

'And where will you lead them?' I asked.

It was a moment before he answered. 'For now . . . Iader. I have another year of service to Rome on this frontier. Then I am to return home.'

'To farm?' I asked, knowing somehow that a peaceful life would make this man happy.

Arminius shook his head. 'To fight. Like you, I was not born to farm, Corvus. We were born to carry a blade, and there is always someone to fight.'

I looked at my hands. Pictured the blood on them. 'Perhaps we can change that?' I wondered aloud, hearing the enormity of that task in the words.

Arminius smiled bravely. 'Perhaps we can.'

The rest of our journey passed in near silence but for the breath of our horses and the tramp of their hooves on the hard-baked track. We saw no sign of the enemy.

'We rarely do,' Arminius had told me when I asked him about it.

I could understand why. They were frightening men, these Germans, and despite their size they were lightning and grace on their mounts.

That question was one of the few things that I did ask the prince. Many more enquiries burned inside me, but I saw a man in deep contemplation, and somehow sensed that his musings would benefit not just myself, but countless others. I had been in the presence of greatness before, and from Arminius came a feeling of calm and confidence. That, despite it all, things would work out for the best. That the chaos of the world would soon be put in check.

I shook my head to clear it of that grand idea. The burden on my horse was proof of the ridiculousness of such a fantasy. Then, with my load in mind, I turned to Arminius. 'The town's three miles further along this road.'

He sensed there was more. Raised his eyebrows.

'I'll meet you at the port.'

I had somewhere else to be. He didn't ask where.

'Do you want an escort?' he said instead.

I shook my head. The harshness of the mountains had given way to rolling hills. I had blades on my hip, and a solid mount between my legs. 'I'll be fine.'

Arminius offered his hand, and looked at me with warmth. He knew that something painful was the cause of my diversion. 'At the port, then.'

'At the port.'

I dug my heels into Balius's flanks, and we galloped towards the green hillsides, familiar places from my childhood. A time where battles had been fought with sticks and the dead picked themselves up from the ground.

A warm wind came to our nostrils as we weaved between the olive trees. There was salt in it – we were nearing the sea. As we crested the ridge, I saw it laid out before us in its blue brilliance. Glittering water, studded with verdant green islands that clung to the coast like crocodiles' spines.

It was the most beautiful place in the world. I had thought so as a child, and I thought so now. I don't know how long I gazed at the shimmering deep, picturing Rome beyond the sea, and what had happened in that unseen city's name, but finally I dropped from the saddle, my sandals hitting the soil that had been a sanctuary to me in another life. It was the refuge of brothers. Our escape when Marcus and I had not wanted to do our lessons or chores. We would sit here; we would talk. His dreams were of conquest, mine of simple happiness. He talked of Rome and, one day, I began talking of her.

'Beatha . . .'

Tears filled my eyes as soon as they fell on the stones that marked her grave. I did not even think to tie Balius off, instead sinking to my knees beside the woman that I loved.

I kissed the stone. '*Beatha.*'

I kissed *her.*

'I've come home.'

42

I sat gazing at the stones that formed the tomb of the woman I loved most and above all others. She had been untainted in a world of wickedness, and though I had adored her purity as she lived, I had only come to truly understand it when she died, and I began to live the savagery that truly defined our empire. I realized now that I had been shielded by my family. Shielded by my town. But above all, I had been shielded by this woman. Hope and purpose had coursed through my veins, hotter than my blood. In a world of despondency, I had been a bastion of happiness. Beatha was my wall. When she died, my defences crumbled.

I looked back at the sea. It was bright in the sunlight, and the hillside about me was a concert of gentle breeze and birdsong. I had chosen well for her in this, at least. Her resting place was fitting of her spirit. And now, it would be a home for my brother.

Balius was happily chewing grass. I called him over, then unloaded the sacks that were tied off on his chestnut flanks. I saw something in the animal's eyes as I tethered him to a tree. I put a hand on his head, and he nuzzled into me. How did he know?

I placed a pick beside the sacks. The last time I had dug into this hillside I had used stone, and my bare hands. My fingers had been bloody long before they gripped my father's throat.

I hefted the tool above my head and set about digging Octavius's grave.

The hill's soil was rich, and I'd soon dug deep enough to bury the parts of my friend that I had recovered from the mountains. I gathered stone. Placed them atop the turned earth. I wiped sweat from my face, and sat between the graves of two people I loved deeply.

'Look after each other,' I made them promise.

I wanted to stay. I wanted to lie down between them, and never rise.

But Marcus was in the mountains, and Arminius was in the town. One needed to be rescued from the dark pit that he'd fallen into, and the other held the rope to do it.

'I'll be back,' I swore, kissing Beatha's stone. 'I love you.'

I rode hard from the hillside before I could change my mind. Behind me, a brave soldier stood watch over the sea, and over the woman I had loved. For once in my life, I knew that I had done something right.

Then, as I spurred my horse towards the town, I thought back to the day of my greatest failure.

43

I pushed open the doorway and stepped into the courtyard. Sunlight bounced back from the white walls. Alongside paths of painted tiles, perfect lines of flowers shimmered in their ranks like armoured soldiers.

I walked to the centre of the square garden, dipping my hand into the cool water of the pond. As I moved my eyes searched for an ambush that I hoped would come swiftly.

There was nothing.

I looked into the pond's calming waters. In the reflection I saw a handsome young man, skin darkened by sun, eyes set alight by life.

I smiled. I was enjoying this game.

I went through the house room by room. It was quiet. My father had gone to visit friends and were not expected back until later that night, when they would be soaked with wine and witless. The slaves had been relieved of their duties for the day, and so my footsteps echoed in the deserted building. There was haste in my footfalls; I wanted to make use of this unexpected privacy.

Twice I searched rooms where window veils played gently with the ocean breeze, dappled light falling across furniture polished as dark as my father's beard. Twice I searched, and twice I was beaten.

I left the house and walked on to the street. I could feel the heat through my sandals, but the breeze drew its fingers across my neck like a caress. A prelude to what I searched for.

Despite the heat, I ran. Sweat began to stain my tunic, but I was young. An athlete. My breath was steady and my limbs were loose. The coast appeared before me, golden sand and a glittering sea. Hot sand pushed between my toes. I looked left and right along a beach that knew my deepest secret.

I was alone. The game was wearing on me, but I was competitive. No matter the sport, no matter the challenge, I did not lose.

I looked at the ocean. The wet prow of a galley glowed golden as the oars beat their way out to sea. I took a moment to indulge my imagination, thinking of her destination. Of Rome. Of endless possibility.

The ship had left the port of my home town, and now I knew that this was where the game would end.

I ran along the sand, stamping it from my feet as I reached the paved streets, picking my way between olive-skinned merchants and haggling slaves. A child caught my eye, and smiled for a coin. I threw him two. I wanted my happiness to be a disease. Contagious. I wanted everyone in the port to feel the same thumping heartbeat of anticipation as I did. The same thrill that flushed my skin, and carried me like an emperor above the heads of those around me.

I knew where the game would end – on the stone pier that drove out into the ocean. It was the closest point we had to Rome. A place where we would sit and dream.

Today would be the day that dream became reality. Today, when the game ended, a life would begin in its place – a priest would see to that. A priest, and a ship, and a fair wind to hurry our love to a distant shore.

I turned a final corner between fishing baskets, the smell of salt and olive oil filling my nostrils, and then I saw the pier. It was a scrum of men, women and children. Sailors loaded a galley that was sitting deep as its hull was filled. Old men cast lines into the water for their dinner. The pier was packed, and yet to my eyes it was empty.

Beatha wasn't there.

Somehow, I had lost the game.

I turned for home. Deflated, my eyes were on the cobblestones as I walked into a thick chest..

'Father?' I asked, confused. Confused because he was supposed to be with his friends. Confused because, for the first time in my life, the man looked down at me with disappointment.

'Corvus,' he said, and I heard a sentence in that word.

I didn't dare ask what. Instead, I followed like a shamed dog in the big man's wake. He strode to our family home. He was silent the entire way, but the rigidity of his posture shouted volumes – I had never seen him like this. My father was not a warm man, but now he seemed so . . . dangerous.

As we walked I hoped that I would see her. Catch a glimpse. I hoped somehow that I could still win the game. I was in trouble, that much was clear, but there was not a shadow of worry in my mind that my father knew about what I had been planning. This was something else – something worrying, but something that could be survived.

It was as we entered the enclosed garden, free of prying eyes, that he hit me.

The blow was unexpected, a force of nature that sent me reeling backwards. I collapsed into a flower bed, the sound of ringing loud in my ears. When I looked up, I saw the furious face of my father looming above me, as dangerous as a cliff on the edge of collapse.

'You fucking *child*,' he hissed, the words filled with hate. 'On your feet!' he ordered me. 'On your feet!'

I struggled to obey. I had barely regained them when his fist crashed into my face. I dropped at once, my vision swimming. I'd never been hit so hard, but it was my father's tone that made my legs buckle beneath me. The first maggot of doubt since he had found me at the port began to gnaw at my insides – did he *know*?

'Up!' he yelled. 'Up!' But despite his words he kicked me, driving all air from my lungs, and turning my stomach into a churning torrent of acid. 'Up!'

He helped me by grabbing my hair and pulling me to my feet. He held me like that, inspecting me as you would a tick plucked from your flesh.

'Corvus . . .' he said. There was sadness as well as anger, now. 'Corvus, you have shamed me.'

He let go of my hair. Pointed to a stone bench. 'Sit,' he commanded of his dog.

I did as I was bid. He was silent, but I felt the heat of the rage that swelled beneath his skin.

'Father . . .' I tried, tasting blood in my mouth.

'Don't say anything,' he seethed. 'Just listen.' I could see then that he was fighting a battle against himself. Despite the damage that he had wrought on me, it was obvious he was holding himself back from inflicting more.

Finally he spoke and, despite the pounding in my skull, it pained me that he did not call me son. 'Corvus, you have shamed this family.'

Not *your* family. *This* family.

The maggot of doubt in my guts became a ravenous snake. I felt sick. Disgrace of this magnitude could only have been caused by . . .

'Explain yourself!'

I said nothing. I held my lips so tightly shut that they pressed more blood from my shaken teeth.

'Boy,' he ordered, stepping forwards with balled fists, *'you will explain yourself.'*

I swallowed blood and fear. 'Of what am I accused?' I asked with a defiant tilt of my jaw.

A backhanded swipe sent my pride on to the hot tiles.

'You are *accused* of nothing!' my father spat. 'To be accused, there must be doubt! And you have left no doubt, you swine! No doubt of your crime, and now, no doubt of your gall!'

I held my tongue. Made sure that it was not between my teeth, for when the next blow came.

Father shook his angry head. 'To steal from your family . . .' he let out in dismay, 'and then to lie to your father's face?' I saw the grief on his own, then. Grief, and misery. 'Did I fail you so badly?'

I realized that there would be no more kicks. No more battery. Anger had passed. In the wake of that storm came my father's bitter disappointment.

'You would have stolen from us, Corvus?' he asked without heat. 'For your own profit, you would have taken a slave?'

The words hit me harder than any of his blows had done. They were like a sword's bite. I felt as though I had been gutted on the tile.

I knew then that the game was over.

'Beatha . . .' I tried.

'Do not speak her name,' my father told me with cold iron. 'Do not ever speak her name again.'

I pushed myself up on to shaking limbs. I trembled with fear, which clawed at every part of my body. 'Where . . . where is she?'

My father breathed deeply, and looked through me.

'Where is she?'

He said nothing.

'*Where is she?*'

The question hung in the hot air. My father's eyes burned over me, and then his shoulders sagged. He was looking at failure. He detached something from his belt and threw it to me.

I caught it out of instinct – a purse. I felt the shape of the coins through the soft leather.

'Run away with that if you want,' my patriarch told me. 'But you will not shame this family by doing so with a slave.'

I heard the coins begin to clatter as my hands shook, the immensity of the disaster gripping me as an earthquake does the countryside. I was not in command of my limbs any more. I felt as though my reason would soon flee, too. 'Where . . . where is she?' I stammered.

'Where else would I sell a slave?' the man grunted with disdain.

I should have hated him then. Should have attacked him. But my mind was consumed. Overrun with one simple thought.

Get her back.
Get her from the slave market.

My father's calls had chased me from courtyard. He told me never to come back, but I had no intention of doing such a thing. I would have forgotten even to breathe in that moment, so single-minded was my need to find my love.

My bloodied face drew stares as I ran like an Olympian to the slave market by the port. It was a small place, just a few pens, and pitiful eyes watched me as I sought out the owner.

'A girl?' he asked. 'Brought here today? What's she like?'

What is she like? The most open and beautiful of spirits. The kindest eyes. A jewel in the crown of all people.

'She's got dark hair. No scars. Seventeen.'

I knew the destination for such girls. So did the merchant. He shrugged his shoulders.

'I haven't had anyone like that today.'

'But you're the only trader in Iader.'

'I am.'

'So she must be here! Can you look?'

Instead the man folded his arms. 'Look, a girl like you're describing? I would remember, and I wouldn't be keeping her here in the pens, do you understand, young lad?'

I understood perfectly well. I wanted to rip his throat out. Instead I pushed by him, and looked into every one of the pens.

'Hey!' he called after me.

'Beatha!' I shouted. 'Beatha!'

She wasn't there. The owner's guard was.

'If you sell her, I'll kill you,' I promised him.

And then I ran.

I ran to the pier, drawing shouts and angry stares as I demanded of the sailors if they had seen or bought anyone matching Beatha's description. I went to every stall in the forum, asking farmers and tradesmen if they had seen the woman I loved. Most looked at me as though I was mad. I saw a flash of sympathy in the eyes of others.

'Oi!' an old soldier of the town's watch shouted at me. 'Piss off and stop bothering people,' he ordered, before he caught sight of my bloodied face, and his eyes narrowed. 'What have you been doing?' But I was already running. 'Oi!'

I lost him in the narrow streets, and stopped at a fountain to wash the blood from my face.

Where could she be? Was the owner of the slave market lying? Could she have been there, but escaped? Perhaps it was my father who was lying, and Beatha had smelled the trap, and already got away? That had to be it! My father had tried to buy my grief. Silver for my silence. He underestimated me – he always had – and he had expected me to remain a broken pile of emotion while he bought the time to seek out my love. But Beatha had escaped the trap!

I ran with strength now, not sadness. I had only to find her. I had money in my hand. We could run. We could sail. Today would be the beginning after all!

As I had done that morning, I looked in all of the places that held secrets for our hearts. I found her at none of them, but I did not despair. It was obvious now where she would be. Beatha was the clever one, and she would have chosen a place where she could see danger approaching. I didn't know how she had learned of our exposure, but I know that she could run ahead of it like a silk sail on fair winds. .

I ran towards our hill that overlooked the sea. As children it had belonged to Marcus and me. Brothers. As I grew and discovered love, it became the first place that I knew Beatha as a woman. It was *our* place, then. A place where we could sit, and plot, and dream of a new life beyond the sea, where we wouldn't be owner and slave, but husband and wife. Father and mother.

I was panting hard by the time I reached the clearing at the top of the hill, my skin scratched from the reaching fingers of harsh brush and branch. It didn't matter. I knew I was close.

As I burst into the clearing, I was smiling.

Beatha lay naked on her back, her own smile staring up at the sky.

It was a red smile, stretched across her throat.

I tried to scream.

Instead I fell.

❧ 44 ❧

When I regained consciousness, I cursed the world that I was alive. I beat my fists against the dirt. Drove my skull against the ground until blood ran into my eyes. I lay helpless as a newborn, the stink of soil in my nose, the beautiful sound of birdsong in my ears as a light breeze teased the trees.

'No . . .'

I made myself open my eyes. I saw her. Cold. Lifeless. Beautiful.

'No . . .'

I crawled to her. I was crippled. Broken. I felt vomit rise in my throat. I didn't fight it. It clung to me. I was a vision of hell. She, even in death, a work of art.

But someone had defiled her. Some beast, for surely no man could have been so vile? Her throat was opened to the skies. There was blood between her legs. Her clothes lay miserable and discarded in the bushes.

With trembling hands I dressed my darling. I whispered a thousand silent apologies as I clothed her. Gave voice to a million promises and curses. I was a broken man, but there was a fuel that kept me going.

It was the fuel of sworn vengeance.

I clawed at the ground with fingernails and stone. The sun had long set before I placed my life into the grave, and kissed her. I had no tears to fall on to her patient face. They were gone. Gone into the soil. I vowed that they would be followed by the blood of those who had wronged her.

Those who had declared war on the world by taking its finest child.

'I will come back to you,' I promised. Her grave was near covered. Only her face remained. I couldn't bring myself to steal her from life. I couldn't bear to silence a voice of reason. A laugh of pure joy.

But neither could I live with seeing her unavenged. 'I will come back to you,' I said again.

I kissed her one final time, then prayed that I could carry out my promises swiftly. I wanted only to be in the ground with her, in the sanctity of this place I had loved so much. The world seemed like a mocking insult now that she had left it.

The final stone went into place on her grave. I kissed it. I kissed her.

I ran hard from the hillside, before I could change my mind.

To the east, dawn was threatening the row of mountains that stood like the lower jaw of a shark's bite. A blood-red disc began to rise behind these vicious peaks.

I took it as an omen. A good omen – the gods approved of what I had planned.

The gods approved of me killing my father.

The sun was high by the time I made it to what had been my home. Now, a place that had held warm memories for me seemed about as inviting as the sands of the arena. I did not want to be here – I wanted to be with the woman I loved – but I had come with a purpose, and that purpose was to kill.

My father. I found him in the garden. Had he even left? From the way that he sat heavily on one of the stone benches, I felt that he had not.

He sensed my entrance. 'I told you not to come back.' Those were his words, but his eyes said different – there was relief in them. Hope.

Cold anger shook my limbs, and held my lips shut. How could he think that I could come back to him after . . . after . . .

'Sit down, son.'

Son? So I was in the fold again? Worthy of love? Worthy of affection? I realized then what was in his mind. Beatha was a slave to him, no more or less prized than a piece of furniture. To him, she was just a chair that had been broken. A table that could be replaced. His ire had been for my supposed theft of property, nothing more, nothing less.

I hated him all the more for it.

'Son. Sit down.'

I walked over. I tried to push it down. All the hate. All the rage. I tried to push it down, just long enough.

It worked.

This time it was *I* who struck unexpectedly, my fist ploughing into my father's dark beard with all the force that I could put behind it.

But the blow did not unseat the man. He took it like a prizefighter, and there was time for me to see the surprise in his eyes before I hit him again, and again, and again.

We landed on the floor. He used his arms to fend off my blows, but threw none of his own. *Coward.* 'Corvus!' he yelled. 'Son! What are you doing? Let me up!'

266

But I would not. Rage had dug its angry tendrils into my limbs, and controlled them as though they were of a separate body. Through a haze I saw myself punch, stamp, kick and thump. I saw blood, I heard bone, and through it all, I said nothing.

'Corvus!' he tried to shout against the tempest. 'Son! Stop!'

But I would not. I was atop of him, my surprise total, and my father could not fight back.

'Help!' he tried instead. 'Cynbel! Cynbel! Help!'

My rain of fury continued. It wasn't my father that I saw below me. Just a bloody mess of wild hair and toga.

And then, I was airborne.

It was only as I slammed on to my back that I saw Cynbel, who had thrown me. There was wild panic in the Briton's eyes. He looked from me to my father, unable to comprehend what he saw. What I saw was the father of the woman I loved. He was as oblivious to her death as I was desperate to cause another.

'Cynbel . . .' I began, but the words would not form. Instead, as I saw my father struggle to regain his feet, I surged forwards like a baited wolf.

Cynbel dropped me as though I was a child.

'Corvus!' he shouted in astonishment. 'What madness is this?'

The madness of grief. The madness of love. I scrambled to my feet. Went for my father's throat. Was put on my back.

'Stay down!' Cynbel warned me.

'Detain him,' my father struggled to say, and the Briton moved on me with sadness in his eyes.

'Don't fight me,' he warned, and I knew that I could not.

He was a yard away when my father made a choking sound, and fell flat on to his face. Cynbel turned to help his master, and in that split second I saw my chance. Without blinking I pushed myself to my feet and scrambled to the wall, pulling myself up, leaving bloody smears on the white paint.

I landed hard on the other side.

'Corvus!' Cynbel called plaintively. 'Corvus, please!'

I thought about shouting back. I thought about telling him the true nature of the man he had just saved, but those words died in my throat as my father showed that there was still life in his.

'Corvus!' he bellowed, voice thick with blood and broken teeth. 'Corvus, get back here!'

Instead I turned on my heel, and fled to my brother.

I fled to Marcus, and a life of death in the legions.

ᕰ 45 ᕬ

I pulled back on Balius's reins and looked at the house I had abandoned as a young man. Now I was a soldier, and I had become proficient in the one thing I had failed to do in the wake of Beatha's death – taking life.

I dismounted and untied my bearskin from the back of the saddle. If my father had survived sickness, then he would not see the return of his son. He would see Corvus, decorated Standard-Bearer of the Eighth Legion. I would make that bastard recognize I had done something despite him.

I left Balius tied in the street, walked to the heavy wooden door set into the white walls, and beat on it as though I were bringing down the great walls of Troy.

It opened after a moment. The man who stood there had aged three decades in less than one. Gone was the barrel chest. Gone the flame-red hair. Gone the life in his eyes.

'Cynbel . . .' I whispered.

At first he didn't know whom he was looking at. I removed my helmet so that my face was less hidden by the shadow of a bear's snout.

Finally: 'Corvus?'

I gave a shallow nod of my head. I felt such sadness to see him like this. The death of his daughter had robbed the world of two great spirits, not one.

'Still my father's slave?' It was hard for me to keep the sneer from my voice. He deserved better.

269

Cynbel shook his head. 'He freed me six years ago.' He spoke weakly. 'After . . . after . . .'

My eyes narrowed. Freeing a slave was an act of kindness, and my father had shown himself incapable of that. 'Why?' I demanded.

'So that I could look for her . . .'

I snorted. I saw that it hurt the man, and his saddened expression stopped me saying what was on my mind – that maybe my father had a conscience after all, and that conscience had forced him to free his oldest retainer in recompense for murdering his daughter.

'You didn't find her,' I said. It was a statement, knowing that only I knew the resting place of my love.

I saw a tremble in his bony shoulders. 'I didn't.'

I made a silent vow to myself then. That I would show my old teacher the grave so that he could honour his daughter.

But first I would kill his former owner. The man who was his master still.

'Show me to my father.'

But Cynbel made no move to get out of my way. Instead, his milky eyes looked into mine. 'You loved her, didn't you?' he asked me quietly.

My jaw twitched as I felt words ready to stumble out. I bit back on them. Tried to keep the mask of Corvus the warrior in place.

But . . .

She would have wanted him to know.

'Yes.' The word came out forcefully. A clipped reply. All I could give. I had come here to shed blood, not tears.

Cynbel only nodded. It was the confirmation of a truth he had long since discovered. I saw in his eyes that he wanted to embrace me.

I took a half-step backwards, and replaced my helmet. My face was cast into fanged shadow: the image of a professional killer.

'Show me to the bastard.'

He lay on his back in bed. He hadn't left it in months, since another bout of sickness. Walking through my childhood home I had felt sick with nostalgia, but now, looking at the shrunken form of my father, I did not know how to feel. Rage was boiling within me, but so too was the frightening realization that death and age came for us all – my father as I remembered him had been as indomitable as the mountains that had claimed my friends. Now he was like shingle on the beach. Tiny. Irrelevant. At the whim of life's waves.

His eyes were shut. Cynbel closed the door behind me. For a long time I looked at him, seeing more corpse than man. I had never killed a sick person. I had never killed someone in their bed.

I supposed that he would be the first.

'Father,' I said. 'Father!' I repeated, louder still.

The old man opened his eyes. In mocking slowness they came to fix on me. There was no surprise in them, or in his words. 'You're alive.' A near grunt.

I folded my scarred arms. 'I'm alive.'

His eyes went up to the bearskin on my helmet, then to the decoration on my chain mail. 'You've done well,' he wheezed. 'I always knew you'd be a fighter.'

I said nothing.

The sick man coughed up something disgusting from his chest. 'We can wish what we want for our children,' he went on, wiping at spittle, 'but in the end we can no more change their nature than we can the weather. I promised your mother I would never let you soldier, and yet here you stand, a standard-bearer. Which legion?'

I was shocked by his words. Never had my father spoken so openly about my mother. Never so openly about their own desires, or wishes, especially for me. Our communication in life had been focused on my lessons. On my athletics. On my accomplishments. Never on my nature.

'You know nothing of it,' I told him flatly.

A smile played at the corner of his dry lips. 'Of course not. What can the old ever tell the young?'

I put my hand to my sword. 'They can tell them that they're sorry.'

His red eyes narrowed. 'Sorry for what?'

'For drawing air when their betters lie buried.'

My father tried to snort. He failed. It came out as a wheeze. A sad, pathetic wheeze. 'It's called survival for a reason.' He breathed deeply. 'I suppose you've come to kill me?' The question was put to me as calmly as any I'd heard. I didn't know if that was from mockery, or bravery. I hated him for it regardless.

I said nothing. I wanted the bastard to fear.

Where was his fucking fear?

'Didn't think it was to show your father your uniform,' he commented, and then tried to prop himself up in the bed. 'I knew you'd come back to do it. It's what I would have done.'

I felt my teeth grind. I'd had enough. My voice came out low, but violent. 'We're not the same, old man,' I promised. 'I carry a blade and a shield in hands that wanted to carry children. That wanted to hold the hands of the woman I loved.'

He shook his head, then. That same look of disappointment. 'The young know nothing of love.' He sighed. 'But I can see you know something of death, so come, son. Come and stick a blade in your father. The gods know I've thought about it often enough, wasting away in this fucking bed while the world goes up in flames around me. Go ahead and kill me. I dare say I'll see you in the afterlife soon enough. Come on. Get it over with.'

But my blade stayed in its sheath.

I had to know.

'Why?' I demanded.

Father didn't look happy with his stay of execution. He scratched at an eye. 'Why?' He near laughed at the ceiling. 'You know why, Corvus. A family can't have a son steal from it. Rome can't have masters making mockery with their slaves.'

I wanted to spit. *For Rome.* Always for Rome.

'I had no idea you were such a virtuous servant,' I sneered.

At my derision, bright fire came into the old man's eyes. He flashed them to my weapon. 'Do not think you are the only one who has suffered in the service of a greater good, *boy.*'

The words stunned me. At any other time in my life, I would have asked him what he meant, but now, the picture of Beatha's grave fresh in my thoughts, there was only one thing on my mind. Only one thing that I had to say, before the end.

'You didn't have to kill her.'

The words were in the open now. Accusation and sentence. With them came the knowledge that I could not leave this room while my father still breathed. Not for what he'd done.

There was scarcely a sound as he surveyed me. When he finally spoke, his eyes were narrow slits in his sallow face.

'. . . *kill her?*'

I held my tongue. My fingers gripped the pommel of my sword. I dared not draw it. Not until I had answers. He would be dead within moments of its unsheathing, I knew it.

'You didn't have to *kill her*,' I growled again, and so deep was my voice that it could have come from the bear that clung to my back and shoulders.

I took a step forwards. His red eyes went to my blade. I could draw it and take his throat in the same heartbeat. I was shaking.

'I should open your neck. I should let you choke on your own blood. Let you know the end is coming, just like you did to her!'

My knuckles were white. His eyes were wide.

But not with fear.

'Corvus, what are you talking about?'

And I saw bemusement in his stare. Uncertainty. My fingers did not loosen on my sword, but in the face of such hesitation the grip of my conviction weakened about my heart.

'You killed Beatha.' I tried to say it with confidence, but failed.

But I saw the truth in his eyes before he said it.

'I didn't harm a hair on that girl's body!' The old man shook his head, and then it came rushing out. 'I took her away from you so that you could overcome your madness, Corvus. I sold her to a friend, so that she could be close to her father when I freed him. We both agreed it was for the best!'

I was staggered. '*We?*'

'Cynbel and I! Left unchecked, only tragedy would have come to you and the girl. I was trying to teach you a lesson.' He sighed. 'Not turn you into . . .'

The killer that stood waiting to draw blood. A killer who shook with grief and questions.

'Cynbel *knew?*'

My father nodded. 'We decided it would be best to keep you apart. Young love is powerful. Dangerous.' As though that needed saying. 'It was best for both of you.'

But Beatha was dead. Raped. Murdered. Through teeth clenched in bitter resentment, I told him as much.

And then, for the first time in my life, I saw true fear on my father's face.

'Son,' he began, and I wondered in that moment if I was to see the miracle of tears on his face, 'the last time I saw that girl was when I sold her.'

I wanted to scream. His treachery and lies were too much, but somehow, I found myself sucked into his game. 'Sold her to *who*?' I demanded, tiring of his fictions.

The old man seemed to shrink. He swallowed.

'The same person that told us about you to begin with . . .'

And with a name, my whole world fell apart.

❧ 46 ❧

I whipped Balius's flanks, hooves clattering against the stone road as we charged from Iader and towards the mountains that held my legion.

At the town's edge, a body of men were waiting for me. *Arminius* was waiting for me. I'd told the bastard that I'd meet him at the port. Despite my haste, I reined in; I would never outride his Germans.

A flash of worry passed over his features as he recognized the bloodlust in mine. 'I thought you'd deserted,' he said simply. 'I'm glad you're here. Very glad. I was going to give you until the morning. Don't want to sit around too long with legion pay chests to look after.'

I had no time to be civil. No strength for it. My entire being had been turned over to darkness. 'I'll see you at the legion,' I told him, kicking my heels hard.

'Corvus!' the prince called after me. 'Corvus, wait!'

But I would not. Then I heard a shout as the German kicked his own horse into action, and soon he was in pursuit. A far better horseman on a beautiful mount, it did not take him long to catch me.

'Corvus!' he called from the saddle. 'Just a moment to talk, that's all I ask of you!'

No.

'Please!'

No.

'Please!'

I turned and saw true worry on his features. The kind I would have seen on the face of Octavius or Varo. Brutus or Priscus. Worry for *me*.

'Just one moment! Please!'

I gave him that. Balius breathed hard as I slowed him to a trot. I felt his ribcage swell between my legs.

Arminius looked me over. He saw a man rash and reckless, and talked straight. 'The road back to the legion is not a safe one, friend.'

My eyes spoke for me – what did I care?

The cavalry officer looked at my horse. 'And he cannot survive you riding him like that.'

I thought a lecture was coming. Some attempt to caution against my haste. Instead, Arminius brought his own horse to a halt, and swung out of the saddle. 'Take mine,' he told me.

I stopped Balius in his tracks, and looked at the animal Arminius was holding. The horse was worth a handsome sum. A mount fit for nobility.

'I can't take your horse.'

The prince shook his head. 'Don't think of it as taking my horse.' He half smiled. 'Think of it as giving me yours.'

I was silent. Arminius rubbed the proud neck of his steed. 'He's always been a loyal friend to me, Corvus, and I . . . I think you need a loyal friend.'

The truth in his words drove like a javelin into my chest.

I didn't want to be alone.

'I'll take your bloody horse,' I growled.

I slid from Balius's saddle and rubbed his nose. I had become fond of him. He deserved better than being flogged to death by me.

I handed his reins to Arminius. 'Look after him.'

'And you?'

'I can look after myself.'

The prince put a hand on my shoulder. I had thought that I would want to react with violence to the familiar action. Instead I calmed.

His blue eyes sparkled with friendship. 'What is it, Corvus?'

I wanted to tell him. The gods knew I wanted to tell him. But . . .

But I couldn't give voice to it even in my head, let alone my tongue. I just knew that I was in the wrong place. That I had heard the wrong things. Only in the mountains could I set it right. Silence the war raging in my mind.

I lifted myself up on to the magnificent horse. 'I have to go.' I looked down at the noble German. 'I owe you a debt.'

Arminius shrugged. 'No doubt you will repay it one day, my friend. Good luck, Corvus. I'll see you in the mountains.'

There was nothing left to say.

'Yar!' I shouted, and my mount leaped forwards to carry me to my end.

I rode over hill and through valley. Past forest, river and waterfall.

I saw none of it. A curtain of red hung before my eyes. It had fallen when my father had breathed a name.

For now, that name had stayed his own execution. I did not want to consider – *I could not consider* that it might be a portent to another's.

Hot tears stung my cheeks as I rode. I wanted to cry out. To scream. To rage against life, and death, and everything I had ever known.

But instead I rode.

I rode to find answers. I rode to find truth. I rode to silence the voice in my head which told me that I had been deceived. That I had made enemies of friends, and brothers of adders.

Somehow, I escaped the valleys and trails unmolested. Maybe the rebels were gone. Maybe they saw a foe so consumed with misery that they considered it better sport to let him suffer.

I found the legion only a little further south than where I had left them. I galloped past the sentries and saw that the force in the valley had swelled.

'What's going on?' I demanded of one soldier. 'Where have these other troops come from?' The young man gulped as he took in my face, the bear snout growling above my savage jaw. 'Tell me!'

'The legate's brought up the reserves, sir!'

'Why?'

'I – I don't know, sir.'

I kicked on to find someone that would. A few of the headquarters staff raised eyebrows at the sweat-soaked mount that I dismounted with haste.

'Where's the legate?'

I was shown to him. With a knot of officers, Hook-nose was looking at a map on a campaign table. Fleetingly, I noticed a couple of weather-beaten scouts standing to attention in the tent's corner.

Hook-nose raised his gaze. A smile pulled at his lips. 'Standard-bearer. Just in time.'

'Sir.' I saluted. 'I'm looking for the Sixth Cohort. Can I take one of these scouts to show me?'

Hook-nose shot me a puzzled look. For the first time he took in my unshaven state. 'Are the pay chests all right, standard-bearer?'

'With Prince Arminius, sir.'

He licked his lips. 'And not with you because . . .'

Shit. I looked at the faces of the other staff officers with him. Their eyes were on me, now. They sensed blood had just dripped into the water.

'I heard the Tenth Cohort had been brought up, sir,' I bluffed, recognizing an officer of that unit. 'I was hoping the eagle had come with it.'

Hook-nose grinned, then. Not a friendly smile, but that of a hungry vulture. 'No holding you back from a fight, is there, Corvus?'

'No, sir.'

He pointed to the map laid out before him. 'Then come and join us, standard-bearer,' he ordered. 'We are about to have ourselves a real battle.'

❧ 47 ❧

The place was a considerable-sized hill fort that clung to a mountaintop like a limpet. Through reconnaissance, and information obtained from the capture of two rebels who had been caught stealing weapons from the camp, and were now crucified in the valley, the legion had identified the place that was home to the men who had been harassing and killing us for weeks. With high walls, and an estimated three hundred rebels to hold them, it would be a tough shell to break, but the men of the Eighth were hungry to sink metal into the meat of their enemy.

It was to this end that Hook-nose had brought up the reserve of the Tenth Cohort. These men were fresh, undrained from the mountains, and would form the spearhead that would rise up from the western slope, Rome's glittering blade of steel. To the east, a secondary attack would be launched by the weakened Sixth and Seventh Cohorts – it was there that I needed to be. It was amongst their ranks that awaited the reason that I had flogged my horse and ridden alone from Iader.

'You'll go with the Tenth,' Hook-nose informed me again as we stood alone in his tent. 'They are our main thrust, standard-bearer. It's the proper place for you.'

I grasped for a reason for me to be on the opposite flank. 'The Sixth and Seventh have been bled on this operation, sir,' I tried diplomatically. 'Maybe they're in greater need of the inspiration of their eagle?'

'Revenge will lead them well enough,' the aristocrat told me, and I hated that his words were true. 'This will be the first real taste of campaign for the Tenth, Corvus. You must be there with them. They'd die for you.'

He saw the disbelief on my face. 'You are a hero in this legion, and beyond,' he explained patiently. 'You're too humble a soldier to see it, but that's the truth.'

The truth? The only truth I cared about was with the Sixth Cohort.

I needed to try one more time. 'Sir, it's just that . . .'

'Speak,' he said with a gesture.

'My brother is in the Sixth, sir,' I told him honestly. 'The only one that I have left.'

Hook-nose brightened at my innocence. 'No, standard-bearer.' He smiled. 'You have an entire legion of them.

I was dismissed.

I sat alone with only an eagle for company. I looked at that prized piece of metal, and vowed that I would hand over a thousand of them if it meant the return of just one of the people that I loved.

Beatha, Octavius and Priscus lay in graves. What of Brutus? Surely by now he had succumbed to his wounds. And if not? Who among us would live through this war? There were hundreds of thousands of the enemy loose somewhere in the two provinces of Pannonia and Dalmatia. Bled slowly as we had been, it was easy to forget that there was a huge body behind the enemy's invisible face, and that body was far superior in numbers to our own. Where were they?

Three hundred were in the hilltop fort that we would assault at dawn. High, thick walls of stone. There would be arrows, and spears. There would be blood, and piss, and shit, and death. Into this fury I would carry the legion's eagle, and the eyes of enemy and ally alike would look to me. My own men for example, my enemy for capture. How I wished I had my comrade Varo beside me, but he too was lost to the mountains – I had asked for him at the hospital, where the air stank of death. I had asked for him at the cohort, where men shook their heads in grief. I had asked for him at headquarters, where the clerk's scrolls listed him as FU on the ledgers of the legion – Fate Unknown.

But his end *was* clear. Like dozens of others, my friend had been captured by the enemy. Doubtless his death was then a thousand times more ghastly than it would have been in any battle.

I rubbed at my eyes. It was the dead of night, and they were red with fatigue and the dust of the road, but I could not sleep. I would not sleep. Not with what was coming with the sun.

I wasn't scared of dying, not now, but I *was* scared of dying with the truth unknown. I couldn't go to the next life with a mind full of hateful accusations and half-truths – *I had to know.*

I got to my feet. There was a wineskin in my hand. It wasn't my first. 'Drink up,' I told Gallus, famed eagle of the Eighth. 'Drink up.'

I poured some of the red liquid over his beak. Looked into his metallic eye. What had this totem seen? What manner of death, and glory, and strength, and weakness?

284

I fought to forget. I fought for comrades. Tradition and virtue had never been the force that moved my shield and blade, but I wasn't fool enough to think that it didn't move other men. That they wouldn't give their all, and more, for an idea. For a distant place. For people who would never know their names or their deeds. Who would know only one of two things: did their sacrifice end in victory, or defeat.

There was no doubt in my mind that tomorrow's butcher's bill would buy another victory for Rome, but this would be no battle talked about in forums and remembered in annals. Too small for that. Three cohorts against three hundred. A mere skirmish in the history of Rome's conquests. Of her enforced peace.

'What do you think to that?' I asked Gallus.

The eagle looked back at me, impassively stoic as ever.

'Well said,' I mumbled.

Gods, I was lonely.

I looked at my pack. Xanthus was there, the wooden horse that had belonged to one of my young soldiers. He had left the child's toy on his bunk to save him from the danger of battle. I decided that I would to do the same, and placed the talisman in the tent atop of what passed as my possessions – a few spare pieces of clothing. A small rock I had taken from the village on the first day that I fought and killed. There was a red smear on it. The blood of one of my first. It was a grisly memento, and I had been proud of it. Now, I wondered about the lives I had ended that day. I had killed them gladly and I would do so again if they so much as threatened my friends, though

I was running ever shorter of such people. But . . . but now I wondered if they had felt that same way. Did they only attack us because we threatened *their* beloved? I had always wondered why they hadn't fled higher into the hills when they first saw our superior force. Why had they stood and fought against odds that they could never hope to beat?

For love, I realized.

But love of what? A wounded comrade who could not be moved, perhaps? The love of their home that they refused to abandon? Whatever the details of their devotion, I had seen enough of war now to know that love is the elixir that the battle-mad drink. It is love of country, or comrades, or plunder, or excitement, but is always the love of something.

A man cannot kill without love.

I felt Gallus's eyes on me. He was judging. Looking for holes in my theory.

'I'm telling you it's true,' I slurred. The wine was rank, but it had a back like Arminius's horse. 'And what the fuck would you know?'

A lot more than me, but I didn't have enough wine to make an eagle talk, and so I was forced to look into stern eyes, and wonder how many men would die beneath her gaze in the morning. How many men would die for their own reasons of love.

At some point thereafter, I was granted sleep.

A hand on my shoulder gently woke me. The tent was dark, but I saw pale hair in the light.

Arminius. 'You're alive,' he said, and seemed happy about that.

I pushed myself up so that I was sitting. Inside my head there was a sound like the clashing of armies.

'Are you all right?'

I sniffed the air. I smelt myself. I could smell horse, and sweat, and the grime of the road. I could also smell . . .

'You're lucky you didn't choke to death,' the man told me, and then I witnessed a prince cleaning up a soldier's vomit.

'I will be soon enough, I imagine,' I told him. 'We're attacking a hill fort at dawn. Three cohorts.'

I saw the man's pale silhouette nodding. 'My men and I are being held as a reserve, to cut off any survivors that try and escape.'

I snorted. 'There won't be any survivors. We're coming at them from both flanks. The other angles are high rock and cliff.'

'Someone always survives.' I saw his smile flash in the gloom. 'How else would we get our stories?'

I said nothing. For a moment, we fell into silence.

'Why are you here?' I finally asked him.

'I came for my horse.'

'Oh.'

'And to see my friend.'

I choked out a short laugh. I was still drunk. 'Dangerous occupation, being my friend.'

'Those who seek to change and better the world are often in the positions of most peril.'

I rubbed my grubby hands over my face. 'Gods, it's like talking to bloody Plato with you.'

Arminius laughed at that. Where my own mirth was dark and desperate, his was rich and booming. 'I *have* been accused of loving the sound of my own voice,' he confessed.

'By who?' I couldn't think that many people would contradict a noble. By openly questioning the word of Rome, I had already stepped over the greatest boundary, so what was one more?

'Her name is Thusnelda,' he told me, and the tent seemed to warm. Not even the darkness could hide the German's glow. 'She has eyes like jewels and hair like gold, and one day, Corvus . . . one day, she will be my wife.'

'She sounds beautiful,' I said dutifully.

'You will have to come to the wedding.'

I snorted. 'You like to dream, don't you?'

Arminius's teeth shone brightly. 'I do, my friend. I dream of great things.'

Experience had told me to laugh at his naivety, but there was something about the German prince that was irrepressible, as though he was beyond the rules that governed the lives of mere mortals. 'I'm sure you will see them all come true,' I told him honesty.

The German placed a hand on my shoulder. 'Thank you, my friend,' he said, and I could hear the sincerity in his voice. 'And what do *you* dream?'

He was smiling. I was not. 'I don't.' I spoke without heat. 'I don't have dreams, Arminius.' I left out that nightmares now raged in their place. 'My dreams died a long time ago.'

For a long time he said nothing. I felt as though he was taking a measure of me. How close he could step to the edge.

Eventually, he dared to tread closer than any other had done. 'One day' – he spoke as softly as wind in the forest – 'I would like you to tell me about her.'

I wanted to growl, then. I wanted to swipe his hand from my shoulder. I wanted to rage, and to accuse, and to throw off the shackles of friendship before another of my betters died and left me.

Instead I simply promised, 'I will.'

There wasn't much to say after that. Arminius rose, and paid homage to the eagle by touching its feathers. By the light of a candle, I could see the devotion in his eyes. This man loved Rome, and his fellow soldiers. I had no doubt he would die to see that totem remain in the lawful hands of those who protected Rome.

At the tent's flap he turned. 'I'll come and find you when it's over. Try to be intact.'

I grunted, but a ghost of a smile played at the corners of my mouth. For a brief moment, this man had helped me forget. 'Take care of yourself, prince.'

He closed the flap. I stood and stretched limbs sore from the road and soaked in wine. I was unshaven, stinking and unsoldierly, but none of that mattered. No one would be looking at me.

'You're the hero here,' I told the eagle.

Under arms and clad in armour, I carried her forth to the waiting slaughter.

❧ 48 ❧

The night air was hot, dark and oppressive, as though I were walking into a cave that led to the underworld. I snorted grimly as I realized that for some of us, it would.

I strained my eyes against the moon-touched black. I felt the movement on the valley floor. Didn't see it. The Tenth Cohort were preparing for battle, but Hooknose had forbidden any torches, lest they were spotted by the scouting parties that the enemy had undoubtedly dispatched. Instead, moonlight was caught here and there by polished armour and helmet. It looked as though some huge, malevolent centipede was stirring for the kill.

I walked through this quiet commotion, Gallus the eagle in my hand. I heard men mutter and curse, prophesy and promise.

'I should have listened to my dad, and been a baker.'

'Watch it! You nearly stabbed me with your javelin, you cock!'

'I'm telling you, they'll run when they see us.'

'I'll watch your back, brother.'

I tried to walk by these pre-battle rituals quickly – it was too much of a reminder that I was without my own battle-brothers – but I carried a famous totem, and she shone in the night.

Voices in the dark. Some between friends. Others for my own ears.

''Ey, look. The eagle.'

290

'That must be Corvus. He killed the enemy general to get that back.'

'Standard-bearer! Sir! Can we please touch the eagle?'

I stopped. That was a mistake. Word spread. Others came closer. In the dark I saw wide eyes, some opened in awe, others in fear.

'There're only three hundred of them, right, sir?' A young lad. A boy.

'Enough for a morning's hard work,' a veteran answered. 'It's an honour to march with you, standard-bearer.'

'The honour is mine.'

And it was. How could it not be? I was opposed to the senseless brutality of the mountain campaign. I was worried for the fate of those Dalmatians I had called friends. I was sick of my own life.

But these men?

They were not Varo and Octavius. Brutus and Marcus. They were not my brothers, but they were cast in the same mould. Born of the same blood. They would die for me, I realized with a stab of humility in my heart. They knew nothing of me save that I was of their legion. Their army.

And they would die for me.

Would I die for them?

I looked about at the eager faces in the moonlight. I saw a gruff soldier put his arm around a wide-eyed youngster. 'Hey,' he said, nodding at the eagle. 'That's what we're fighting for, lad. Just follow the eagle, and we'll be all right.'

And by following the eagle, they would be following me.

How could I not die for them?

291

'Keep your shields tight and high when you reach the wall,' I advised them, fumbling for words that I felt duty-bound to give. 'Watch your shins as you go over.'

Armoured skulls nodded in the darkness.

'I must be going.' What to say? 'I'll see you at the top.'

A promise to strangers. An oath to brothers.

'See you at the top,' they echoed. 'See you at the top.'

I found the front line of the Tenth Cohort and met its commander. He was a tall man with a thin face cast into deep shadow by the late hour and the cheek-plates of his helmet. His name was Paulus, and he was hungry.

'We've been sitting on our arses for weeks waiting for this call,' he told me. 'Don't get me wrong, I've drilled the men from dawn till dusk, but to be in camp when the rest of the legion is slitting throats? Insufferable.'

There were worse things in life to suffer than sitting out combat, but that wasn't something to say to an infantryman. With little surprise, I realized that I too was anxious for the coming battle. Anxious for the single-minded chaos of kill or be killed, to be away from the torment that had raged inside my mind since my father had uttered his bitter words.

A man on horseback approached. 'I'm looking for the standard-bearer,' a harsh voice asked.

'Over here.'

The rider reined in before me. I could smell the stink of his horse. Sweat, and leather. His accent was unmistakably Italian. Not one of Arminius's Germans. A dispatch rider, I guessed. 'Standard-bearer, I have a message for you.'

I felt my teeth clench and stomach tighten. No word that this man carried could be good for me.

'What is it?'

'You have a comrade,' he said, almost as a question. I was not ready for what came next. 'Brutus? I was asked to send word from his wife.'

My stomach churned. *Brutus?*

I forced myself to be flat. To be steel. 'He's dead?'

The horse tried to pull away. Maybe it sensed my unease. My capability for violence. The rider tugged back on her reins as he answered. 'I don't know,' he told me honestly. 'She says that you must come back with the eagle.'

'That's it?' Come back with the eagle? 'What about Brutus? What word from him?'

The horse trampled the ground. It was as anxious to move on as the rider. 'I don't know, sir. Would you like me to carry word back?'

'No,' I said after a moment. 'Thank you.'

The rider turned and left, leaving me with questions.

Come back with the eagle? Why? *Why?* Was she simply wishing me good fortune, or did Brutus live? Was he dying? Did he wish to see the totem before he died? Or was he already in the next life, and Lulmire simply wanted him to be honoured by the eagle visiting his grave?

I snarled. I wanted to be angry, but the truth was that sending messages via the dispatch rider was an uneasy affair. Words had to be passed from mouth to mouth. Messages must be simple. Even then, they could be forgotten. At least her message was clear: *Come back with the eagle.*

Come back to Brutus, dead or alive.

I sensed movement, then. Someone was coming along the lines. I heard words in the darkness. 'Remember your training,' an aristocratic voice was saying. 'Kill the bastards, boys. Kill them for Rome.'

'The legate,' Centurion Paulus whispered beside me, and I could hear a grin in his tone. 'I'd recognize the silhouette of that nose anywhere.'

'Men,' the commander of the legion greeted us. 'All ready?'

'All ready, sir.'

I saw Hook-nose turn in the saddle as he attempted to look over his force hidden in the mirk of night. 'Stealth won't do us much use given that they appear to already be on high alert up there, but I'll take every inch of advantage in war,' he said. 'Standard-bearer, you'll march with the First Century.'

'Yes, sir.' There was no other place for the eagle to be. It couldn't inspire men if it cowered behind their backs.

'Commander, if your cohort is prepared, proceed and march them out to the forming-up point.'

'Oh, we're ready, sir,' the soldier promised with feral purpose. 'Tenth Cohort, by the centre, quick march!'

We stepped off into darkness. Beside me, Paulus chuckled happily. 'Oh, I do love my fucking job.'

The pace slowed as we broke from the track in the valley floor and took the trail that led into the mountains. There was the occasional voice of a section leader or centurion in the gloom, but for the most part the cohort advanced as the disciplined professionals that they were – silently, and with deadly intent.

I was glad when we began our upward climb. The footing could snag an unwary man, and so it needed all of my concentration to keep myself and Gallus upright. Focusing on putting one foot in front of the other left me with little time to think about anything other than the sweat that trickled from inside my helmet and into my tired eyes. My hair itched, my gut was soured from too much wine and my knees hurt, but it was all preferable to thinking about what my father had said.

'See yourself through the battle,' I told myself repeatedly. 'Live, if you want answers. Die if you don't.'

A simple choice.

We marched. We climbed. Above us, black sky was giving way to slate grey. Eyes now long accustomed to the gloom sought out the jagged fangs of the other peaks that surrounded us.

'Not much further, sir,' I heard a scout tell the commander of the Tenth. Then, 'We're here, sir.'

'Form battle lines,' the officer ordered immediately and, as the word was passed, his men began to move seamlessly into position.

'We trained hard for this,' their leader said, pride in his voice. 'You will fight beside me, standard-bearer?'

A curt nod of my head. 'I will.'

I felt a hand on my tired shoulder. 'It will be my greatest honour.'

We fell into silence as the centuries shuffled into formation as best as they could on the mountainside. It was impossible to see our full position, but we had been briefed on it – we were on a slope two hundred yards wide, five hundred yards beneath the enemy hill fort. The way ahead of us was clear but for the occasional rocky outcrop – our formations should hold well until we reached the wall of stone. It was ten feet high, but we had a plan. A plan where men would die, but in the rivers of their blood others would be carried to victory. I had no doubt that by noon the field would belong to Hook-nose and the Eighth. It was what was to come after that truly terrified me.

I looked up the slope for distraction, hopeful to see what awaited us. I saw only forbidding black peaks, rising like hungry titans in the darkness.

Behind and about me, I noticed that all was near silent save for the splash of piss and spit on rock as men relieved themselves of fear and bad luck – the Tenth Cohort were ready. On the opposite slope, the fort between us, the Sixth and Seventh should now be in their own positions.

There was nothing to do but wait for dawn.

Wait for death.

The hot light of day crept over the mountains with hesitation, as though it was aware of what was to come, and wished to play no part in savagery. But, like the men who were soon to die, the light could not change nature. It could not change what had always been. Night then day. Peace then war. Like the hours in which we slept, peace was only ever a temporary truce. War was never far away. The idea of lasting peace was a fantasy. A wishful thought that there could, and would, be a final reckoning. A decisive campaign that would establish dominance and hierarchy once and for all.

We were about to prove how stupid such notions were.

I looked up the slope before me. It was steep. Steep enough that my lungs burned just to look at it. And across that obstacle in itself was the wall, an ugly scar of slate on the mountainside. It was too dark to see the men that doubtless stood sentinel there, but light enough to see that many of the men around me would soon fall.

I looked at their leader, Paulus. He was not much older than thirty. He didn't have the old eyes of the mountains. His look was eager. Hungry. He wanted this fight.

He felt my gaze, and my question – what do you think?

The centurion shrugged his armoured soldiers. 'I've seen worse places to die.'

A year ago, perhaps I would have laughed.

I put out my hand. 'Good luck.'

'Good luck.'

I chanced to look over my shoulder at the ranks about me. Young faces. Old faces. Scared faces. Excited faces. Pale faces. Flushed faces. No man the same, yet all a part of the whole. The body. The entity that would creep up this hillside to visit death in the dawn.

And what of those who stood against us? Now came the first cries of panic. The men on the walls had spent their nights dreaming of lovers, of family and of terrors. When the morning light revealed the latter, the defenders of the hill fort began to shout with dread.

'Listen to them bleat, boys!' Paulus snarled to his men. The need for stealth was gone, now. 'Shall we say good morning?'

At his words, five hundred men raised a vicious cheer, and beat their shields with their fists and javelins. It was an ugly, barbaric sound. A symphony of savagery.

I saw the officer turn his head. He was looking at a ridge that made itself evident as a black smudge still cast in the shadow of a larger mountain. Suddenly, a dozen fire arrows arced up from it, and into the grey sky.

It was the signal to begin death's dance.

'Tenth Cohort! Prepare to advance!'

A cheer. A promise. Of pain. Of victory.

'Advance!'

I stepped off with them, my legs suddenly heavy from nerves. I held Gallus in my left hand, and pulled my sword free with my right, cursing as the man behind me caught something on the back of my helmet and pushed it forwards almost into my eyes. Instead of hill fort I saw bear-snout, but the man must have recognized his error, for I felt it being pulled roughly back into place.

I twisted to face him. I don't know if I planned to thank him or curse him.

It didn't matter.

In that moment, I felt and heard the hot air scream beside my face, followed immediately by the slap of wet meat.

The soldier behind me went down with an arrow in his face.

It was the first of dozens launched from the walls. Lightning fast, black against a grey sky. Hunters, looking to fell an eagle.

I tried to stamp on my fear.

'At the half-pace, raise shields!' Centurion Paulus ordered – he had already caught one arrow in his own.

Hide and steel clashed and thumped as his men reacted to the command. Where there had been open slope and stone in front of my face, now I was a prisoner in a cell – a welcome one. I heard the padded smack of arrows as they hit our tight formation. I heard screams from somewhere in the ranks as others found their mark.

But they did not stop the advance – not even close – and the Tenth Cohort inched its way up the slope. I counted the paces in my mind. Counted down the distance to the wall. There were the slaps of arrow against steel. There were a few shouts of pain. But largely we went on unmolested, cocooned in our shields, our own fangs yet to show themselves.

I counted another ten paces. By my tally, we were over halfway to the wall.

That was when I heard the shout: 'Break ranks! Break ranks!' A command thick with panic.

I looked at the centurion beside me. Beneath the shields, his face was confused, and angry.

'Hold your ranks!' he hollered. 'Hold your bastard ranks!'

But somehow we felt discipline falter. A ripple through the formation as men pushed and pulled their way into other ranks and files.

I heard the cause a second later. There was a terrible shout of horror. A rumbling crash. Hideous screams.

'I need to see!' the centurion shouted to no one but himself, pushing free of the securing shields.

Instinctively, I did the same. I swallowed at what I saw.

Two boulders half the height of a man rolled with terrible speed and intention towards our ranks. I looked up at the wall ahead, and saw the enemy cutting ropes – there were more of the terrible weapons tethered at the top of the slope.

'Gods . . .' I heard Paulus utter. 'Hold the line!' he shouted at his men. 'Brace!'

But you can't brace against a boulder that's had two hundred yards to build up pace, and I watched open-mouthed with horror as two crashed into our ranks like Hannibal's elephants, sending sword and shield and soldier into the air, a bloody red smear carved through our ranks.

'Close up!' The harsh voices of centurions and optios. 'Fill the ranks, you lazy twats! Come on, what's wrong with you? Scared of a bit of blood?'

I gritted my teeth. We pushed on. Another boulder hit, then another. With each impact, Paulus's face grew darker with anger, but his men held their discipline, and stepped over and through the tattered remains of their friends. Behind us, we left screaming those whose feet and legs had been pulped by the assailing stones.

A hundred yards to go. The arrows continued to rain and hammer shields, but it was the boulders that held true terror.

'They only have two left,' the centurion growled, watching them cut the ropes. Desperate to be at the people who were killing his men.

I scanned the wall. He was right.

Two left.

Both in the centre of their lines.

Both aimed at the centre of ours.

I saw the enemy swing their axes, then scamper.

The boulders were loose.

The soldier on my left: 'They're coming straight for us.' I looked at him. He was grey. Even his skin seemed to shake.

'Hold the line,' Paulus snarled.

'Hold the line!' the strongest soldiers echoed.

I watched the balls of stone as they picked up speed and came towards us like chariots at the games. They were closing fast. Less than five seconds before I lived, or died.

It didn't look good.

'Hold the line! Hold the line!' Paulus's face had changed. He looked resigned to his fate.

He knew that he was going to die.

I looked at the tumbling weapon, and realized the same. I was about to meet stone with skin. Boulder with bone. I would be pulp. A smear on a mountainside. My flesh would be matted with the fur of my bearskin. My guts would be smashed into the wood and metal of the eagle.

I had a half-second to smile at that irony. Death was at hand. I wasn't surprised that I almost welcomed it.

I watched the rolling rock. Prepared for its embrace.

And then I saw it hit a half-buried stone in the slope. It skipped. It was the smallest of actions, the most minimal of manoeuvres, but it was enough.

A second later, the boulder ploughed into our ranks. I shielded my eyes as the blood of Grey-face beside me went spurting out of his body like he was a trod-on wineskin.

I remembered then what brave Varo had told me on my first battlefield.

Don't look down.

This time I listened.

Beside me the ranks closed. I heard a struggle: 'Move, you prick! I'm fighting next to the eagle!'

'I've served longer than you, you bastard! I'm fighting next to the eagle!'

I wished Brutus could have heard the words. The need for honour will always walk alongside death and misery.

'Tenth Legion!' Centurion Paulus called. 'Form bridging formation!'

We were at the wall.

Arrows hammered against the shields held above our heads: a rain of terror. Now we were at the foot of the wall, those loosed by the strongest bowmen had the power to puncture shield, and screams echoed beneath our faltering sanctuary. Then, like the drumming of an angry child, came a wild rhythm of beaten steel and wood as stones began to fall on our heads like Titan's hail.

'Front rank, kneel!' Centurion Paulus commanded, and the front line of his men put their knees into the stone, the shields above their heads pulled tight to rest on their backs and shoulders.

'Next rank up!' And the soldiers behind them followed on, building a floor of ramped shield that others could climb. Within moments, through the cement of flesh and shield, Paulus had begun to build a bridge that would crest the enemy defences.

Spear, arrow, rock. They killed, maimed, crushed. They drew blood, but not panic. The Roman war machine had arrived on the enemy's doorstep, and the Empire's killers had the scent of blood in their nostrils.

'Carry the wall!' Paulus screamed, moving himself on to the ramp of his men. 'Carry the wall!' he repeated.

I looked about me. Saw a man take an arrow in his shoulder. Saw another have his helmet knocked clean off, an astonished look on his face as he realized he was alive. All about me was blood, screaming, oaths and death. At the top of the wall I saw the shapes of the enemy, stabbing, throwing, firing and dying. The Tenth were amongst them now. They were at the wall's top.

I should be with them.

I spat to clear the fear from my throat. I thought of my friends. Brutus, a lingering end. Priscus, fallen on the battlefield. Octavius desecrated. Varo vanished. I raised the eagle high.

'Fear the Eighth!' I hollered. 'Fear the Eighth!'

My heart swelled with pride as I saw my beloved friend's battle cry rip through the ranks like fire. 'Fear the Eighth!' they cried in bloodlust. 'Fear the Eighth!'

I gripped the eagle tightly – I had honoured my friends.

Now I would kill for them.

I charged up the ramp of shields, and threw myself at the enemy.

Within moments, Gallus was slick with blood. I hadn't intended to use the eagle as a weapon, but as I reached the top of the wall an enemy fighter came at me from the right, and I swung Gallus into his livid face, the precious metal splintering bone and skull. 'Fear the Eighth!' I roared. 'Fear the Eighth!'

Maybe they did fear us, but they fought like cornered mountain lions. All about me was the ringing of steel. The screams of challenge, or pain. Behind me, a sea of rolling red shields glinted in the rising sun. We had the wall. We had the numbers. The day was won.

Now we just had to kill.

I found a victim. He didn't come at me looking to win an eagle. He came at me like a startled rabbit, bouncing from one skirmish to the next, desperate to escape.

I ended his flight as I drove my blade into his ribs. 'No!' he begged as he died. There was an edge to his words. An accusation of unfairness. It caught me, and the distraction was almost my own end.

I felt blood spurt across my arms. Saw a bearded man drop by my feet.

'Stay sharp, standard-bearer.' Centurion Paulus, smiling like a wolf with a bloody snout.

'Thank you.'

'The wall's ours. And over there. Look.' I followed his outstretched arm and sword. On the opposite side of the town's dwellings I saw red and gold gleaming in the sunlight – the other cohorts were carrying their own fight. 'I want that,' the officer then told me, and I saw that his eyes were set on a banner in the centre of the enemy's camp. It would be as precious to them as our own eagle. A worthy prize for whichever man claimed it. 'I'll be fucked if I let the other cohorts get there first,' he growled, looking about him – the fight on the wall was over. A few of the enemy lay moaning as they were dispatched by hungry blades, but the majority of the enemy were retreating into the centre of the hill fort.

'Form battle line on me!' Paulus called, and I knew that my place was at its centre.

Why? To kill? For glory?

No. For answers.

I wanted to be the first to reach the other cohorts. I knew who would be at their head. I knew who would be cutting through the enemy as though they were naught but bleating goats.

'Tenth Cohort,' Paulus commanded, 'by the centre, advance!'

We stepped off. I don't know who began beating their sword against their shield, but soon it was rolling thunder in the mountains, announcing the immediacy of death. Ahead of us, the enemy cowered in shaking ranks. There were at least a hundred of them in a tight knot of bristling spears and pale faces.

'I'm gonna skull fuck your corpse!' a man shouted from our ranks.

'I'm gonna put my babies in your daughters!' another promised to savage laughter.

I saw them, then. The civilians that cowered in the centre of men and arms. Their plaintive wails hit me at the same moment. It was the kind of sound to drive a man mad. No wonder the soldiers around me were eager to silence it with their blades.

I looked at Centurion Paulus. His pace was quickening. He wanted the enemy's banner. He wanted glory. It was only as one of the enemy broke from their ranks, unarmed and seemingly unafraid, that the officer ordered his men to halt a mere fifty paces from their enemy. 'They want to talk?' he said almost to himself.

That was exactly what they wanted. It came in a shout of Dalmatian, and I wondered if I alone understood it.

'He says they want to surrender,' I told the officer beside me. 'He says the men will surrender if the women and children are not harmed.'

Paulus laughed violently, and made a show of looking around him. 'You're not in a position to be negotiating!' he called. After a moment, I translated. As I did, I looked at the fearful faces of the enemy – young and old. Pale and tanned. There, undoubtedly, a pair of brothers. From the grief-stricken look on one man's face, it was his wounded son he knelt beside. All of them had wide eyes fixed on the machine of death that had overcome walls and now stood in splendid, bloodied ranks before them.

The Dalmatian leader said nothing back. I expected at any second that Paulus would order the charge.

Instead I heard him sigh. 'I don't want to lose more of my men for a battle already won,' he confided in me. 'Tell him to get his men to lay down their weapons, and then we'll talk.'

Surprised, I shouted the words. I could feel the Dalmatians' hesitation. Behind him, on the far wall, the sound of fighting had ceased.

'You will spare the woman and children?' he asked, recognizing that his own life was forfeit.

He didn't ever receive his answer for, at that moment, a harsh voice cried out from our left flank. 'The other cohort's over the wall!' the man shouted urgently. 'They're in the town, sir!'

That did it. Paulus raised his sword. He would not see others take his share of glory. 'Fear the Eighth!' he bellowed. 'Fear the Eighth!'

I had just a moment to see the looks of resignation and abject terror pass through the cluster of our enemy before the Tenth Cohort charged past me, hollering the words of my friend as they ploughed into ranks of man, woman and child.

I did not take part in the charge. Instead I let it run by me, a violent torrent of hate and power. I heard the steel sing. I heard the cries. It was all a blur, the peaking sun now burning into my eyes. Eyes that stung with tears.

They were not tears for the butchered, nor tears for the butchers.

They were tears for the inevitable. For the pain I could no longer ignore.

The hill had been carried. The day belonged to the Eighth, and to Rome. There was no longer an enemy force standing, and so I sheathed my sword; it was questions that I must wield, and the answers to them would be as deadly as any blade.

'I don't want to do this,' I said out loud. 'I don't want to do this. *Please*,' I pleaded with my own conscience.

I tried to shut my eyes. To shut my mind.

But Beatha was always there. Naked. Raped. Murdered.

Under the stare of her lifeless eyes I found my courage.

'I'll do it.'

I wanted to sob. But no tears came. Just a shaking in my limbs, and bile in my gut. I fought to stay upright as a wave of nausea passed through me. I fought to be the man she had always thought me to be.

Through her I found my courage, and against a backdrop of screams, I went to find the answer to my own.

Individuals among the enemy fled through the buildings like whipped dogs, their eyes huge and wild. On their tails were packs of Roman soldiers, and when they caught their quarry they dragged them viciously to the floor. The men they butchered. The women they raped. The children . . . it depended on the age.

None were spared. In the eyes of the victor, all were guilty by association.

But it was not my fight. Not in this moment. I strode through the bloodshed like a centaur, with only one aim in mind.

To know the truth.

I found the man who possessed it on the far wall. His back was turned to me, but even in his arms and armour, I would recognize him anywhere. I had seen that silhouette grow from a boy to a man, and then from a man into a soldier.

I climbed steps of stone. Placed the bloodied eagle against the rampart. The man made no movement at the sound. He was looking out over the mountains. I followed his gaze. The wicked slopes were cast soft yellow in the morning sunlight. It looked like a king's hoard of gold. Endless piles of treasure. There was no sign of suffering. No sign of the evil that had changed this man.

'Marcus?'

He didn't turn. Instead he pulled his centurion's helmet from his head and laid it atop the stone of the objective his men had fought to take. Evidence of their sacrifice lay all about. A carpet of bodies. A slick paint of blood.

'Marcus . . .'

He turned, and I expected to see the face of my brother.

I tried not to shudder.

This wasn't the man I knew. This wasn't the boy that I'd run with through woods and over hills. This wasn't the brother who knew my secrets, fought by my side and promised me eternal friendship. This was the cold face of a stranger. Dead eyes like a shark's, a fresh scar painted along his jaw.

'Marcus . . .' I began again, but the next words caught in my mouth.

I had come here to speak words that sounded treasonous to our brotherhood. Thoughts that had been like knives in my mind. I had sought him to seep poison, and to have him laugh at the accusation, but now, as I saw the death in his demeanour, my stomach soured to acid, and I realized that I could have been wrong about everything.

Marcus wiped a hand at the sweat and dirt on his face. It left him with a grotesque, bloody red mask.

'You went to Iader,' he said, his tone like the stone of the mountains that loomed about us, spectators to our tragic theatre. 'I didn't ever think that you'd go back to Iader.'

I tried to speak. Fear and thirst held my tongue. I tried to control my limbs. They were beginning to shake.

'You spoke to your father?' There was something in his eyes, then. Not guilt. Not pity.

Anger.

He snorted, and spat. 'I should have killed your father.'

It was too much. The word burst forth from me like a spear-point from my chest. '*Why?*' I demanded.

He looked through me.

'Why, Marcus? Why should you have killed my father?'

For honour, I wanted him to say.

Because he's a liar.

Because he killed your beloved.

But he said none of that. He simply stared.

'*Why should you have killed my father?*' I raged against the dawn.

But we both knew why.

Because he had talked.

Because he had given me a name.

My father had talked, and given me the name of the man who had bought Beatha, and promised to keep her safe.

'Tell me you lied to me, brother!' I suddenly pleaded. 'Tell me you lied!' I struggled for words. 'Tell me you . . . tell me you bought her, and sold her! Tell me you bought her, and sold her, and set her free! Tell me . . . tell me . . .'

I saw fire in his eyes. Anger on his face. I was no longer looking at my brother. This was not Marcus of Iader. This was the leader of the Barbers. This was a killer.

He always had been.

'*She was a slave, Corvus!*' Marcus suddenly hissed. '*A SLAVE!*'

My vision swam. I staggered. I put my hand against the wall to steady myself as white light began to push against my vision.

'*You* betrayed *me!*' I heard him snarl through the ringing in my ears. 'We were supposed to be brothers, Corvus, but you chose her over me! A slave over your brother! A slave over Rome!'

Every word was a war-hammer to my chest. I sank back against the wall. Felt puke in my gullet. Hot blood tingling through my body, but no anger – just a revolting sense of loss.

Beatha was dead, and my brother had died with her.

'Tell me it isn't true,' I croaked.

He stepped forwards then. As he came towards me, I didn't see the man I knew. I saw the soldier I feared.

'If you did it, just kill me,' I uttered. 'Just kill me, Marcus. Just kill me.'

Instead he stared through my soul, then spat on to the bloody stone.

'You never were a soldier, Corvus,' he accused me with bitter disappointment. 'You never were a soldier.'

I saw the anger in him then. I expected the blade.

Instead, words fell from him like the executioner's sword: 'And you were never my brother.'

The ringing in my ears became a roar. The white crept over my eyes like a tide.

And then, I suffered no more.

❧ 50 ❦

When I opened my eyes, Marcus was gone.

Looking about me, I saw that my only company was the dead. Already, the crows were taking eyes.

'Yar!' a commanding voice from below shooed them away. I heard steps on the stone.

I didn't push myself to my feet. I didn't care for life, let alone my appearance.

A blond head appeared at the top of the steps.

'Arminius . . .'

The German prince took in my sorry state, and hurried to kneel beside me. 'You're hurt?'

I shook my head. I wasn't injured – I had been gutted. I felt hollow. Numb. My brother was the architect of my life's pain. I should feel anger. Terrible anger. Instead I felt . . .

Nothing.

'I keep meaning to die,' I said honestly.

It took a moment for the prince to assess my words. When he had, he said, 'The gods do not want you yet. You have a part to play for them, brother.'

Brother?

'My name is Corvus,' I said with too much heat.

Arminius gave an apologetic smile.

I saw hope in it.

I dashed that promise against a rock in my mind, and pushed myself to my feet. All about me lay the dead. Roman. Dalmatian. Dozens upon dozens, and for what?

This was no town. This was no great victory. It was a bleak home in the mountains, now laid to waste to supposedly protect those who dwelt in these lands.

'I've had enough,' I suddenly growled, sweeping out my arm. 'Of all this! They won't listen,' I told Arminius. 'They won't change! It will be like this, over and over! Romans die. The natives die. And for who? For what?'

'For the glory of Rome?' the prince suggested, but I could see that he was testing me.

'*Fuck Rome.*'

The words hung in the dead air. Arminius looked into my eyes. What he saw in there scared him, and he looked quickly away.

To the dead.

He moved beside a legionary whose young face was turned up to an uncaring sky. Then he turned his attention to a Dalmatian – he was about the same age as the enemy he had died fighting. Arminius sighed sadly. 'These men were both recruited, trained and told to fight for Rome. Now they are enemies, when they should be friends. They have been turned on each other to line the pockets of rich senators and a distant emperor. Does that seem fair to you, Corvus?'

I said nothing.

'But such voices can only be heard through violence. The rebels need to stand long enough to be heard. Maybe then they can have a voice. Maybe then this sacrifice will have been worthwhile . . .' He looked at me. 'But they'll never do it without the right leadership.'

There. Open treason.

I knew what he was saying. I knew what he wanted.

'The rebels need leadership, Corvus. Leadership, and treasure. You can give them both.'

The legion's coffers. I felt as though they were weighing on my chest as I answered. 'I can't turn against my brothers.'

That bastard. He almost smiled. He almost fucking smiled, and I did not hate him for it. 'Which brothers do you have left, my friend?'

And he was right.

Arminius left me, then. He left me with a pat on my shoulder and my eyes on a bloodied eagle. All about me was death, and betrayal. I had thought that my life's hopes died in the mountains, but now I realized that they lay butchered in my adolescence. Butchered by the one person I had thought I could trust. Could I live with myself if I did not avenge Beatha's murder? Would she forgive me if I *did*?

'Enough!' I screamed from the top of the wall, my words caught and dying in the stone of the mountain. '*Enough,*' I pleaded.

No more questions. No more thoughts. Arminius was right. I had no brothers, only misery, and it was time to take action. Deceived by my empire, my family and my greatest friend, what other choice was there for me? What hope of redemption?

None.

None save for the sword, and knowing that I could never set eyes on Marcus again, I knew that there was only one choice left to me.

I would leave the Eighth.

I would turn against my empire.

I would become a traitor.

Author's Note

Legion is the first book that I've self-published, and it felt right that this new beginning should take us to the start of Corvus's own journey, before he was found in a German forest, and given the name Felix.

In ad 6, the famed Tiberius was poised to launch a huge invasion across the Danube and into the lands of the Marcomanni. To aid him, the local chieftains of the Roman-controlled Illyricum were ordered to raise large numbers of levies to serve as auxiliaries. (Illyricum was later to be split into the provinces of Pannonia and Dalmatia, but I've used these later titles for simplicity's sake throughout the series.)

As described in this novel, this impressive force raised for Rome turned against its 'master' at their marshalling grounds, putting a huge enemy army at Tiberius's back. It would force Rome to call off the invasion across the Danube, and instead the Empire faced brutal conflict within its borders.

Soon after declaring their intentions, the rebel leaders broke their force into three main contingents, with one fighting in their home territories, a second invading the Roman province of Macedonia, and a third attempting to invade Italy. It's this final contingent that Corvus and his comrades do battle against in the valley.

According to the Roman historian Velleius Paterculus, who took part in the war as a cavalry officer, half of a Roman legion was surrounded by twenty thousand of the enemy, but somehow defeated them. I've let my imagination fill in the blanks on how that happened. It's often the case that when a smaller number rout their enemy then some kind of trickery or unusual tactics are involved. Given how excellent the Roman soldiers were, there is always the possibility that the outnumbered legionaries simply butchered the rebels in open battle, but I like to think that there was more to it than that. I doubt that we'll ever know, as there is very little evidence from this period, and that which does exist must be looked at with a critical eye; propaganda and 'fake news' are not modern inventions, and many of the 'contemporary' sources of the period were written with political ambition in mind, often at a great distance from – and years after – the events that they chronicled.

Regardless, it's likely that the half-legion who survived the battle against such heavy odds were then sent to the coast, where Roman settlements were coming under siege. It makes sense to me that in doing so they'd need to protect their supply lines, and the way to do that would be by going into the mountains and taking the fight to the enemy. It certainly seems to be the case that the rebels tried to avoid pitched battles after that initial blood-letting, and it is established that the campaign largely descended into what we would refer to today as guerrilla warfare.

As I have said before, I am a storyteller, not a historian, and you should take what I write with a grain of salt. I am, after all, a soldier, and we never let the facts get in the way of a good tale. I write historical *fiction*, and I write it for an audience in the twenty-first century. For me, the story comes first, and I believe that is best served with prose and dialogue that is more relatable to the reader. I believe that the less someone is taken out of the moment by unfamiliar words and patterns of language, the more they can engage with the emotion on the page. I probably get the balance wrong more often than not, but this is what I strive for.

Corvus and his comrades are fictional characters, but if studying and serving with soldiers has taught me anything, it is that the character of the warrior transcends time.

Legion is chronologically the first book in my series about Corvus/Felix, and it takes us to the point where we first met him in *Blood Forest* (which has since been relaunched under the title *Ambush*). I love writing this series, and so long as you want to read it I will keep telling the tale, until it reaches its conclusion.

With the entire region aflame in open rebellion, and Corvus betrayed by the one friend he had left, there is still a lot more blood to shed.

Acknowledgements

Although I have self-published this book, I would still like to offer great thanks to the team at Penguin who worked with me on *Blood Forest (Ambush)* and *Siege*. Without them there would be no series. Thanks also to the publishers who have made Corvus's story available in several other languages.

Nothing gets done without the support of my family and friends, and my agent Rowan Lawton. That is also true of the historians who give me the skeletons of my stories through their hard work and research.

Thank you to my wonderful cover designer and copy editor, who gave *Legion* its professional polish.Finally, thanks to you, the reader, for encouraging me to continue this series. Reading a book is a commitment of your most precious asset, time, and I hope that I've repaid your trust.

Geraint Jones

Printed in Great Britain
by Amazon